"DRAGON FANS REJOICE . . ."*

Praise for the series by Allyson James

THE BLACK DRAGON

"One of my favorite authors. A unique and magical urban paranormal with dragons, witches, and demons. Will keep you enthralled until the very last word!"

—Cheyenne McCray, *USA Today* bestselling author of *Forbidden Magic*

"Tasty and tempting reading! HOT." —**Romantic Times*

"Begins with a bang and the action never lets up, not for one single, solitary, wonderful moment. I devoured this book in just a few hours . . . So overwhelming that I couldn't even consider putting this book down. The story is unusual, wonderfully original, and filled with intriguing characters . . . Dragons, magic, and a fight to save the world—Allyson James has a winning combination that makes *The Black Dragon* a story to remember!"

—*Romance Reader at Heart*

"A book destined to leave a smile on your face and dragons in your dreams. Get your copy today."

—*Romance Reviews Today*

"[Allyson James] keeps the sexual tension up to the point of boiling . . . Such an incredible talent."

—*Two Lips Reviews*

continued . . .

DRAGON HEAT

"A new series filled with magic, humor, and excitement. Exciting and passionate, this story is gripping from beginning to end." —*Romantic Times*

"[A] delightful romantic fantasy . . . A fun tale of life between a mortal and her dragon." —*The Best Reviews*

"Ms. James's imaginative story is exceptionally intriguing . . . Highly sensual." —*The Eternal Night*

"This story has a wonderful fairy-tale feel about it. Allyson James does an outstanding job of creating and bringing these mystical creatures to life with characteristics and emotions that you can't help but fall deeply in love with; even the so-called *evil* black dragon with his cocky, bad-boy qualities will make the reader hum in pleasure and clamor for his story." —*Two Lips Reviews*

"A sexy, funny romantic romp . . . A truly mesmerizing read. The chemistry between Caleb and Lisa is searing and the love scenes are wonderfully entertaining."

—*Romance Reader at Heart*

Berkley Sensation Titles by Allyson James

DRAGON HEAT
THE BLACK DRAGON
THE DRAGON MASTER

THE DRAGON MASTER

Allyson James

BERKLEY SENSATION, NEW YORK

THE BERKLEY PUBLISHING GROUP
Published by the Penguin Group
Penguin Group (USA) Inc.
375 Hudson Street, New York, New York 10014, USA
Penguin Group (Canada), 90 Eglinton Avenue East, Suite 700, Toronto, Ontario M4P 2Y3, Canada
(a division of Pearson Penguin Canada Inc.)
Penguin Books Ltd., 80 Strand, London WC2R 0RL, England
Penguin Group Ireland, 25 St. Stephen's Green, Dublin 2, Ireland (a division of Penguin Books Ltd.)
Penguin Group (Australia), 250 Camberwell Road, Camberwell, Victoria 3124, Australia
(a division of Pearson Australia Group Pty. Ltd.)
Penguin Books India Pvt. Ltd., 11 Community Centre, Panchsheel Park, New Delhi—110 017, India
Penguin Group (NZ), 67 Apollo Drive, Rosedale, North Shore 0632, New Zealand
(a division of Pearson New Zealand Ltd.)
Penguin Books (South Africa) (Pty.) Ltd., 24 Sturdee Avenue, Rosebank, Johannesburg 2196,
South Africa

Penguin Books Ltd., Registered Offices: 80 Strand, London WC2R 0RL, England

THE DRAGON MASTER

A Berkley Sensation Book / published by arrangement with the author

PRINTING HISTORY
Berkley Sensation mass-market edition / November 2008

Cover art by Aleta Rafton.
Cover design by George Long.
Cover hand lettering by Ron Zinn.
Interior text design by Laura K. Corless.

ISBN: 978-0-425-22471-7

BERKLEY® SENSATION
Berkley Sensation Books are published by The Berkley Publishing Group,
a division of Penguin Group (USA) Inc.,
375 Hudson Street, New York, New York 10014.
BERKLEY SENSATION and the "B" design are trademarks of Penguin Group (USA) Inc.

PRINTED IN THE UNITED STATES OF AMERICA

10 9 8 7 6 5 4 3 2 1

This book is dedicated to Hannah,
our friend of twenty years who passed away
during the writing of this book.
Thank you for all the joy, love, and laughter.

1

He didn't know where he was, or who he was, or *why* he was. He stood upright in a naked human body in a dark, cold place that smelled metallic, damp, and oily.

The only light came from a crude lamp set high on a wall, a flickering orb surrounded by insects craving brightness. He didn't blame them. A few moments ago, his world had been one of heat and light, and now he stood in terrifying cold and darkness.

The dim light showed dirty walls and hard stones with letters scrawled beside a solid door. For some reason he could read the letters, though they made no sense to him.

MING UE'S DIM SUM.

He went toward the windowless door, the dragon magic tangled across it nauseating him. He had been summoned by a Dragon Master once before, long, long ago, and he tasted the rage of it still.

He moved along the wall to the door, his bare feet aching from the sharp pebbles strewn across the ground.

He heard voices coming from behind the door, and he cocked his head to listen . . .

"I won't do it, and that is my final word."

Tiny Ming Ue stood with her back straight, hands on her cane, eyes flashing black fire.

Carol clenched her well-manicured hands and tried not to lose her temper. Ming Ue was half Carol's size and wrinkled and gray, but she wielded all the power in the room, and she knew it.

Ming Ue's nephew Shaiming quietly sipped tea at another table in the closed restaurant. He pretended to be absorbed in his cup, but the twitch of his eyes betrayed his interest.

Carol dropped her voice to reasonable tones, the ones that persuaded hard-hearted venture capitalists in the financial district to sign fortunes over to her. "It won't be much of a change, Grandmother. You'll be doing the same things, and I know you'll welcome the help."

"I don't need any help. I've run this restaurant for thirty years, not to mention raising you nearly all that time. Your mother entrusted you to me when she died, and this is the thanks I get."

Ming Ue spoke in her sharp Cantonese, the language with which she bullied the great and terrible. Carol loved her grandmother, but sometimes, her stubborn insistence in clinging to the old ways drove Carol crazy.

"All I ask is that you add a few things to the menu to bring it in line with our other restaurants."

"*Your* other restaurants. I let you run those as you please, but you will not turn my dim sum house into an over-Americanized, make-believe-Chinese tourist trap. My dim sum is the best in San Francisco—the best in California. People come from all over to try it."

It was true that the restaurant with its plain cream-colored walls and small tables did attract those who wanted to try real dim sum. The only pictures on the walls were artful cut-paper dragons and flowers, and the tablecloths were all bright red, a lucky color.

Unfortunately, nowadays people expected more flash and glamour in a restaurant, and the many-times-washed white plates and dim sum cart with the squeaky wheel didn't quite measure up.

"Grandmother, please be realistic. You're losing business here. If we don't modernize the menu, we'll never raise the customer base. And with a manager—one you'll supervise, of course—you'll be able to take it easy. Maybe even retire and look in on the restaurant when you want to."

"Retire?" Ming Ue screeched, and Carol realized she'd miscalculated. "I'm only seventy-six years old. Why should I retire?" She jabbed her cane at Carol. "You are a smart young woman, and I love you, but I will not let you turn my restaurant into no better than a fast-food joint. I own Ming Ue's, not you."

Carol closed her mouth in frustration. She'd built her portfolio to great heights by knowing when to stop arguing with difficult investors, but Ming Ue always seemed to win. Business at Ming Ue's had slacked to almost half in the last six months, never mind how much lucky magic her grandmother claimed had seeped into the restaurant's walls.

Dragon magic, Ming Ue said. *The luckiest kind of all.*

Shaiming only drank his tea, knowing better than to get involved in an argument between the women of his family.

"All right, Grandmother," Carol said, trying to sound reasonable. "We'll talk about it later. I have an important meeting first thing in the morning, so I'll go on home."

Carol would bring over the proposed changes to the restaurant after lunch, when Ming Ue was sure to be full of tea, dim sum, and happiness. Lunch drew the best crowd, and Ming Ue was always content after chatting with her regulars.

"You do that," Ming Ue said with a scowl.

Carol turned away. Back off now, save up arguments for later, that was the way to win over a reluctant client.

"And you'll not make me change my mind!" Ming Ue shouted after her. Carol rolled her eyes. She walked out of the restaurant, very carefully not slamming the door behind her.

Carol made herself feel better by muttering very unprofessional curses under her breath as she made for her car parked a little way down the alley. She wasn't afraid to be out here alone—no one with any sense would bother the alley behind Ming Ue's. Whether it was lucky magic or Ming Ue's iron personality, thieves and those who extorted "protection" from small businesses steered clear.

She fished for her keys, still fuming. The investors she'd meet with tomorrow were enthusiastic about taking Ming Ue's restaurants nationwide but worried about the low profits of the original restaurant. If Carol could persuade them she could turn Ming Ue's around and show them her detailed outline to do so, she could save the day.

She heard a step behind her, but she didn't turn.

"She'll be all right, Shaiming," she said, assuming her mother's cousin had come out to try placation. "I won't push her too hard. I know her health is frail, no matter what she says."

Another footstep, and no answer. Shaiming was ordinarily quiet, but the silence behind her made the hairs on the back of her neck prickle. She turned around.

A tall man she'd never seen before stood directly behind her. The streetlight at the end of the alley glinted on red hair, night-dark eyes, and the gleam of naked muscle. He was huge and powerfully built, his shoulders massive, pectorals hard and flat. He also wasn't wearing a stitch of clothing.

Carol dragged in a breath to shout for help, but he put his hands on her shoulders and shoved her back against the car. He smelled like wind, sweat, and clean air, and he was enormously strong.

Carol fumbled in her purse and whipped her canister of pepper spray in front of the man's face. He knocked it out of her hand, and the stray squirt she managed to get off didn't seem to affect him in the slightest.

His eyes were pools of shadow, black all the way across, and a tangle of red hair framed a harsh, hard face. "Why did you summon me?"

"What? Let go of me."

He shook her. "I smell your power. Great power." His hands hurt her wrists, but his eyes were full of fear. "I won't serve you."

She had no idea what he meant. She only knew that he was strong enough to snuff her life out if he wanted without breaking a sweat.

Still, a spark in his eyes seemed to call to something deep inside herself. She felt that thing within stir and respond, and the spark flickered. He tilted his head in surprise and studied her, in a manner that reminded her of someone she couldn't think of right now.

The alley flooded with sudden light, and Ming Ue marched into the glare with Shaiming close behind.

"You there. Leave her alone."

"Grandmother, go back inside! Call the police."

"Release her, *now*." Ming Ue struck the ground with her cane, a tiny thunder crack that echoed up and down the alley.

The red-haired man stared at Ming Ue and abruptly let go of Carol. Carol slid out from under him and dashed back to Ming Ue.

The man faced them in the floodlight's bright circle.

Except for his mane of wild hair and his not-right eyes, he had a perfect male body, like a sculpture come alive. Every limb rippled with muscle, perfectly proportioned and raw with strength. His phallus, as proportionate as the rest of him, hung heavily from a thatch of red hair.

Ming Ue regarded him without fear. "Who are you?"

He only looked back at her, dark eyes glittering under the light. He made no move to run away or to attack; he simply watched the three of them huddled together with the wariness of an animal.

"Grandmother, we should call the police."

"No, we shouldn't. I've already called Malcolm."

Malcolm was a tall man with black hair and silver eyes on whom Ming Ue doted, claiming he had powerful and lucky magic. Ming Ue also claimed Malcolm was a dragon.

Malcolm did have strength, both physically and in personality: Carol couldn't deny that. She'd be thrilled right now to have his bulk between her and the large man in the alley.

Ming Ue jabbed her cane toward the red-haired man. "*This* is a dragon, Li Mei," she said, calling Carol by the pet name she'd gone by as a little girl. "I don't know what kind, but he obviously has no idea where he is or why he's here."

The old human woman unnerved him far more than the other two—the silent man and the young woman who smelled so good. When he'd had the young woman's body under his for a few seconds, he'd had the strangest and strongest feeling that she belonged there.

As his mind cleared, he'd realized that this was the human world, and that he'd responded to the binding call of a very powerful witch or a Dragon Master.

Which of them had called him? The old woman glittered with power but not enough to trap a dragon. The man had only a glimmer of magic. There was a deep glow inside the young woman, a flame she hid, something enormously powerful. But when she'd looked at him with her soft, dark eyes, he'd seen nothing of the arrogance of a Dragon Master, no evil.

Of course, the three of them could have banded together, pooling their talents to bring him here. Enslaving him . . .

He balled his fists and took a step forward. He shouldn't understand the human speak of this time and place, but magic had quickly adapted his senses.

"Why do you want me?"

"We don't," the old woman said. "What's your name?"

She didn't mean his true name. She meant, *What should we call you?*

Other dragons gave themselves human-sounding names, but fire dragons never did. They rarely interacted with other dragons, or even with their own kind. They lived in blissful solitude until they chose to mate, then they knew their mates so well, bound in thought and body, that there was no need for names.

"This one is different," the old woman said to the other two. "Not like Caleb or Malcolm."

"I can see that," the young woman replied. She was nervous and afraid, yet her voice was strong.

"What kind of dragon are you?" the old woman asked. "A great one, obviously."

The fire dragon simply looked at her without answering. If they didn't know what kind of dragon they'd called, it was their own fault. *They* should be slaves to *him*, not the other way around.

"He's coming," the old woman announced.

Lights pricked the darkness behind him, followed by a

strange squeal and a metallic taint in the air. A vehicle much like the one the fire dragon stood next to halted some distance away, and a large man rose from it.

A black dragon. The fire dragon's fury boiled over.

Black dragons were ice-cold creatures who cared for no beings but themselves. The ancient beasts lived inside mountains of stone, poring over incomprehensible and strange calculations. They were powerful, not because of their fighting strength, but because their minds were sharp as steel.

The black dragon's human form was as tall as the fire dragon's, but he had a fall of long black hair, and his eyes were silver. He moved with confidence toward the fire dragon, but the fire dragon regarded him with contempt—the black dragon had answered a summons by these humans.

A woman emerged from the vehicle behind the black dragon. She was small, but her magic burned like a bright white flame—a witchling. *She* could have summoned the fire dragon, though he felt no binding threads from her.

The black dragon cocked his head, looking the fire dragon up and down with his bright eyes.

"Damn." His voice was soft, almost silken.

"What's the matter?" the witch behind him asked. "Do you know him?"

The black dragon shook his head. He held his hand out to the witch, giving her a look that spoke of tenderness. He might be talking to a mate, but dragons and witches didn't mate.

"He's a fire dragon."

Give the mighty black dragon ten points.

The old woman sucked in her breath. "Truly?"

"What's a fire dragon?" the witch asked.

"I've never seen one before," the black dragon said. "They are elusive and volatile and don't interact with other dragons. Some dragons think they're only legend."

"Like the silver dragon?" the witch asked him.

"Not quite, but almost."

The old one clasped her hands. "How wonderful. You see, Carol? Dragons always find me, even the rarest of them. I am the luckiest woman in Chinatown."

The beautiful woman with the deep flame stood tall in front of the old one. "This has gone far enough, Grandmother. I want the police."

"That would be a bad idea," the black dragon said mildly. "Let me take care of this."

The fire dragon knew that the black dragon—Malcolm—was the strongest being in this alley, the one he'd have to get past to stay free.

"Why are you here, black dragon?" he snarled. "In this form, summoned by these mages? Do you belong to them?"

"I protect them," Malcolm answered.

"Enslaved." The accusation sounded hollow because the fire dragon knew he'd been enslaved himself.

"I protect them by choice. Why have you come here?"

The fire dragon put his fists to his bare neck. "Harnessed. Dragged here. Did you do it?"

"Not me, but I know what it feels like to be ripped from Dragonspace, believe me. So which of you summoned him? Shaiming?"

The silent man jumped, then beamed a smile and shook his head.

"None of us did," the old woman said. "We wouldn't know how. He just showed up in the alley."

Malcolm's eyes narrowed. "Now that's very interesting."

Curiosity was a black dragon's weakness. The arrogant creatures could lose a battle because they'd stopped to investigate something trivial.

Malcolm drew close, and the fire dragon growled, feeling the need to challenge. He drew every ounce of power he had deep inside himself and willed the fire to take over.

His body heated white-hot, and he felt the triumph that came with the change. *Yes!*

The small group collectively gaped as he became living fire, a string of incandescent light that blasted back the darkness of the alley. Malcolm started for him, but the fire dragon sailed out of reach.

The fire dragon swooped and swirled around the tiny old woman then the lovely, flame-filled young woman at her side. His flame called to hers, and she stared up at him with fear and wonder in her eyes.

"What are you?" she breathed. She lifted a slim-fingered hand toward him.

The fire dragon flitted out of reach, sensing that if he touched her, she'd bind him forever.

The strange human world pulled at him, and he rose in an arrow of flame over the glittering, odd-smelling, alien city.

2

He was here.

The fire dragon—the only dragon powerful enough to help him—was in the human world.

In his prison, the Dragon Master, Sying, shivered. So close, so close.

The years of silent work, of not letting his enemies know he'd stockpiled his power bit by tiny bit, were over. Sying had managed to summon the fire dragon. And just when he'd seen the flame searing the walls beyond his prison, the fire dragon had jerked away and vanished.

At first Sying had been bewildered, but then he realized what must have happened. Another Dragon Master had intercepted the call and pulled the fire dragon to him.

Sying sagged against the wall. All the centuries of imprisonment had almost come to an end. And then his key had disappeared.

He'd thought the ancient Order of the Black Lotus had killed the only Dragon Master left twenty-five years ago.

The young Chinese woman, her husband, and her baby daughter had died, the line ended.

The Order had survived all these centuries by the power of their demon-god, their members passing secrets from generation to generation. They were thorough and could not have missed another Dragon Master, but it seemed that they had.

After so many years—failure.

Sying pressed his hands against the glasslike walls of his prison and closed his eyes.

When Carol needed to cope, she groomed herself. After she left Ming Ue's, reassured that Malcolm would keep her grandmother and Shaiming safe, she drove home, locked herself into her apartment, and started her ritual.

She washed her hair, pumiced everything that could be pumiced, trimmed and filed her nails, shaved her legs, exfoliated every inch of skin, and ended by slathering herself with body lotion. She pulled on a Chinese silk robe with red dragons that had belonged to her mother, and lounged in the expensive soft chairs in her living room with a hot cup of tea.

But her grooming ritual hadn't stopped her shakes. What she'd seen in the alley had been unreal and intense, and Carol Juan liked only the real.

She'd worked her way through Stanford, returning to San Francisco after she'd obtained her MBA to manage Ming Ue's tiny restaurant. She'd grown the business, made Ming Ue's Dim Sum a household name in the city, and opened seven more Asian-Pacific restaurants that were now booming. She was a smart, successful, well-respected businesswoman, and she'd done it all herself.

Carol knew odd things happened at Ming Ue's, especially after her grandmother had become friends with

Caleb and Lisa, and Malcolm and Saba. Ming Ue claimed that Caleb, Lisa, and Malcolm were dragons and that Saba was a powerful witch. Carol went along with it, but she never really believed—until tonight.

The red-haired man in the alley had radiated power; even she, without her grandmother's interest in the supernatural, had sensed that. She remembered his hard body against hers in the dark, the jolt he'd sent through her. He'd smelled clean and sharp, like wind and rain and dust, as though he'd come from somewhere far from San Francisco.

And then he'd turned into living flame.

Carol couldn't deny what she'd seen. She'd been to every Chinese New Year celebration since she'd been born, and watched fireworks displays grow more sophisticated each year. But she'd never seen anything like that, and she couldn't pretend that his transformation had been fireworks or special effects.

When the stream of flame had circled her, she'd smelled again the wind and dust that had clung to his human body. She'd also felt another spark jump between them before he'd torn himself away and disappeared over the city.

Malcolm had wanted to chase the string of fire, but Saba begged him not to. Saba and Malcolm had just become parents of an adorable little girl that kept them jumping, and Saba wanted to get home to her. They'd been out tonight at a nearby restaurant, the first time they'd gone out alone since little Adara had been born, which was why they'd been able to answer Ming Ue's call so quickly.

Carol picked up the stack of magazines on the table beside her and flipped through the latest issue of *San Francisco Magazine.* She always felt better looking at the big, glossy full-page ads for Ming Ue's restaurants. No photos of stereotyped rooms crammed with Chinese symbols and a plateful of pot stickers, but shots of an upscale restaurant with subtle lighting and discreet décor. The dim sum carts full of Chinese delicacies were pushed by well-dressed young women who were charming, gracious, and intelligent. They had a full menu at each restaurant as well, cooked by nationally recognized chefs.

At the bottom of the ad was the gold symbol awarded to Carol by the Chinese American business community. She was very proud of that award.

Carol tossed the magazine aside, hands still shaking. Her teacup was empty so she went back to the kitchen and brewed herself another pot of crisp oolong tea infused with orange blossom petals.

As she replaced the metal canister in the cupboard, her living room exploded with incandescent light. The tea canister crashed to the floor, spilling black leaves and white petals across her clean tiles.

A shaft of white-hot flame was rising from her living room carpet to the ceiling, then the flame condensed before her eyes into a living, naked man with fire-red hair and intense black eyes.

Carol stared at him from the kitchen door, heart racing in fear. Again something inside her reached to him, like a faint music she couldn't quite catch.

"Why did you summon me?" he demanded.

"I told you, I didn't."

"Liar." His voice grated as he came to her. "Who are you?"

"This is *my* house. Who the hell are you?"

He cocked his head, studying her with eyes both volatile and curious. He'd done that before, and she realized he reminded her of Malcolm, who often looked at people as though he were learning them, sizing them up.

She pictured the comforting shape of the phone hanging in the kitchen and her cell phone in the bedroom next to her bed. This man had grown tense around Malcolm, the only one he'd backed down from.

His hand closed around her wrist as though he'd read her thoughts. "Do not summon the black dragon again. I will kill him this time."

"Kill him? You can't kill Malcolm."

"He is no match for a fire dragon."

She fought the hysteria that welled up inside her. "What is a fire dragon? I don't even believe in dragons."

"They exist. Fire dragons are the most powerful and magical of all the great dragons."

"Now you sound like Caleb."

"What is a Caleb?"

"A golden dragon, if you believe my grandmother. He says golden dragons are the most powerful." She'd always thought the golden-haired man's declaration was some kind of running joke between himself, Malcolm, and Ming Ue.

"A golden. How many others have you enslaved? How many can you hold at one time?"

"Why do you keep saying *enslaved*? They're not slaves. They're friends."

The man scowled. "Mages and dragons are not *friends*. Mages envy the power of dragons and seek to bind their magic for their own use."

Carol tried to pull out of his grip, but he was too strong. "No one has enslaved anyone. You are the one who followed me home and broke into my house. I don't know who or what you are or why you're here, but I didn't have anything to do with it, and neither did my grandmother."

He pressed closer. "You are strong with your power, maybe even a Dragon Master. Why else would I have ended up in a magical place?"

"Magical place? You mean San Francisco?"

"The dark space marked with dragon and mage magic. You and the old woman and the man came from it."

"Ming Ue's Dim Sum is a magical place?" She wanted to laugh. "Wait until I tell my investors."

"Are they mages, too?"

Another hysterical laugh bubbled to her lips. "I hope not. I'd never convince them I could turn Grandmother's restaurant around if they were." She drew a breath. "There's someone else I could call to sort this out. Grandmother always asks for her advice—claims she's a silver dragon or something."

His fingers bit down. "A lie. There are no silver dragons—they are legend."

"In that case, you'd have nothing to worry about. *Please* let me call her."

He gave her a skeptical look. "If you can summon a silver dragon, then you are indeed powerful."

"I don't know about summoning. I was just going to ask her to come over."

He abruptly released her and stepped back. "Ask her then. I want to witness it."

Carol rubbed her wrist where he'd crushed it and thought rapidly. Lisa was not a physically strong woman, but she seemed to have a way of putting everything right. Caleb, her husband, would likely come with her, and he was, like Malcolm, a large man of reassuring bulk.

The man gazed at the marks on her wrist with a puzzled expression. "I hurt you."

"It's what happens when you grab people and push them around."

"I did not think a Dragon Master would be so fragile." He sounded stunned.

"I guess I'm happy you didn't break my arm. Stay there while I get my phone and call Lisa."

He watched her, still casually naked like he didn't notice it.

Carol didn't like men who made her want to step back—or worse, step toward them. She liked men in buttoned-up suits on the other side of a negotiation table with her in charge. She'd built up her portfolio and her power by never giving an inch and never being intimidated by sex or sexual attraction. Men she worked with might have been sexless androids for all she let herself notice them.

This man wasn't about to be a blank. He had a powerful presence, and not simply because he was tall and well sculpted.

Carol wrenched her gaze away from him long enough to scuttle into the bedroom and grab her cell phone. She punched Lisa's number as she walked back out, silently begging Lisa to pick up.

The man had moved to the window and pulled back the blind to look out over the city. Her view from Russian Hill was to be envied, her apartment taking up the top floor of a tall, elegant house that overlooked glittering city lights. The dragon-man was staring out as though the sight dismayed him.

He half turned from her, showing her a tight backside and a black tattoo of a flame stretching across his hips and up the small of his back. The sight mesmerized her until she realized that anyone passing outside could look up and see him standing naked in the window.

She slammed the blinds closed just as Lisa's voice mail answered. "Hello. I'm not here, but please leave a message."

"Lisa, it's Carol. I'm at home, and I have a problem. A *dragon* problem."

The man regarded her with suspicion as she clicked off. "With that device, you summon dragons?"

"Why do you keep talking about summoning?"

He snatched the phone from her and before her eyes crushed it down to its circuitry. Bits of black plastic rained from his fingers down to the carpet.

"Damn it, what did you do that for? I had a hundred contacts on that phone—I *need* it."

The fire dragon glanced at his blood-coated fingers in surprise. He dropped the last pieces of phone and held up his hand, staring at the scarlet liquid as though he'd never seen blood before.

"So fragile." He looked at her with stark fear in his eyes. "Why did you do this to me?"

"I didn't do anything to you."

He caught her by the shoulders, his blood seeping into the white of the robe. "Why have you made me so weak?"

"You're not weak, believe me. You're ten times stronger than I am."

He curved his warm body over hers, but his touch softened and his thumbs caressed her through the silk.

"This weakness. It makes me afraid."

Carol should be the one afraid of this very strange man who'd appeared out of nowhere. But she sensed his confusion, a warring of incredible strength with fear. He could be rough, like he'd been in the alley, or hold himself back as he did now, his touch almost gentle.

He tilted his head again to look at her, his tangle of red hair brushing his neck. His dark eyes took in everything, and deep inside them was the spark that had jumped between them before.

"You need to wash off your hand," she said.

He looked at his fingers again. The blood had started drying, but the plastic pieces had left a mess of cuts. "It is not so painful now."

"You still need to clean it."

She took him by the unhurt hand and towed him into the kitchen. She snapped on the water in the sink and stuck his bloody hand under the cold flow. "Just rub it clean—don't use soap yet."

He stared at the faucet. "What magic is this?"

"There is no magic in this house, and none in me, all right?"

"You are wrong, mage. The flame is inside you. You burn with it."

Carol wanted to retort that of course she didn't, but she kept silent. She'd felt the spark when he'd leaned against her in the alley, a stirring of something she didn't understand.

Carol had always been a realistic person, but she'd learned not to deny what her instincts told her. Her instincts told her now that he was powerful but responded to her for some reason.

"What am I supposed to call you?" she asked.

The water rushed over his fingers, dissolving and washing away the blood. "A name like your black dragon has given himself? What is it—*Malcolm*? That isn't his true name."

"It's true enough for me."

Carol snapped off the water. Most of the blood had gone, and she dabbed the water from his hands with her kitchen towel.

His grip tightened on her hands through the fabric, this time not crushing. "If you were the mage who summoned me, you'd know my true name. You'd sing it with glee."

She blinked up at him with her dark eyes as she continued to wipe off his hands with the cloth. He liked her touch, competent but gentle.

"Obviously, I don't know your name then," she said.

"Then why did I appear to you?"

"I haven't the faintest idea."

Her eyes held such innocence, dark brown and filled to the brim with fire. Her black hair spilled in a straight, sleek wave to her shoulders, as shining and beautiful as silk.

As a dragon he would have found her strange, if he'd even noticed her at all. As a human he liked the way she smelled, fresh and clean with a hint of something flowery, as though she'd been walking through a garden. Her hair was damp, and for some reason he wanted to press his lips to it.

When he'd been called to the human world long ago, he'd remained in his dragon form, and he'd not had all these thoughts and sensations. The sensations especially startled him.

He touched her cheek, enjoying the feel of her petal-smooth skin. "If a rival mage called me and I came to you instead, he will come looking for you. He might try to kill you."

Fear sparked in her eyes. "Terrific."

"I would not like to see you slain."

"I wouldn't like to see me slain either."

"If you are not my enemy, then I will keep you safe."

"Says the man with no name who broke into my house and assaulted me outside my grandmother's restaurant."

"Seth," he said.

She blinked, her lashes brushing his fingers. "Sorry?"

"Seth. You will call me that."

"The name just came to you, did it?"

"It is not my name, but the sound pleases me."

She stared at him a moment, then said it. "Seth."

The word sounded even better in her voice. He wanted to taste it, especially when her tongue poked between her teeth. He leaned down and licked her parted lips.

Another spark leapt between them, and she gasped. "Why did you do that?"

He felt exhilarated for the first time since he'd landed in this place. "Say it again."

"Why?"

"I want you to."

"No."

She tried to step away, but he cupped his fingers around her face, and she stilled.

"What do I call you?" he asked. "The old one said it." He replayed the scene in his memory. "Carol."

Her name had music, gleaming threads that shone from her as she responded. It wasn't her true name, but close, one given to her by someone very special. He caught the notes of it and wove it back around her.

Carol.

What are you doing?

Seth stopped in surprise. "You felt that?"

"Like something tight in my head? Yes."

A non-mage should not be able to feel a dragon mark. A dragon could bind a lesser being with the flick of a thought, and the lesser being would not know until it was too late. But not only did her mind keep him out, she pushed back so hard he felt his skin depress.

"What are you?" he demanded.

"What do you mean, what am I? The strange one in this room is you, not me."

He reached out to her again, but her thought threads battered him away. "I've never encountered anything like you. You have a flame worthy of a dragon."

"I suppose that's a compliment."

He studied her tall, slim body, the resilience of her, the way her flesh curved into shadow beneath the silk robe. He stepped closer, wanting to nuzzle her neck and inhale the goodness of her. The taste of her lips had warmed his skin, and now he was hard with wanting.

A dragon shouldn't want a human, but he did. She was different, he told himself, special enough that he found her interesting. Physically, he was stronger than she was—it would be an easy matter to force her down on the floor and take her.

These were human thoughts that his human body understood, alien to a dragon. This body knew what it wanted, knew how to brush her hair back from her forehead, understood the warmth in her eyes. She wanted this, too, and tried to make herself not want it.

"I'll not hurt you," he whispered.

She stilled under his touch, her skin heating where his fingers brushed it. Her lips parted, red and lush, her breath sweet.

Seth wanted this woman, and he ached with it. Was it one more way she pulled him to her, a witch wanting to be serviced by her slave?

The blood pounding in his veins didn't care. He slid his fingers along her cheek, flicking his thumb softly across her lashes.

"Are all human women as beautiful as you are?"

Her brows quirked in surprise. "Beautiful?"

"That is the word, isn't it? Beautiful, desirable—so many words for wanting."

"You learned a lot of vocabulary in one night."

"My mind seems to know the words."

When he'd flown as fire over this vast and glittering city, he'd felt the lingering pull of the woman called Carol, which had dragged him unerringly to this tall, narrow house squeezed between other tall, narrow houses. Her flame had called to his, and now he was here as though he belonged with her.

His first instinct had been to hate her, but at the same time the urge welled up in him to *protect*. Fire dragons, more territorial than most, had the instinct to curl up around what was theirs and keep it safe. They mated for life, fighting and flying side by side with their mates for centuries.

Seth hadn't yet mated, and the need to wrap himself around this woman both worried and exhilarated him.

He leaned to taste her lips again, and her eyes half closed, her body relaxing.

A thumping sound from the other side of the room made her jump. "That's Lisa."

Seth suppressed a snarl of disappointment as Carol slid out from under him and hurried toward the door.

The aura coming from the hall outside was strange and heavy and definitely not dragon. Seth went after Carol and held her back.

"That's not a silver dragon. It's not a dragon at all, or a human."

She stopped, worried. "What is it then?"

"It smells—different. Wrong."

A gruff, male voice sounded through the door. "I heard that. Open up, Carol."

Carol exhaled. "It's all right. It's Axel."

She sounded relieved, but the aura Seth sensed was bizarre, like nothing he'd ever encountered. He gestured for Carol to unfasten the locks he didn't know how to work, but he stepped in front of her when she opened the door.

A black-haired, brown-eyed man bulky with muscle stood on the threshold holding a large box. He wore a leather jacket and had his hair pulled back in a short ponytail, but he wasn't human. His aura was similar to that of an incubus, though that wasn't quite right.

"Demon," Seth growled.

"Sort of. I like the term *imp*, personally, and you can call me Axel. Can I come in? This box is heavy."

Carol opened the door wider. "Of course."

The man strode inside and gave Seth a hard look before he dropped the box on the sofa. "Lisa can't leave the kiddies right now, so she sent me. They're teething, and that's bad enough for human children, but these are dragons. Lisa says she knows the fire dragon is here, and will you please look after him until she can figure out why?"

Carol stared. "Look after him? What does she mean, *look after him*?"

"She said she's not sure what's wrong, but something's bad, and this guy's probably the key. So could you keep an eye on him while she looks into things, and she'll get back to you as soon as she can? She says he won't hurt you." He gave Seth a pointed look. "Will he?"

"Axel, I have a crucial meeting with investors tomorrow morning. I thought Lisa and Caleb would come over and take him somewhere."

Axel shrugged. Seth sent dragon threads toward him, finding an eclectic aura of white, black, and red. "What are you?"

"A friend," Axel returned. "You probably guessed Axel's not my real name, but I don't have to respond to the dragon true-name shit. The only people who can summon me are kiddies with nightmares, or Lisa when she's pissed, and Saba, because I like her. I use *Axel* because it's easier to pronounce. I think it's Norwegian, and I'm Japanese, but like I say, I embrace all cultures."

"Axel," Carol interrupted sharply. "Tell Lisa I don't have time for this. Maybe you and Malcolm could take him back to wherever he came from?"

Axel shook his head. "Hey, I'd love to help out, but I have places to go, nightmares to eat. Caleb sent along some clothes. He figured the fire dragon would wear about the same size he does."

"*Axel.*"

Axel lost his good-natured look, and Seth saw in his thought threads the fearsome beast he could become. "We need you, Carol. This is no time to be stubborn." The beast-like nature abruptly faded, and he dug into the box, pulling out a large shirt with writing on it. "Hey, I like this one. Think Caleb would mind if I borrowed it?"

While their attention was focused on the shirt, Seth quietly coalesced into fire and slid out the open doorway. He flowed down the stairwell and out the door below, finding his way out into the night.

In the sloping green space across the street, he felt the presence of the black dragon, Malcolm's mathematically sharp threads touching Seth's. Seth morphed back into solid human form in front of him, ready to fight.

"I know what it's like," Malcolm said. "You feel yourself squeezed through a hole in space, crushed into this form. You resist with all your strength, but your power deserts you. You wake up alone and weak, with a hatred in you so fierce you want to kill whatever you see. And you can't."

The black dragon knew. Malcolm might be bound to the witchling that held him, Seth realized, but he hadn't forgotten the pain of being summoned.

"What happened to you?" Seth asked him.

"Witches tore me out of Dragonspace and trapped me here to punish me. I got free, with the help of Lisa, Ming Ue, and my Saba." The harsh silver eyes softened. "Trust them."

"And you? Why should I trust you?"

"Because I've lived eight hundred years in this place and I know how to walk among humans." His gaze flicked briefly over Seth's nakedness. "I'll teach you how to be less conspicuous."

"I've been to this world before."

Malcolm's brows rose. "You have?"

"Long, long ago. But it was very different, and I remained a dragon."

The black dragon shook his head. "The world has changed. You need to learn it all over again."

"Why would you help me? A black dragon is my enemy."

"Because Lisa thinks you're important, and I've learned the hard way to listen to Lisa." Malcolm tossed a wad of fabric at Seth. "I'll teach you how to put these on, and then I'll show you what you've gotten yourself into."

3

In the morning, Carol walked into the offices of Juan Enterprises with burning eyes, an aching head, and a raw throat.

After Seth had vanished, Axel slammed out to go look for him, and Carol made herself go to bed. She'd not slept, starting at every sound, expecting Seth to manifest in her living room again. She was not sure whether she was afraid he would or whether she wanted him to. The doubt bothered her.

He never did return, and the alarm went off just as Carol finally drifted into slumber.

The office phone was ringing as Carol pushed open the glass door of her suite in a financial district high-rise. The receptionist, Francesca, a fiftysomething woman with sharp-edged red spectacles, answered the phone and held the receiver out to Carol. "It's Lisa Singleton."

Carol switched her briefcase and raincoat to one hand and took the phone in the other.

"Carol . . ." Lisa's voice came over the phone in a tone of reproach. "I really wish you had kept the fire dragon with you. Malcolm went after him, but Saba hasn't heard from him since one this morning. We need to know why he's here, and what's going on."

Lisa and Carol had been friends since childhood—both of them taken under Ming Ue's wing as babies. Carol's parents had died in a car accident Carol didn't remember, and Lisa's grandmother and Ming Ue had been best friends.

Carol and Lisa had played together, gone to school together, talked about their first boyfriends together. They'd grown apart after college, Lisa pursuing a culinary arts career while Carol had started running Ming Ue's restaurant.

They could always speak their minds to each other, but since Lisa had met Caleb she'd been different in a way Carol hadn't been able to pin down.

"If Malcolm has him, then everything's fine," Carol said. "I have a meeting in five minutes, so I'll have to talk about all this later, all right?"

"Carol, this is more important than Ming Ue's restaurants."

"You're kidding, right? *Nothing* is more important than Ming Ue's restaurants. I've got to go. I'll call you back and we'll talk dragons all you want."

She cut off Lisa's protesting *Carol* by leaning over the counter and slamming the phone onto the receiver. Francesca raised her plucked brows as Carol swung her water-spotted raincoat onto the coatrack.

"If she calls back, tell her I can't be disturbed. In fact, don't put anyone through today who wants to talk about dragons—and that includes my grandmother."

She snatched up her briefcase and started for her office, but Francesca sprang from her seat. "Wait, I meant to tell you. There's a man in your office, and he *does* want to talk about dragons."

Carol's heart skipped a beat. Seth?

She pictured his tall, raw-muscled body, his coarse red hair, his eyes like pools of night. His touch on her face had been gentle, wondering, and when he'd flicked his tongue across her lips, she'd melted in hot response.

If Axel hadn't arrived when he did, what would have happened? She'd lain awake last night wondering about that, too.

Francesca went on apologetically. "He said he was a friend of your grandmother's. He sailed on in and I haven't been able to pry him out."

"That's all right. I'll talk to him. Call me in about ten minutes, all right?"

Under Francesca's surprised look, Carol gripped her briefcase, clicked her way across the gleaming marble floor, and opened her office door.

The man inside wasn't Seth. He was an elderly Chinese man she'd known since childhood as the Junk Man—his real name was Zhen . . . something.

He ran a junk shop in one of the back alleys of Chinatown, and he and Ming Ue had been friends since the mists of time. Carol's cousin Lumi, who owned a bicycle shop, often bought bicycle parts from the Junk Man or sold parts to him.

Zhen sat upright on one of the chairs in front of Carol's desk in his usual garb of old-fashioned dark gray trousers and a Chinese jacket of the same fabric. His face was a mass of wrinkles, and a gray-white braid hung down his back.

He got to his feet as Carol walked in, his usual smile absent. "I have much to say to you, Li Mei. Please, it is very important."

"No one calls me that anymore," Carol said without closing the door. Her grandmother had given Carol the nickname *Li Mei* when she was very small, which roughly translated to *pretty little plum blossom.*

Carol hadn't minded mind being called Li Mei by her grandmother or Ming Ue's friends, but when she'd left for college, she'd adamantly insisted on Carol. She'd learned early that Americans in business were far more comfortable dealing with other Americans, and were happy when the young Chinese woman who turned up at meetings spoke with no accent and introduced herself as plain Carol.

"I would not have come, but it is too important," Zhen said, clasping his gnarled hands. "You are in very great danger."

Carol tried a smile. "I'm sorry, Zhen, but I'm expecting people this morning for a very important meeting. Come to Ming Ue's tonight and have tea. You're an old friend, and it will be nice to have you join in the celebration."

Zhen didn't change expression. He flicked his fingers, and the door behind her slammed shut.

Carol swung around and tried to open it, but the door wouldn't budge. She rattled the knob. "Francesca!"

"She can no longer hear you."

Carol turned back. Zhen looked the same as always, a faded old man with oil-stained fingers and serviceable clothing, but a faint light seemed to glow around him.

"Stop this," Carol snapped. "I've had enough for one day."

Zhen glanced at her immaculate desk, then all the pens in her pen tray suddenly shot into the air, whirled around one another, and coalesced into the pattern of a blossom.

A forgotten childhood memory tapped her, of herself very small, playing under Zhen's worktable while he and her grandmother talked. Zhen had sent a handful of hex nuts dancing through the air, making her laugh.

"How did you do that?"

She reached out and gently touched one of the pens. It quivered, then the entire arrangement collapsed back to her desk.

"These are minor tricks," Zhen said. "Trifles to amuse children. What you face, Li Mei, is far more dangerous, deadly dangerous."

"Why, because a naked man who can turn into fire is following me around? He's gone anyway. Malcolm has him."

He shook his head. "Child, you are a bigger fool than I thought you were."

"I beg your pardon?" Carol said, affronted.

"I know you think of me as only Zhen the Junk Man, while you are the grand Carol with the MBA from Stanford. Your grandmother is so proud of you for that. But what you may learn from a school is nothing to the wisdom of real life."

"I do know real life," Carol countered. "When I took over Ming Ue's, it was a struggling neighborhood restaurant. We barely had enough to make ends meet, and Shaiming and I washed dishes at a bigger restaurant to bring in extra money—on top of working all day at Ming Ue's. Don't tell me I don't know about real life."

Zhen pursed his lips. "This is not what I meant. You know much about money and profits, but you know so little about truth. Why do you think a fire dragon, a magical and mystical being, came to you, of all people?"

"I keep saying I haven't the faintest idea why he came to me, and no one seems to believe me." She gave a short laugh. "I used to think I was the only sane one while everyone else was crazy, but now I'm thinking it's the other way around."

"No, I'm afraid you are very sane. But you must stop being sane and come with us into the world of magic and dragons, where things don't fit into the neat entries in a ledger. If you don't, it might be the death of you."

"And everyone is saying dire things about danger and death."

"Because it is so."

The clock on her desk clicked to nine, and the butterflies in her stomach fluttered. "Zhen, I really, really have to go. This meeting is the most important one of my life. You wait here, and I promise I'll come back and talk to you when I'm finished. I'll have Francesca make you tea—real oolong tea. All right?"

"I cannot let you out."

Carol snatched up her desk phone and punched the button that would buzz Francesca, only to find the line dead. She glared accusingly at Zhen. "What did you do?"

"If I let you go to this meeting, Li Mei, it will be your death."

"What are you talking about? I'm the one who called the meeting. I have to be there."

"Have you ever heard of the Order of the Black Lotus?"

"No. Is it an organized crime gang?"

Carol loathed Asian organized crime, which some people still called Tongs. They terrorized small-business owners, picking on recent immigrants who were often afraid to go to the police. In some countries, the police were just as vicious as the crime gangs, and newcomers weren't yet brave enough to fight back.

Asian gangs had never bothered Ming Ue's, which Ming Ue attributed to dragon magic. They never bothered her cousin Lumi's bicycle shop or Zhen's junk shop either. Lumi had gotten involved in gangs when he was in high school, but he'd quit, and now they left him alone.

"They guard many secrets, one of which is a Dragon Master. You must not face them, or him, until you are strong enough."

"Seth said something about a Dragon Master. What the hell *is* a Dragon Master?"

"You are. It is also what you will become."

Carol sank into her fine-tooled leather desk chair.

"Zhen, if I don't show up to this meeting without a damn good reason, they're going to think I'm a total flake, a ditzy woman, a poor risk. I worked for years for this—Ming Ue's can go national on this deal."

"I'm sorry, Li Mei, but what you truly are is much, much more important than spreading your small Chinese restaurants across the United States. Your mother, she would have told you all this had she not been killed too soon."

She looked up sharply. "My mother?" She didn't like anyone talking about her mother.

"Lian Juan was a Dragon Master. The talent, it manifests from time to time in your family, and has passed from generation to generation for thousands of years. Ming Ue does not have the talent, but it manifested in your mother and also in you."

You are strong with your power, maybe even a Dragon Master, Seth had said in his dark voice.

"The talent does not always shine forth," Zhen went on. "When Caleb and Malcolm came to us last year, you showed no sign of blossoming. You had never shown any signs near Lisa or her grandmother either, and they were silver dragons. That did not surprise me as much. Silver dragons are very different." He sent her a faintly apologetic smile. "Your mother might have learned much from her."

"I wish you'd stop talking about my mother. She's been gone a long time, and I'd like her to rest in peace."

"What do you know of your mother's death?"

Carol looked away. The terrified grief of a small child had given way to the anger of a teenager, then the sadness of an adult. Her mother's and father's death had been a waste, and she'd never stopped wishing the past had been different.

"She died in a car accident with my father. I was in the backseat, but I was only three and don't remember it. I'm glad I don't remember. I survived, and Ming Ue took me in and raised me."

Zhen gave her a sad look. "No, Li Mei, this is only what you have been told. Your father, he died in the accident, but your mother was killed by the Order of the Black Lotus. They pulled Lian still alive from the car they'd caused to crash, and beat her to death. It was terrible, and it grieves me still. And now, Li Mei, the same Order hunts you."

Seth folded himself into the shadows and watched the men come out of the building Carol had gone into. Their auras were sticky, black, and unclean, and made his skin crawl.

They were demons, but a different kind of demon than he'd ever seen before. He was used to incubi, mindless soul-suckers that fed on dreams, but these were something new.

Malcolm stood next to him, a steaming paper cup of coffee in his hands. He'd explained coffee to Seth and offered him some, but Seth had taken one sniff and declined.

The night before, Malcolm had taken Seth all over this strange city of metal and stone, teaching him about it as they went. It was very different from the old villages of wood and mud in the place Malcolm called China—a different world, as he'd indicated.

When the dawn broke, the city had been drenched in rain, fog collecting around the spires of the bridges that connected the peninsula to the mainland. Malcolm had taken him to the street where he said Carol worked, and they'd arrived just as she emerged from a taxi.

Seth had watched her long, sleek legs as she'd climbed out of the car and slammed the door, the rainy street reflecting the shadow of her umbrella and blotch of yellow taxi. He'd liked watching Carol last night, with her eyes wide, her hair mussed, and her naked body warm under the silken thing.

Not long after Carol had gone inside, the demons had come out. In their black suits, umbrellas popping open against the rain, they looked no different from other men on the street, but the stink of them fouled his throat.

He and Malcolm exchanged a glance, and Malcolm nodded. Malcolm dropped his cup of coffee into a trash can, shoved his hands in the pockets of his jacket, and strode up the street in the direction the demons had gone, head bent against the rain.

Seth joined a group of people streaming into the building, and scanned the crowd for more men with demonlike auras.

The inside gleamed with glass and polished stone, and the air smelled stale and flat. A slab of granite rose from the middle of the floor, and a neatly groomed woman behind it looked Seth up and down, taking in his T-shirt, jeans, and calf-length raincoat.

"Can I help you?" she asked coolly.

"Carol Juan, where is she?"

The harsh echoes of his voice rang back to him, and the woman raised her brows. "If you mean Juan Enterprises, perhaps I could call for you. Your name?"

"Tell her that Seth has arrived."

The young woman half turned from him and spoke into a device hooked to her ear. When she turned back, her eyes held uncertainty. "The receptionist says would you please go up right away. Fifteenth floor. The elevators are behind me." She waved impatiently at them and turned to bathe someone else in her cool stare.

Malcolm had showed him elevators the night before, and he barely flinched when the metal doors closed and the box rose swiftly upward. When he reached the fifteenth floor, he strode through narrow passages until he found JUAN ENTERPRISES painted on a glass door.

"Are you Carol's friend?" a woman with red glasses asked as he entered.

"Yes, where is she?"

"In her office." The woman came around her tall desk and hurried to a smooth wooden door. "She won't answer the phone or open the door. An old man was waiting for her in there. I thought it was a family thing because he's Chinese, but she missed her meeting, and I was about to call security . . ."

"Carol is in here?" Seth put his hands to the door, sending thought threads through and encountering—nothing.

"Yes. I've been knocking, but I can't hear anything." She wrung her hands in agitation. "But if what she's talking about is important enough for her to miss her meeting, she'd never forgive me for interrupting."

"And if she is dying or dead, *I* will never forgive you."

"Dying?" she repeated in alarm. "But wouldn't the old man call for help?"

"Unless he is the one who hurt her."

"He's about eighty, looks like he couldn't pick up a paper clip without straining himself."

"Size is deceiving in a mage." Seth sent a spurt of his dragon fire into the handle and shoved.

The door fell open in a splinter of wood to reveal Carol standing behind a desk, her face ashen, and an old man sitting stiffly in a chair.

The woman rushed in. "Carol, are you all right? Should I reschedule the meeting?"

Carol jerked her attention to the woman, blinking. "Yes. Yes, do it now. Tell them I had . . . a family emergency."

"What happened?" Seth demanded.

"What are you doing here?" Carol shot him a glare filled with anger and grief. "*How* did you get here?"

"Malcolm brought me."

"Why? Francesca, stop standing there and get on the phone. Get them back as soon as you can. I'm fine."

Francesca nodded, shoved her glasses up her nose, and scuttled out of the room. Carol switched back to Seth.

"What do you want? Where did you go last night, and why did you come back?"

The Chinese man broke in excitedly, "He is a fire dragon, Li Mei. You drew him to you." He made a gesture at the outer room, and Seth felt magic flow to the phone Francesca had picked up. Francesca stared at it and started rattling buttons.

"The phone is dead," she called.

Carol muttered something and pushed past Seth and out of the office. She snatched the phone from Francesca, then turned an accusing stare to the old man who had followed her. "Stop doing that."

"You must not meet with them," the old man said in a pleading voice. "I have told you."

"If you mean the demons, I saw them come out," Seth said. "I don't know what they were, but they are something evil and dangerous."

The old man nodded. "She is not yet strong enough to fight the Order, or the Dragon Master."

Seth's eyes narrowed. "What Dragon Master? There is another?"

Carol slammed down the phone and swung to face them both. "Will you two stop talking about Dragon Masters?"

Seth sent his fiery red thought threads to her, and she jerked her focus to him. Then, as she had the night before, she pushed back.

He softened his touch, making it soothing, not intrusive. He'd never in his life touched another being with tenderness, but with Carol he thought he'd never tire of weaving his threads through hers, saying her name with his dragon music.

"Carol, do you want me to call or not?" Francesca broke in. "I'll use my cell or go downstairs."

"What? Oh, hell, it doesn't matter. Forget it. I'll have to start all over again."

Her eyes were wet. She wiped them with the heel of her hand and came around the desk. "I'm going out."

"You have another meeting at eleven," Francesca said quickly.

"Cancel it. I don't know when I'll be back."

She snatched up her coat and marched out the door. Seth followed two steps behind her, catching up to her at the elevator.

"I want to be alone," Carol said without turning around.

"No." Seth followed her in, and the doors closed behind them.

"Do you mean no, you won't leave me alone?" Carol asked, an edge to her voice.

"Not with demons hunting you."

Carol wouldn't look at him, and they rode to the ground floor in silence. She slid into her coat as they exited the building, then she walked quickly along the sidewalk, climbing a steep hill.

Seth strode next to her, his hands in his pockets.

Houses and buildings lined the road, blocking them in like cliffs. Seth looked back down the hill and saw rain-soaked streets flowing behind them to meet a gray sheet of ocean. One of the bridges rose to their right, a dark weight against the rain.

Seth liked watching Carol's body move, liked watching her hair glisten in the light rain. His thought threads still wove around her, and the fact that she'd stopped pushing them away pleased him.

He could tangle for a long time with this woman, so different from any he'd ever known. Her body was lithe and strong, and he'd seen a sweet glimpse of breasts in the gap in her blouse as they rode down the elevator.

After a time Carol turned a corner and walked across a paved flat space with a statue in the middle. A large number of people milled about despite the wet, but a quick scan of the crowd showed none of the demonlike humans Seth had seen come out of her building.

The rain slackened, a wind coming from the ocean to break the clouds. Carol walked to the middle of the square and sat down on a bench, easing her feet out of her tiny high-heeled shoes.

"I should have changed these." She wiped tears from her eyes as she spoke the matter-of-fact words.

Seth crouched in front of her, thighs stretching the fabric of his jeans. He closed his big hands over her slender foot and lifted it to his lap.

He liked the feel of her fine-boned foot under her thin stocking, her toes forming a gentle curve. He drew his thumbs along the arch and massaged her heel, then he leaned down and gently bit her ankle.

She jerked away with a gasp. "You can't do that in the middle of Union Square."

"Why not?"

She gave him a confused look. "I don't know. I'm sure there's an ordinance."

"Dragons don't have ordinances, whatever they are."

"*Please* don't talk about dragons right now."

Her black threads of rage and grief spun around him, touching him with sorrow. He released her foot and sat on the bench next to her, lacing his arm around her shoulders. She went stiff, but her body needed the comfort and began to relax against him as though she was unaware she did so.

Seth was very aware of *her* pressure on the planes of his chest. As a dragon, he'd never mated; as a human, his body seemed to know what it wanted.

He drew his thumb under Carol's chin and turned her face up to his. She gave him a startled look before he touched his lips to her open mouth.

He tasted the dark spice of her tongue and the soft cushion of her lips. He deepened the kiss, and Carol responded to him, her breath hot and sweet.

"You have to stop," she whispered.

He nipped her lower lip. "Why? Is there an ordinance?"

"I don't know. My life has just gone to hell—I don't want to think about kissing."

"Why has it gone to hell?" He stroked her neck under her hair and kissed her one more time.

"Not because of the meeting." She wiped tears from her eyes again. "Not only that. The Junk Man told me . . ."

She trailed off, her attention moving across the square to the elderly Chinese man tapping his slow way toward them.

"He told me that my mother didn't die in a car accident like I've believed all my life," she said hollowly. "He told me that this Order of the Black Lotus, whoever they are, had her taken from the car and beaten to death."

4

Carol didn't know why she felt better blurting out the horrific tale to Seth, but Seth's arm was solid and steady around her, his hand on her neck soothing.

"They always told me paramedics rescued me and called my grandmother," she went on. "But Zhen says he took me before the fire department and police got there, so this Order wouldn't know I survived."

Music played through Carol's head like faint chimes as she spoke. It brought the sound of wind and water, the chill of high mountains, the pungent smell of pine.

"I am sorry, Li Mei."

Carol raised her head to see Zhen standing on the pavement in front of her, gazing at her in sorrow.

Her anger flared. "If you've known all these years about my mother, why didn't you tell me?"

"Because it was terrible knowledge. The talent didn't manifest in you, and we thought that if it never did, you'd never have to know. Now that your talent has arisen, you need to be warned of the danger."

"Does my grandmother know?"

By Zhen's hesitation, she knew what he would say. "Ming Ue thought it best we kept how your mother died a secret."

Carol balled her fists and got to her feet. Seth rose beside her, as though he didn't want her to move an inch away from him.

"So you and my grandmother decided what I'd believe."

The old man looked even more sorrowful. "My warning is not enough. I must train you to resist the Order when they come for you. They will want to use you for . . . many things."

"It didn't help my mother, did it?"

"Your mother, she did not want her heritage. She wanted her husband and you—*a real life*, she called it. But your family is not usual, Li Mei. Your ancestors were powerful Dragon Masters, and you are, too. You can see and speak to the dragons; you can call them to you as you called this one." He stabbed his cane at Seth.

"And I keep telling you, I didn't call him. I wouldn't know how."

"The other Dragon Master summoned him," Zhen said. "When he did, the mage in you awoke and pulled the fire dragon to you instead."

"That is why I can't put my mark on her," Seth rumbled as though understanding something. "I can't mark one who enslaves me."

"Are you back to the slave thing? Even if this were all true, I wouldn't enslave anyone."

Zhen shrugged. "And yet, he belongs to you."

"He's not a stray kitten," she snapped.

Definitely not. Wherever he'd been all night with Malcolm, Seth had obviously shaved and cleaned up at some point. His sleek red hair no longer lay in an unruly tangle, though it wasn't completely tame. Damp red strands curled across his forehead and down his neck, dark now with rain.

She had a sudden and vivid image of him standing before her naked and wrapped in chains. In the vision he faced away from her, his hands manacled in front of him and a chain hanging from a collar down his back. He looked over his shoulder at her with a sinful smile and wickedness in his eyes.

Carol gasped and shoved the picture from her mind. Carol Juan *never* thought of things like that. Sex to her was done discreetly with the lights dim after a dinner in the finest of her restaurants. Mutual pleasuring, then sleep, then both of them saying over breakfast, *Oh, I have to go, need to be in the office by nine*. Perhaps there would be another encounter, perhaps not.

She had the feeling that sex with Seth would be nothing like her previous affairs, not that there had been many of those. With Seth it would be basic and raw, with sweat, noise, and the bed torn apart, then drowsing in a pool of sunshine afterward. While part of her backed rapidly from that, another part of her whispered, *Wouldn't it be nice?*

She dragged in a breath of mist-soaked air. "Let me think about one thing at a time, all right?" She turned to Zhen. "Leave me alone for a while. I need to be alone."

"But alone is what you must not be. Both you and the fire dragon must be guarded."

"Guarded against what?"

"The Dragon Master and the Order—"

His words cut off as Seth gave a strangled cry. The music in Carol's head became clanging and discordant, then Seth's body jerked as though he were a marionette on strings. Then he began to *fade*.

"No," he said hoarsely.

One moment, he was as solid as the buildings around her; the next, Carol could see rain glistening through him.

"Quickly, Li Mei, you must call him back," Zhen said in agitation. "Do not let him be taken, or he will be turned against you—he will be a weapon against us."

Carol barely heard him. Seth writhed in agony, his body growing fainter as the musical chiming untangled and tore out of Carol's head.

She had another vivid vision, this one of a dark room brushed with red light, a man with black eyes and a narrow face standing inside what looked like a column of glass. His mouth moved, but she couldn't hear what he said.

The vision snapped away as quickly as it came, rain-soaked Union Square rushing back at her. But she understood one thing—no matter what, she couldn't let Seth go to the dark place with the being that radiated evil.

She held out a shaking hand. "Seth. Stay with me."

His body was insubstantial, but Carol closed her hand around his wrist. "*Stay with me.*"

Under her touch, Seth's arm solidified. Rain gleamed through him, then suddenly it didn't, and she felt the heat of his skin. The chimes in her head grew louder but smoother, the harsh cacophony giving way to sweet music.

San Francisco ground on around them, shoppers and businessmen hurrying across the square, umbrellas firmly overhead. They talked to one another or on cell phones, not noticing Carol desperately trying to hold on to Seth near the Victory statue.

Seth closed his hands over her elbows and rested his forehead in her hair. He breathed hard, and she was shaking and sweating.

"You did it, Li Mei," Zhen crowed. "You called the fire

dragon back; you kept him true to your summoning. He belongs to you now."

The music inside Carol's head rose to a ringing crescendo, the chimes both frantic and triumphant. Seth leaned down and put his lips to her ear, his hands tightening on her arms.

"Enslaved," he whispered.

Zhen left them, tapping slowly up the hill that would take him back toward Chinatown. He'd done the duty that his ancestors had been charged with, and he should feel better, but he didn't.

Poor little Li Mei. He wanted to warn her of all the dangers, but he was compelled to go only so far. His job was to protect the Dragon Master, had been for centuries, and that meant protect her from everyone, including the fire dragon.

Ming Ue understood. She stood by him.

The fire dragon was amazing. Seth was a mixture of so many things: arrogance, curiosity, protectiveness, rage, and best, or maybe worst, the ferocious power of his dragon fire. He had as much potential for destruction as Carol did, and Zhen wondered if Seth knew it.

At the top of the hill, he turned the corner to Bush Street, heading for Chinatown, when he was surrounded by five men, one of them a hard-faced crime lord called Danny Lok.

"You warned her."

Zhen held up his hands. "I did not tell her everything. I promise."

The men were hired thugs—he knew that—who didn't care what he said.

At a nod from Lok, they grabbed Zhen by his bony shoulders and hustled him into the nearest house, where two men proceeded with his punishment. By the time the rest of them had reached Union Square and spread out, Carol and the fire dragon were nowhere to be seen.

Carol found herself in the circle of Seth's arm as they walked up the hill from Union Square. His body was scorching hot, hotter than a human's had a right to be.

"Are you well, Carol?"

"No. I have a headache, and I'm about to puke." She shuddered. "What was all that? I had this vision . . ."

"Of the imprisoned Dragon Master. He was trying to summon me, but you called my true name and pulled me back."

"I called you *Seth*—is that what you mean?"

"No." The notes in her head jangled. "My true dragon name that no one knows but me."

"We had this conversation last night. I told you I don't know it."

"Something in you does. You are singing it now."

Carol tried to suppress the music blaring in her head, but she couldn't. Some part of her psyche wanted to embrace the jingling sounds and pull them close.

"Is that what that is?"

"My true name and my dragon thoughts tangled in you." His voice was hard. "You have the power to use me as you wish."

"Which is completely ridiculous." But after everything Carol had seen last night and today, the ridiculous and the real had become one and the same.

This man is my slave. The words didn't even ring true. He watched her with the wariness of a caged predator, but at the same time his arm was strong against her back, supporting her.

"If I did enslave you, it wasn't on purpose. Go wherever you want, and I'll take a taxi home. All right?"

"It's not that simple." His dark eyes held a mixture of anger, confusion, resignation, and restlessness. "The name will bind me to you until you release me. When you sing it, I must do as you wish—fight a battle, perform labor, pleasure you—and I must do it without choice."

Carol had the swift picture of him naked in chains again, but this time, he wasn't smiling.

"Whatever you want," he said, his gaze intense. "You can make the vision in your head come true."

Whatever you want. Carol shivered. She'd always prided herself on keeping herself in tight control, and here she was envisioning erotic bondage scenes with a man who could turn himself into living fire.

Remembering their kiss wasn't good either—the salty tang of his lips, the strong delving of his tongue.

She shoved the thoughts away.

"Why isn't it simple?" she asked. "If I've enslaved you, then I'll set you free." She flicked her fingers. "There, you're free."

The chiming in her head increased, and Seth shook his head.

"My true name is wrapped in you, and your power is wrapped in me." He stepped away and gestured to the air between them. "Can you see it?"

"See what?" Carol peered where he pointed and saw nothing but gray Sutter Street in the rain. Then as her vision cleared she discerned tiny raindrops glittering in midair, clinging to gossamer threads. The threads were red, gold, and black, and stretched between him and her. When she put out her hand to brush them, she touched nothing.

"What are those?"

"Thought threads, mine tangled with yours. Only dragons and witches and mages can see them."

"How do I untangle them?" She waved her hand back

and forth through the threads, but they didn't change. "They're not really there."

"I don't know," Seth said. "I've been bound once before, and I was only released when the Dragon Master died."

"Oh." *Nice thought.* She shivered. "I'll undo it. I'll find a way."

"How will you?" Seth asked skeptically.

"I don't know how." Carol stuffed her hands in her pockets. "But I know someone who might." She started walking again, and Seth's long stride quickly caught him up to her. "When anything crazy goes on around here, Grandmother turns to Lisa. Lisa always seems to know what to do."

"The one you claim is a silver dragon."

"Grandmother claims she is. Of course, it turns out there's a lot that Grandmother hasn't told me." She clenched her fists in her pockets. "One thing at a time. We see Lisa and ask her how to get rid of these dragon thread things. Grandmother comes after that."

Carol was used to putting everything on a schedule and following it with precision. That was how things got done and money got made. In her life, event followed event in a smooth, planned succession that took her to the top, one small step at a time. That was her secret.

Seth's arrival and Zhen's revelations had blown her precisely planned life to pieces. Carol strode to the curb and hailed a taxi to take them to Lisa's house on California Street. Her legs were still wobbly, and only Seth's strong hand on her elbow kept her from falling.

Seth smelled the golden dragon long before the tall, hulking man came out of the door at the top of the stairs.

"Hello, Caleb," Carol said, hurrying up to him.

Seth's protective instinct made him want to pull her

back. This was the golden dragon's territory—his marks shimmered over every door and window.

Carol went to the warrior dragon and hugged him without fear. The golden returned the hug, then his thought threads touched the tangle of Seth's and Carol's, and his blue eyes widened.

The dragon-man lifted his hands carefully from Carol, conveying that he would not touch what Seth considered his. Seth nodded briefly, and the tension eased the slightest bit. There would be no battle done, at least not today.

"I'm sorry to drop in on you unexpectedly," Carol said, oblivious to their wordless communication.

"We are always happy to see you, Carol," Caleb boomed. He gestured her into the apartment and stood back and waited for Seth to enter.

Seth's skin tingled at the huge concentration of magic in the small space, a mixture of golden dragon and a strange power he'd never felt before. He could barely breathe under the weight of it, but Carol didn't seem to notice at all.

"Is Lisa here?" she asked, peering into the kitchen.

"No, she took Severin to the doctor."

Carol turned, concerned. "Is he all right?"

"He will be. Lisa says he has an ear infection, but it will be healed."

Caleb broke off as a very small dragon zoomed across the room at them. Its elongated body was a mixture of gold and silver, its eyes wide and blue.

It angled itself straight for Carol, but the golden dragon reached up and snatched it out of the air. "Gotcha."

The dragon shimmered and became a human baby with red-gold curls, blue eyes, and a huge smile that revealed one tooth. She popped her thumb in her mouth and regarded Seth with interest.

Carol stared at the baby, eyes wide in shock. Seth was surprised as well. "She is your offspring?" he asked.

The golden dragon's stance relaxed into one of pride. "This is Li Na, twin to my son, Severin. Is she not beautiful?"

The girl had a dirty face, tangled hair, and a sunny smile. Dragons usually hid their offspring until they were able to hunt for themselves and fight off enemies—a dragon never showed his child to another dragon. The dragons in human form were violating rules that had been steeped in dragon consciousness for eons.

"The black dragon, Malcolm, also has offspring," Seth said. He took off his coat and draped it over the back of a chair. "Is that why you two were snatched into the human world—to mate?"

Caleb grinned. "I wish. I was forced here by witches to protect the silver dragon. Witches also trapped Malcolm. Finding our mates was a fortunate happenstance. Very fortunate."

Seth looked at Carol. "Is that what you want? Offspring?"

Carol pulled her astonished gaze from small Li Na. "What?"

"Do you want to mate with me? When I kissed you in the square, you seemed to want to."

Her face turned bright red. "*Seth.*"

Caleb chuckled. "Humans are embarrassed about mating. I don't know why. I enjoy it. It's much better than dragon mating." He looked Seth up and down with a blue gaze that pretended to be more vacant than it really was. Goldens had nowhere near the intelligence of black dragons, but they were cunning, and none was better at fighting and battle strategy. "Are you really a fire dragon? I never believed they existed."

"We exist. It's silver dragons that don't exist."

A smile split Caleb's face. "Yes, they do, and one is coming now. Don't tell me you can't feel that."

Something incredible was making its way up the stairs. Wild music like nothing Seth had ever heard before burst through his mind like harsh wind and silver laughter, a cross between a fierce storm and soft summer rain.

Carol went rigid as a slender human woman came through the door with a child in one arm and a shoulder bag slung over the other. The woman had dark red hair and brown eyes of almost the same shade as Carol's. Her smile was at once full of wisdom and innocent wonder. The whirlwind of sound continued, coating the air and winding its way first around Seth, then Carol.

"Lisa," Caleb boomed. He enfolded the woman in a hug, and she transferred the baby from her arm to his as he did so. "Carol has arrived with the fire dragon."

"I can see that."

Lisa dumped the heavy bag on the red sofa and turned to study Seth. "A fire dragon. Fascinating."

"Lisa," Carol said in a strangled voice.

Lisa turned to her, arms out, and they embraced. Humans liked to do that, he'd noticed, wrap their arms around each other and hold each other close.

"It happened, then," Lisa said, sounding almost sad.

"*What* happened? I've known you since we were babies, Lisa, but you look—different—somehow."

"You're seeing the silver dragon. I'm sorry, Carol. I know this is hardest on you."

The presence of the silver dragon was daunting, almost terrifying, although Lisa looked like any other innocuous human in the city outside. Seth sensed the silver of her thought threads, the incredible power that rippled through her. He also glimpsed silver dragon magic in the baby daughter, a faint copy of her mother's power.

Lisa faced Seth, hands on hips. "I've always wanted to

see a fire dragon. At least, the silver dragon in me has. I didn't even believe in dragons until a couple of years ago, when I found Caleb stuck in my spare bedroom."

"The first dragon you met was a golden?" Seth said, trying to cover his nervousness. "Poor woman."

Caleb scowled. "Careful. This is my territory."

"It's *my* territory, too," Lisa broke in. "Cease fire, Caleb. This is too important."

Instead of being contrite, Caleb chuckled and pressed a kiss to his wife's hair. "Don't worry, my love. We won't do battle yet." He eyed Seth. "I wouldn't mind a good fight, though, to see what you can do."

"You'd regret it, golden boy."

"Maybe, maybe not."

Carol had wandered to a window that overlooked a sea of tall houses and a wide smudge of green trees beyond that. Her thoughts were snarled and unhappy, the music of them doleful.

Seth moved to her and couldn't stop himself running his fingers through her sleek hair, liking the warm, silken sensation. The bond between them was tighter since she'd dragged him back from the other Dragon Master, and her sorrow tugged at him, dimming his own brightness.

"Carol is afraid," he said, trying to weave comfort through the threads. "She does not understand what she is, or what she has to do. She came here for your help."

Lisa looked Carol up and down. "I know she did. But in this case, I don't know if I can."

5

Seth's hand was warm and soothing. Carol had already noticed how much he liked to touch her hair, lifting strands to rub between his fingers.

It was as though he worked her through his senses one by one: studying her with dark eyes, cocking his head to listen to her voice. Then touching her, leaning to put his nose to her skin, moving his tongue to taste her. She had no idea how to respond, or even if she should.

Carol had known love most of her life—Ming Ue was a kindhearted woman, and her quiet cousin Shaiming had taught her to tie her shoes and ride a bicycle and other fatherly things. But she'd never been close to anyone, never let herself get close. She'd studied hard in school, graduated at the top of her class, then came back to San Francisco and worked ten hours a day to make ends meet.

There hadn't been time to get close to anyone, and no man had ever looked at her the way Seth did now, seeing Carol the woman, not Carol the academic or Carol the workaholic. Seth didn't care about her top honors or her MBA or the fact that she'd made her family prosperous. He looked at *her*, and she had a hard time understanding how to react.

She turned her head so her hair slid from Seth's grasp. He let go but not with any kind of submissiveness.

"I can see it in you," Lisa said. She cocked her head and looked Carol over, very dragonlike. "The power is amazing. No wonder you're disoriented."

"None of this surprises you," Carol said a little resentfully.

"I knew you had the potential for the Dragon Master talent, but it's come out far greater than I ever imagined it would."

"Did my grandmother tell you? And why didn't she bother to tell me?"

Lisa's voice gentled. "Ming Ue explained everything after I became the silver dragon. She said you would be safer not knowing if you never manifested. I agreed with her."

"So you kept it from me? Your best friend?"

"Answer me honestly. Would you have believed me?"

Carol started to snap that of course she'd have appreciated the truth, but stopped. No, she wouldn't have believed it.

Until yesterday Carol had never believed in anything she couldn't see or touch, and certainly not dragons or magic. She'd tolerated her grandmother's stories over the years and ignored the evidence of her own eyes.

Carol had always reached for the real, burying herself in school and work to forget that she'd lost those closest to her in a cruel accident. Dragons and magic hadn't saved them.

"It's irrelevant now," she said in a hard voice. "We just have to fix the problem. Seth says I can't set him free simply by telling him to go. Is he right?"

Behind her, Seth put his hands on her shoulders, his

touch hot through her jacket. His music swirled through her head, the chimes almost sweet.

"He's right," Lisa answered. "You can't stop thinking his name?"

The music swelled in response, and Seth's fingers tightened.

"Every time I try, the music gets more intense," Carol said.

"That's the way of it. But I've removed dragon bindings before—don't worry. Look into my eyes, Carol, and don't look away, no matter what happens."

"No matter how weird or scary," Caleb put in from across the room. He cradled a baby on each arm, all three watching with interest.

"Thanks, Caleb," Carol said shakily.

"I meant that you should trust Lisa."

Seth growled, his touch growing heavier, more possessive. "Will it hurt her?"

Lisa hesitated in a way Carol didn't like. "It shouldn't."

"I don't care if you are the silver dragon," Seth rumbled. "If you hurt her, I'll stop you."

"I'll do my best not to. I promise."

"Just do it, Lisa," Carol said. "We'll talk about how scary it will be afterward."

Lisa gave her a tight smile at the variation of the phrase Carol has used all her life—*Let's do it first and talk about how hard it will be later.*

Lisa laid her palm against Carol's cheek. Her fingers touched Carol's temples, her thumb curving against her cheekbone.

Carol looked into Lisa's eyes as requested and bit back a cry. Lisa's irises swirled with silver that spun into a vortex with dark pools in the center. Carol wanted to follow the spiral down, down, to whatever waited there.

Something inside her snarled, resisting the pull. At the same time she heard of cacophony of wind chimes, the metallic ones in Lisa's living room combining with those ringing and spinning inside her own head.

A light, merry voice overlaid Lisa's own, as though two Lisas spoke at the same time. *It is difficult.*

Carol felt a sharp tug on her scalp as though something jerked it forward. The skin on her face moved under Lisa's fingers, followed by sudden pain.

Over the din of the warring chimes, she heard Caleb growl and the soft mewling of the babies. Fire pierced Carol's eyes like a thousand stabbing pins, and she felt cool droplets of blood slide down her face. The tangled threads in her mind ripped apart like muscle from bone.

Carol screamed. Behind her, Seth snarled, then his hands jerked from her shoulders, and she heard him hit the wall with a sickening crunch.

Rage blurred her vision. She flung Lisa's touch from her face and backhanded her across the jaw.

"Leave him alone," she shouted, her voice dark. "He is mine."

Lisa stared at Carol in shock. Caleb deposited his children on the sofa and came at Carol, his eyes glittering with mindless fury.

Air whooshed, and Seth became a string of incandescent fire, encircling Carol in a wall of flame.

Caleb kept coming, the good-natured man suddenly a snarling warrior. Lisa grabbed him. "No."

"She hurt you."

"Don't touch her," Lisa said rapidly. "She's a Dragon Master. She can hurt you far worse that you can her, and she can bind you. Let her be."

Seth's opaque flame blurred Caleb and Lisa, but Carol smelled their fear. A very small part of her rejoiced at it.

The rest of her was shocked. "Lisa, I'm so sorry. I'd never hurt you, or Caleb."

"Maybe not on purpose," Lisa said. "I can't remove the mark. I can't reach the part of you that's holding Seth without hurting you and possibly killing him. Or you. I don't know why."

Seth's flame flared and then he resolved into his human form. He stood right in front of Carol, which gave her a nice view of his naked buttocks and the flame tattoo across his hips.

"You will not touch her," he said fiercely.

"I guess I won't. Are you all right, Carol?"

Carol wiped her eyes, surprised no blood came away on her fingers. The pounding in her skull had receded to a faint headache, and she badly needed a glass of water.

"I think so."

"What happened, exactly?" Caleb demanded. He moved back to the sofa and picked up his daughter. Severin looked up from the couch with wide blue eyes, fingers in his mouth. "You can't be stronger than Lisa. No one is stronger than Lisa."

"Apparently, Dragon Masters are," Lisa said, rubbing her face where Carol had hit her.

Carol's body throbbed in a cross between pain and anger, but a distracted part of her couldn't pull her attention from Seth. Neither Caleb nor Lisa seemed surprised by or even seemed to notice his nudity, but Carol's gaze was riveted to Seth, and something in her ached.

He is yours, a voice whispered. *The power of a fire dragon, to do with as you please.*

She had another vision, this one of Seth over her in the dark, his face twisted in passion. Her passion answered back.

As though he sensed her thoughts, Seth turned to her. His front was as nice as his back, hard pectorals dusted with red-gold hair, his skin tanned evenly as though he spent all day in the sun.

Which of course he didn't. He was a dragon; he'd never been human before last night. She saw the wanting in his eyes as he gazed at her and felt the answering wanting in herself. His music wound around her again, its touch as delicate as a lover's.

Behind Seth, Caleb still sounded worried. "What is a Dragon Master exactly? How can one have power over the silver dragon?"

"I don't know," Lisa said. "The silver dragon has never encountered a Dragon Master. Ming Ue said she thought the potential might have skipped Carol, so the silver dragon didn't pay much attention. That, and I was always busy with other problems," she finished with emphasis.

Carol heard her friends in the background but dimly. Ignoring them, Seth touched Carol's cheek, his fingers finding the hurt left by Lisa's fingers.

"You're bruised."

"I'll be all right."

Seth continued to stroke her face, and she had to force herself not to melt into him. She rarely let herself react to men, and truthfully, she'd not found one worth much reaction. But her body swayed to Seth's as he bent his head and brushed his lips over hers.

She again felt a searing bite, as though a touch of his fire rippled through her body. Music tingled in her head, and their thought threads smoothed and became tight once more.

"I want to show you what I am," Seth said. "Will you let me?"

Suddenly, Carol wanted to know very much. She wanted to know everything about him.

She touched his face. "Yes. Please."

Seth looked at Lisa. "You have a way here. I feel it." He

pointed to the apartment's second bedroom, which Carol knew held the cribs for Severin and Li Na.

Lisa's brows went up. "Are you sure?"

"I will protect her," Seth said. "I am compelled to, but I would anyway."

"This might not be wise."

Seth balled his hands, which did wonderful things to his biceps. Carol couldn't resist running her fingers up and down his arms, tracing every corded muscle.

Carol felt Lisa's gaze on her, and she clasped Seth's hand protectively. "I have no idea what you two are talking about, but if Seth wants to go in there—Lisa, please let him."

Lisa sighed. "All right. But while you're there, Carol, don't stray one foot from his side. It's a dangerous place already, and it might be doubly dangerous for you." She bit her lip. "Maybe I should go with you."

"No," Seth and Caleb said at the same time.

Lisa glanced at Caleb, who scowled as he cradled Li Na. The baby watched with intelligent eyes as though she followed every nuance of the conversation.

"I'll stay," Lisa conceded. "But if you need me, call me. Promise?"

Seth didn't answer, his gaze intent on the door. Carol couldn't imagine what danger lurked in the babies' bedroom aside from stray toys, but she nodded at Lisa.

Lisa walked to the bedroom door and opened it. Caleb stood like a sentinel by the sofa, Li Na securely in his arms, Severin peeking around his legs.

Carol caught a glimpse of the bedroom Lisa had redecorated for the children in bright hues of blue, red, and yellow, the two cribs perpendicular to each other against two walls.

Lisa raised her hand and drew her finger down the open doorway. Silver magic tingled and jangled, and the hairs on the back of Carol's neck stood up.

The air rent like fabric. Under Lisa's finger, the black tear grew, revealing darkness beyond and a wind so cold it took Carol's breath away. Her hair danced in the sudden breeze, and the wind chimes in the living room spun and clanged.

Seth grasped Carol's hand and strode to the door, his eyes widening into voids as black as the nothing beyond the tear. His voice swam in her head. *Don't let go of me.*

She was about to ask why when she found herself falling into blackness at sudden sharp speed. Her insides twisted, and she opened her mouth to scream.

Something solid formed around her and under her, and then she felt herself being lifted straight into a cold, starry sky. She saw scales and wings and a flash of bright red-orange, as the fire dragon arrowed himself across a rocky plain.

"Seth?" she gasped.

Don't let go.

Good advice. Carol closed her hands around the huge talon in front of her and held on tight.

Flying was freedom. Seth spread his wide wings and let the updraft catch him, reveling in the feel of the thermals.

He smelled the dry air of his home, and inhaled, letting the glory of it fill his lungs. Mountains rose above mountains, the sky stretched to eternity, and there wasn't another soul in sight.

He barely felt Carol's grip on him, but the flame of her presence was unmistakable. She still bound him with his name, but here that didn't seem to matter as much. He wanted to fly, and he could protect her only if she flew with him.

Her rapid heartbeat came to him through the thought threads and her fear. He swooped low over a green forest and up against vast cliffs, wanting to show her the beauty of this place.

She bleated an expletive.

Are you well, Carol?

Dragons didn't emit human-speak from their mouths, but he could project his thoughts to her through their bond.

"No," she shouted. "I'm terrified. Where are you taking me?"

Home.

"Where's that? Is it far?"

I will show you.

Seth slid through Dragonspace, finding folds in the atmosphere that took him quickly across the vast world. His heart throbbed with joy when he saw the empty spaces of his own territory, the rock-strewn plains, the red cliffs soaring thousands of feet above it.

There was water here, hidden deep underground, bubbling to the surface in springs only he knew of. His cave was tucked high in the cliff's surface, the opening almost invisible from the ground. He felt his lair call to him, and heard the singing of the stones inside.

Seth landed in the shadow of the cliff and gently set Carol on the ground.

She brushed off her skirt and looked around, staying near his body. "This is where you live? No wonder you're uncomfortable in San Francisco."

It's cold there.

"Not always. In the summer, the days can be warm and soft, downright hot sometimes." She scanned the rolling stillness of the desert. "It's nothing like here, though."

No.

Carol leaned her hands on Seth's nose. "I don't like it any more than you do. I'll do everything I can to fix this."

I think you can't while the other Dragon Master exists.

The power in you didn't call me to save me from bondage to him. You wanted the power of the fire dragon.

"For what?"

To kill the other Dragon Master, perhaps. I don't know.

She absently stroked his nose. "I've always been so sure of myself, so in control, and now something strange is inside me, doing what it wants. It's terrifying."

Seth wove his music around her. *You do not need to be afraid.*

"Why not? My life is falling apart, and I'm standing in a world that can't exist, talking to a dragon. If Zhen is right, then this Order that the other Dragon Master is involved in killed my mother and won't be happy that I survived."

I will not let anything hurt you. You have bound me, and that means I protect you.

"Against your will."

Seth drew back so he could look down at her. She was so small to him—he could crush her without thinking about it, but he knew he never would. *I would want to protect you whether you compelled me to or not.*

"I don't want you to have to protect me. Life was so easy until yesterday. All I had to do was prepare for an investors' meeting."

If you had gone to that meeting, you would have had to battle for your life. The demons were ready to take you.

"If you and Zhen are right about that, why didn't they break down my office door to get to me? They just left."

Perhaps they were sent to see how strong you are. The demons would take you if they could, but if you proved stronger and defeated them, well, they are only demons. Dispensable.

"You think they'll try again, then."

They will try until they get what they want. I've had dealings with this Order before. The old man said he would train you to use your mage powers. I think you must believe him.

"This is all so wrong. I can barely take in what Zhen told me about my mother. I didn't just lose her—she was taken away from me."

Tears wet her eyes. Seth nuzzled her, and she leaned against him as though liking his warmth.

Seth had never wanted to be touched before. Only mates touched. He'd not begun the hunt for his mate, but now his dragon self was reacting as though he'd already found her.

But Carol was human and had enslaved him, and Seth couldn't trust his instincts.

Carol ran her hands over his shoulder. "I thought dragons would be cold and scaly, but you're so warm. You're a beautiful dragon."

Am I?

Carol stroked him slowly. "You're not really red. You're iridescent. I can't decide if you're yellow or orange or red or black."

All those. He nudged her again, realizing there was some compensation when he was stuck in the human world—he could touch Carol as much as he wished.

She asked, "So you were here minding your own business, when suddenly you were yanked away to the alley behind Ming Ue's?"

He twined his frustration through their thought threads. *I was angry. So angry.*

"No wonder you accosted me in the alley."

Seth closed his eyes, narrowing his focus to her scent and the warmth of her hand. *Your world is too crowded for me, especially now. I am hemmed in on all sides and feel powerless.*

"What do you mean, *especially now*?"

I was there before, a long time ago. I don't know how long, perhaps a few thousand years of your time. A Dragon

Master summoned me and several other dragons. We had to do his bidding, and men of the Order of the Black Lotus were there, too. The Order killed him.

He felt her blanch. "And that's how you were freed?"

Yes.

"So you could just let the Order kill me, too."

Seth's dragon brain processed this, wondering why he hadn't simply stood back and let her be taken. But he'd rushed into her building when he'd seen the demons, his first instinct to protect her.

That could be part of the binding—he'd tried to protect the first Dragon Master who'd called him, too. But he hadn't been human then, hadn't grieved for him.

I'll not let them hurt you, he promised.

"Why is the Order so down on Dragon Masters anyway?" she asked. "What did a Dragon Master do to them?"

Nothing. They want power and will get rid of anyone who stands in their way. The Dragon Master killed their god, and they punished him.

"Killed their god? How do you kill a god?"

He was a demon-god. I don't know how the Dragon Master did it, or if he banished it instead of killing it. The Dragon Master used my power and that of the other dragons to help him, but I remember little of it.

Everything had been a blur of fire and pain. When he'd awoken from darkness, Seth had been free and back in Dragonspace. He never learned what had happened to the other dragons.

"If that was a few thousand years ago, why is the Order still around, and why are they killing Dragon Masters now?"

I don't know, Seth said unhappily. Something was very wrong, and it annoyed him that he didn't understand what.

Something disturbed the energy at the boundaries of his territory. Seth raised his head, testing the wind. He scanned with his dragon thoughts while Carol watched, worried, until he brushed against a cold and ancient mind.

"What is it?" Carol asked.

Black dragon. Seth slid the words through Carol's head then snatched her up and launched himself into the clear, dry air.

Malcolm waited one wingspan outside Seth's territory, stopping just short of violation. The black dragon was huge and ancient, three thousand years old at least. His wingspan was twice that of Seth's, but Seth knew he could outfly him. A fire dragon didn't need wingspan to be fast.

I tracked the demons to their source, Malcolm said without greeting them. *As I thought, they are incubi, but not quite. I'd guess from what they did and how they spoke that they were bred from incubi and demons from deeper hells, ones with intelligence.*

Smart incubi, Seth finished. That wasn't good. *Where are they now?*

A warehouse south of the city.

Did you follow them in?

Malcolm snorted. *By myself in human form with no backup? I went to Lisa's to report. She suggested I find you and bring you back, and we investigate together. We dragons, I mean. We'll pick up Axel and my Saba on the way.*

Every time Malcolm said *my Saba,* his voice went soft, and gentle purple threads shot through his aura. His Saba, his mate.

Carol broke in. "I take it you aren't including me in this expedition?"

You'd be a risk, Malcolm said. *We know nothing about your power and would have to spend too much time protecting you.*

"I'd be insulted if I didn't partly agree," Carol said.

"Where am I supposed to twiddle my thumbs while you're out finding these smart demons?"

At Lisa's, Malcolm answered. *Her house has the strongest protective magic in the city. Anywhere, for that matter.*

"Fine." It wasn't fine, Seth could tell. "But don't you dare finish and go out for pizza without telling me. I don't want it to be midnight before someone looks around and says, 'Oh, did anybody call Carol?' "

We'd more likely go out for dim sum, Malcolm said, and Seth realized in surprise that he was joking. A black dragon who knew how to joke—would wonders never cease?

Malcolm led the way back through Dragonspace, and Seth slowed his own slipstreaming so he wouldn't leave Malcolm in the dust. He held Carol securely against him, feeling the bond between them strengthen with every mile.

They approached the rocky ledge, the strange pull of the human world compelling Seth toward the door set into the cliff. Malcolm went through first. A bright light surrounded him and changed his dragon shape to human male, his dragon essence shrinking and warping into a black tattoo that folded around his bicep.

Seth felt his own body compressing, a sensation he already hated. The first time it had happened, the pain had been horrific, and he'd fought like a mad thing. This time, his flesh adapted more quickly, his dragon self sliding into the human pattern it now knew. His dragon essence seared into the tattoo across his lower back, then the pain was gone.

He stepped through the door with Carol in his arms and found himself in a strange dark place that looked nothing like Lisa's apartment.

6

Carol slid to her feet. "Where are we? What happened?"

Behind Seth, the way to Dragonspace snicked shut. They stood alone in a huge room that was bone-chilling cold. Rafters extended toward a high roof that was lost in darkness, and a faint reddish glow came from the right. Other than that, the place was empty.

"Malcolm?" Carol whispered.

Seth moved close to her. The weight of the black dragon's thoughts had vanished along with the heat of Dragonspace. "He's not here."

"I know this place."

Seth knew with icy certainty that he did, too. He recognized the red glow, the cold, the fear. "Do you?"

"I don't mean I've ever been here before. When you were called away from me in Union Square, I saw this. Red and black, with something horrible in the middle of it. Like a man behind an opaque bubble, but it wasn't a man—at least I don't think so."

"I saw it, too."

Seth started forward cautiously, keeping Carol's hand in his. The floor was freezing to his bare feet, and his breath fogged in the air.

"Is this a warehouse?" he asked. "The place Malcolm spoke of?"

"This would be one. An empty one. The red light is from an emergency exit sign over there."

She pointed. Seth noted the glow from the words and the red bulb that spilled down into the darkness. A very ordinary, mechanical, human thing, but it didn't seem quite right.

"We should leave," he said.

"I couldn't agree more. Though how I'm going to find a taxi in the warehouse district with a naked man, I don't know." She sighed. "Maybe someone left behind some work clothes or something."

She released his hand and began walking deeper into the shadow.

As though she'd sprung a trap, Seth felt the sudden weight of evil swirling out of the dark. "Carol, no."

She turned back just as the shadows lit up with dancing red light. Five incubi, including the two that had gone into Carol's office, appeared out of nowhere, guarding a glasslike column in which a man floated.

Seth couldn't see much of the man, who rippled and shimmered as though he were under deep, oily water. But he felt him. The being's aura was thick and black, threads crawling along the underside of the glass and trickling out to encircle each of the incubi.

"That's what I saw," Carol whispered.

A wave of darkness came from the glass, pushing past the incubi straight for Carol. At the same time Seth heard the music of his true name turn to a disharmonic snarl.

Carol pulled back at Seth's name, and he suddenly felt himself being ripped in two.

"Carol," he rasped.

Carol tried to untangle herself from his name, fighting the threads, but she only succeeded in ripping him more.

Seth's tattoo seared, sparking like the fire it represented. Drawing the last of his strength, Seth grabbed Carol and wrapped his arms around her. "Hold on."

"What are you—?"

Carol's startled words cut off as Seth became flame, his human body meeting the fire that lifted from his back. He surrounded and bound Carol with it and shot off with her high into the warehouse, seeking the open window at the top.

Seth sailed hard and fast across the sky that had become inexplicably dark during their absence, angling across the glittering city to the place Carol lived.

The street was deserted, the house dark as he shot in through the open front door of the house on Russian Hill. He flew up the twisting stairwell to the top, then unwound from Carol and flowed into his human self again.

Carol leaned against the door frame, breathing hard. "That was—different. How did that work?"

Seth didn't care *how* it worked; he only cared that it *had* worked. He braced his hand on the wall next to her and leaned down to kiss her.

Carol went rigid, then her lips softened to his, and she wound her hands around his neck. He flattened himself against her, feeling every inch of her body with his.

Something white-hot jumped from his mouth to hers. It flashed back through his body, and Carol jerked away.

"What was that?" she asked, eyes wide. "That happened before."

"I've never been human before. I'm learning this, too."

She slid out from under him, and his body was suddenly cold without her against him. "We need to get inside before one of my neighbors comes out and sees me kissing a naked man." She patted her jacket in dismay. "Except my keys are at Lisa's. I left my coat and purse there."

Seth softly touched the locks. He sent a tiny trickle of dragon fire through them, and they clicked open.

Carol scuttled inside and pulled him in after her. "Nice trick. Can all dragons do that?"

"I don't know. I haven't asked them."

She shut the door and did up the locks, then tiredly flicked a switch that lit up the room.

"So why is it night now when we only left Lisa's at ten in the morning?" she asked. "We weren't in your place that long—were we?"

Seth closed the curtains over the window across the room. "Time moves differently in Dragonspace. It was a bright afternoon when I was dragged out of it, and I landed in the alley in the middle of the night."

Carol folded her arms, which pushed her breasts into a curved shelf. "So it could be a different day?" She looked at blue numbers on a machine opposite her sofa. "No, same day. We need to tell Lisa what happened to us, why we didn't come through with Malcolm."

At the moment Seth didn't care about Malcolm, or the silver dragon, or what they'd seen. Carol was beautiful watching him with her eyes the color of the coffee Malcolm had drunk that morning. Her skin was creamy with a tinge of olive, a fine contrast to the black hair that swept back from her forehead.

He went to her and touched his fingertips to her lips, which parted, her eyes darkening. Seth brushed her skin bared by the top buttons of her blouse and found it incredibly smooth. He let his hand slide down and around to her backside, liking how the full curve fit into his palm.

"Really should call Lisa," she rasped.

Seth ran his hand up her torso and along her chin, releasing her with reluctance. "Call her, then."

Carol made for the phone in the kitchen, rubbing her arms as she walked. As she punched numbers, Seth couldn't stop himself coming up behind her and sliding his hands to her hips.

He heard Lisa's voice through the device. "Carol, are you all right?"

Carol began speaking rapidly, explaining to Lisa what had happened.

"Malcolm told us about the warehouse," Lisa said. "You stay put while he, Caleb, and I check it out." She hesitated. "I don't like that this being, whoever he is, could call you through a door of his own, canceling out mine. No one should be able to do that."

Carol didn't answer, her eyes going remote as though she'd realized something. Seth kissed her cheek, but Carol didn't pay any attention.

"Carol, are you still there?" Lisa asked.

Carol jumped. "Yes, sorry. Be careful, Lisa. Those incubi or whatever they are looked dangerous."

Lisa's laugh sounded like silver chimes. "They should be careful of *me.* And Malcolm and Caleb. Trust me, Carol, we've done this before. Don't go anywhere, and tell Seth to stay with you. I don't want you unprotected."

Seth was busy biting Carol's earlobe. "I don't think he wants to go anywhere."

"I didn't think he would." Lisa sounded amused. "I'll call you later and tell you about it. *Stay put.*"

"Fine by me," Carol said, and clicked the phone off.

She went still again, staring off into space as she held the phone absently in her fingers. Seth nipped the earlobe a little harder, and Carol started and looked around.

Seth stroked her cheek. "Something troubles you."

Carol's dark eyes held fear and confusion. "Lisa said she didn't like that whoever that was could pull us to the warehouse and override her door like that."

"I heard her. I don't like it either."

"Except . . ." She gnawed her lip, then looked up at him, the fear in her eyes deepening. "I don't think he overrode the door, Seth. *I* did."

Seth's dark gaze was enigmatic as he studied her. Carol's body still flushed from his hands on her skin and his mouth on her earlobe. She'd never had a lover want her so *thoroughly*, a man who wanted to touch, lick, and nip every part of her.

The fact that he wanted her was almost as unnerving as discovering she could bind dragons and open doors from an alien world to her own.

And yet, it felt natural in an odd sort of way, as though she'd always known how to do these things. She felt like someone picking up a musical instrument for the first time and discovering she was a virtuoso. The talent had to be nurtured and developed, but it had always been there, biding its time.

Carol thought of the evil she'd sensed inside the rippling column, the awful power that had snaked out to strike them. Seth had carried them swiftly to safety, but Lisa and her friends were walking right into danger.

"I can't let them face that alone," she said.

Seth let go of her and straightened to his full height, his strong, tall body like a reassuring wall. "If she is truly a silver dragon, she is the most powerful dragon in the universe. So the legends go."

"But this evil being that's been summoning you is a Dragon *Master*, isn't he? Isn't it logical that all dragons are in danger of him? If he can figure out your true name, can he do that to Caleb and Malcolm, too? Maybe Lisa as well?"

"If he harnesses the warrior strength of a golden dragon,

or the intellectual power of a black, he will be strong indeed."

"Plus he could hurt them."

Seth nodded, his black eyes intense. "The power of the true name is painful. The worst pain there is."

"Do you think you can find that warehouse again?"

"Yes."

He came to her, his naked body solid with muscle, ready to wrap her in his arms and take off again. She put up her hands to stave him off. "I think we should drive this time."

Seth cupped her face in his hands, and once more his lips brushed fire into her. He smiled slightly. "If you insist."

They drove south of the city in Carol's dark BMW. Seth, dressed now in more of the clothes Axel had brought last night, sat uncomfortably in the soft leather seat beside her.

The car was nothing short of luxurious. Carol had bought it for herself as a reward when she made her first million. She had much of that million still salted away in growing retirement funds for Ming Ue and Shaiming as well as a cushion for the restaurants.

Seth, she realized, didn't give a damn about money or cushy cars. She understood better his impatience and anger at being tied down in this world now that she'd seen the wild beauty he'd left behind in Dragonspace. He could fly across that world in the blink of an eye—no doubt he thought her method of transportation slow and dull.

Maybe when she figured out what was going on and things got back to normal, she would have Seth take her flying in Dragonspace again. Carol had been born and bred in San Francisco's Chinatown, but something about the wild beauty of Seth's home called to her. She longed to soar again over broad mountains and rocky deserts, breathing in the fresh, sharp wind of emptiness.

Seth couldn't tell her exactly how to get to the warehouse, because he'd flown away fast. He could only point and say, "That way," and Carol had to navigate streets to orient them in the appropriate direction.

After a long time of driving and backtracking, Seth finally indicated a huge building sitting in the middle of an unused portion of docks. Carol pulled up alongside a smaller car that belonged to Saba, but her friends were nowhere in sight.

Seth wouldn't let her out of the car until he'd come around and opened her door for her. Carol shivered as she emerged and studied the deserted parking lot. Rusted cranes towered beyond the warehouse, used in their day to load containers onto waiting cargo ships. A container, likely empty, still hung from chains on one of them, drifting in the breeze like a hanged man.

The huge metal doors to the truck bays were closed, a glass door that led to what had been an office broken long ago. Black graffiti covered the outside walls, blotting out most of the original color of the brick.

Seth found another door tucked in a narrow passage between buildings. The metal door was ajar, the padlock rusted through.

Before they could open it, Malcolm yanked it back from the inside and came striding out. His silver eyes gleamed eerily in the darkness, the breeze stirring his long hair.

"They're gone," he said.

Carol craned her head to look past him but saw nothing in the inky darkness. No shimmering column, no incubi, no red light. Carol couldn't even see the exit sign, which, come to think of it, couldn't have been lit, because no electricity flowed in this building. It was dark, silent, and deathly cold.

"What happened?" Carol asked him.

"Nothing happened. We arrived, but the Dragon Master had gone."

"That was him, then, inside that column thing?"

Malcolm nodded. "They must have moved him."

"Who? The incubi? Or the Order of the Black Lotus?"

Malcolm looked from Seth to Carol. "What do you know of the Order of the Black Lotus?"

Carol shrugged. "They don't like Dragon Masters."

"It's also a fraternal order of some of the most prominent men in the city," Malcolm said in a grim voice.

Carol looked at him in surprise. "I'd never heard of them before Zhen told me about them."

"It's a deep, dark secret. Membership in the Order is inherited, and the only way to become a member is through the death of the previous male heir."

She digested this with some disquiet. "If it's such a secret, how do you know?"

"He's a black dragon," Seth said. "They pride themselves on being know-it-alls."

Malcolm looked annoyed. Seth placed his hands on Carol's shoulders, his music in her head changing to wariness and caution.

"Where are the others?" he asked Malcolm.

"I sent them away. Saba didn't want to leave Adara too long, even with Ming Ue babysitting her. I elected to stay and wait for you."

Carol blinked. "But you didn't know we were coming."

"I calculated the odds of you not being able to stay home at about ninety-seven-point-nine-to-one. You are a woman who likes to take charge of situations, even situations you don't understand."

"Forgive me for worrying about my friends. I realized that dragons hunting down a Dragon Master wasn't a good idea."

"And that is true." Malcolm's intense gaze raked over

her, then Seth. "There are three ways to bind a dragon. A witch may learn his true name by trickery, which is what happened to Caleb and myself. Or a dragon's true name can be read from the *Book of All Dragons*, if the person knows how to get past the securities in the Dragon Archive. The third way is through a Dragon Master."

He gave her a pointed look. As his meaning sunk in, Carol's mouth grew dry, but something deep inside her gave a satisfied chuckle. *The great dragons fear you.*

"I'd never hurt you," she said hurriedly. "You're the same as family."

Malcolm answered without changing inflection. "Dragon Masters can call the true names of any dragon, and a very strong master can enslave several dragons at once. We don't know what your powers are at this point, but we do know you can't control them. That means none of us is safe from you."

Something inside Carol flared in sudden anger. She reached out with gray-black thought threads without realizing it and touched the silver threads of Malcolm's aura.

Without effort she followed the threads down to the essence of Malcolm's being, where, at the bottom of the tangle, his true name lay. All she had to do was reach out and take it.

She sang a note, and Malcolm looked at her in horror.

No!

The air shimmered with black dragon energy, Malcolm ready to change into his dragon form. The power within Carol moved to the next note, and the next.

She closed her eyes, clenching her teeth. "Stop," she shouted. "Malcolm, if you become a dragon, I'll snare you. I can't stop myself. Get out of here."

Malcolm hesitated a fraction of a second, then the energy diminished. "Talk to Ming Ue," he said.

"Just go."

Carol heard Malcolm's boots on the echoing floor as he walked with measured stride out of the warehouse. After a moment, the car outside started, the sound loud in the silence. Carol opened her eyes.

Seth was watching her, his gaze intense.

"He's right, isn't he?" Carol asked, a coldness inside her. "I wanted to trap him; something wanted to prove I could."

"Dragon Masters are powerful. They are very rare, but all dragons fear them."

"And now dragons fear me. Including you."

Seth only watched her, his thought threads still jangling.

Carol had never been uncertain before. In her life she'd seen clear paths and made conscious decisions to follow them. Never had the way been murky or the path strewn with obstacles she didn't have the confidence to navigate around.

For the first time in her life, she looked at another living being and said, "What am I going to do?"

Seth didn't reply. She knew he wanted to get as far away from her as fast as he could, like Malcolm, except he couldn't. Even now, the Dragon Master in her clasped the chains that held him and tightened them a notch.

Seth's body jerked in response, and he rumbled in his throat.

Carol let go, but the *thud-thud* of his heart reached her through their bond.

Something detached in her wondered why the other Dragon Master had called a fire dragon specifically—not a golden, a black, or whatever other colors were out there. Of all the dragons in Dragonspace, and the three dragons already in this world, he'd called Seth. Why?

Carol looked pleadingly at Seth. "Help me."

He hesitated a long time. The power in her urged her to snatch him to her—he'd have to obey without question. Carol banished the thoughts with effort.

Seth walked quietly to her and took her hand. His touch was warm against the chill, and for a moment she clung to him and enjoyed it.

They left the warehouse together, Seth silent as they went to the car. He helped Carol in, then climbed into the passenger seat, still not speaking.

Seth laid his hand on her knee as she drove back to the street, his touch comforting. But Carol couldn't relax and let him soothe her, because she had no idea whether he touched her because he sensed her distress or because he'd been compelled to through the bond of his true name.

7

Carol went to bed when they reached her apartment, but Seth knew she didn't sleep. She hadn't spoken on the drive home, and now she lay alone in the bedroom, her breathing light and shallow, wide-awake.

Seth stood at the window in the living room, watching the street outside. He saw nothing but humans of the city walking briskly home in the dark, a small group of them laughing and talking as they made their way up the hill. Vehicles bright with lights swept up and down the street, becoming fewer as the night wore on.

The Dragon Master he'd seen in the shimmering column puzzled and worried him. The man who'd called him long ago should have been dead and dust by now, but the voice had been similar, though not the same. The old Dragon Master had been cruel, but he'd been human, not tainted with otherworldly evil as the being in the column had been.

Seth thought about what had happened all those years ago. The Order had wanted the Dragon Master to call forth their demon-god so they could beg him for more power. The Dragon Master refused. The Order put pressure on the emperor, who in turn commanded the Dragon Master.

The Dragon Master had used Seth and four other dragons to release the demon, in a horrific scene that Seth had never forgotten. The sticky threads from the column gave him a similar chill, stirring old memories.

The Dragon Master had then turned on the Order and either killed or banished the god once it came forth. How he'd done it, Seth still wasn't sure. The Dragon Master must have used Seth's fire, but it was all a strange blur.

He only knew that suddenly he'd felt the bonds of his true name lift and disappear. He'd groped along the threads, bewildered, but he'd found the gossamer strands of the Dragon Master snapped and withered.

The only explanation for that was that the Dragon Master had died.

Seth hadn't waited around to ask questions. He'd felt the pull of Dragonspace, his fire had created a door in the thin way between the worlds, and he'd gone.

He'd later mildly wondered if the other dragons had escaped, and he assumed they had. He hadn't much cared—he'd been a young dragon then and the only thing that mattered to him was to make certain his territory hadn't been taken over.

Now Seth wondered about the fate of those dragons, whether they were happily sunning themselves in Dragonspace or had died at a dignified old age or had remained trapped in the human world.

Back then, the walls between the worlds had been thin, and he'd been able to exist as a dragon here. Now the fiber between the universes was thick, and this world didn't want to see him in dragon shape. He imagined the reason he could still turn to fire was because shooting fire could be explained as long as no one looked too closely.

But this summoning and binding was different, and not only because of the passing of time. Carol's touch, her music, the look in her eyes were completely different from that of Sying, the middle-aged Chinese man who'd made Seth feel every moment of his slavery.

Carol had loved Dragonspace. He'd felt in their connecting threads her dart of joy when he'd flown with her over his home.

He tried to tell himself it was all illusion. Carol had proved she could tighten the bond whenever she chose. It was dangerous to trust her, and yet he craved her every moment.

Seth had never touched another being in his life. Even when he'd been here before, he'd allowed no one to touch his hide, and he'd stayed as far away from humans and the other dragons as possible. It was what dragons did.

Now that he'd touched Carol, he didn't want to stop. He couldn't believe that human body temperature could be so *warm*. His own fire could flare to incandescent, but it was nothing to the warmth of Carol's hand on his cheek.

He liked her smell, her taste, the smoothness of her skin. He wanted to lie against her and savor the feeling of her along his body.

He had no way of knowing whether these needs were true or part of his enslavement. The doubt made him hesitate to trust himself.

Her plea for help in the warehouse had nearly killed him. He'd wanted to scoop her up and carry her to Dragonspace where he'd curl around her and protect her forever.

As it was, all he could do was hold her hand until she felt calm enough to drive home, and then stand here in her window like a guardian while she finally slid into sleep in the other room.

Seth saw something that wasn't quite human move in

the darkness. It came stealthily but purposefully up the sidewalk, then entered the house through the door below.

He recognized the demonlike aura and opened the door of the apartment, waiting as Axel climbed the stairs.

"Everything all right?" Axel whispered as he entered. "Carol sleeping snug?"

"She is now," Seth answered in a low voice. He closed the door. "It took her a long time."

"Poor kid. Her grandmother expects her to bear up, doesn't remember that Carol is still so young."

"Carol is stronger than anyone understands," Seth said. "Even herself."

Axel moved to the kitchen and opened Carol's refrigerator. "What about you? I'm a creature of the night, but dragons have to sleep sometime."

"I don't seem to need to yet."

"You're still adapting. How's that going?" He rummaged through the refrigerator. "Huh. No beer."

Seth leaned against the counter as Axel turned to explore the cupboards. "The black dragon showed me much of the city."

"Well, Malcolm knows all about the human world. He was stuck here for eight hundred years. Witches bound him to get their revenge. Poor guy."

"Now his mate is a witch," Seth observed. "And he lives here by choice."

"One of life's little ironies." Axel peered into the open cupboard. "You know, she has nothing to drink but tea, water, and white wine. How does she live like this?"

Axel started to explore another cupboard, but Seth closed his hand on Axel's shoulder. "Don't."

"Hmm? Oh." Axel's smile flashed, revealing pointed teeth. "I like you being so protective. Makes my job easier." He opened the refrigerator and quickly extracted a bottle of water.

"What is your job?"

"To make sure we don't have to protect her from you."

Axel gave him a pointed look and wandered back into the living room. He planted himself on the sofa and crossed his booted feet on the coffee table. In his leather jacket, jeans, and motorcycle boots, he looked much like the young men in a Japanese gang Malcolm had pointed out to Seth last night. The only thing that set Axel apart was that he didn't have the same young anger and arrogance in his eyes.

"I'd never hurt her," Seth said.

He remembered that he already had hurt Carol, had bruised her arm when he'd clasped it the first night. But he'd not understood then how much physically stronger he was than she.

"Yes, well, Carol's pretty special," Axel said. "She has a brain, and she doesn't understand all this paranormal stuff. If her grandmother had prepared her from childhood, she'd have been ready to step into her power, instead of having it blindside her."

Seth agreed with Axel, but he also understood Ming Ue's fear of seeing grief in Carol's eyes. "The old woman was trying to shelter her."

"I know." Axel guzzled some water and wiped his mouth with the back of his hand. "Something I wanted to ask you about dragons. I know that goldens are warriors, so I can understand why a mage would want to capture one. Black dragons have intelligence that would put anyone in Mensa to shame. But what do fire dragons do? You can change into flame—very interesting, but what advantage does that give a mage?"

Seth knew exactly what a fire dragon could do for a mage or a Dragon Master. Carol didn't know, and he sensed that Ming Ue, for all her knowledge of dragons, didn't know either.

"We have great magical ability," he said.

"I figured that. What kind of magical ability?"

"Nothing I can explain."

Axel's dark eyes narrowed. "But a mage who enslaved a fire dragon would have a huge advantage?"

"Yes."

"And that's all you're going to tell me?"

"That's all." When Carol was ready, she would know, and then Seth would truly be in her power. Either that, or the power of the fire dragon would kill her.

Inside the bedroom, Carol's breathing changed. He felt the shift in the threads swirling in his brain, the shimmer of them dimming.

"She's dreaming," he said.

"I'm staying put then." Axel leaned back. "Incubi slide in on dreams."

Seth nodded. He was so wrapped up in Carol, he'd feel if any incubi tried to reach her through her dreams, and he'd be ready. He almost wished they would come so he could have the joy of killing one. Demon bones crunched so satisfactorily.

Carol dreamed of boulders. She drove along a stretch of highway, skirting a high, dark cliff. She passed a yellow WATCH FOR ROCKS sign and glanced up at the metal mesh that covered the naked side of the hill.

She'd been driving this road for years and had never seen so much as a pebble come tumbling from above. But tonight the slice of her BMW's headlights caught a trickle of gravel, and then several boulders flew down toward the car.

Carol shrieked and swerved, plunging the car into the ditch on the other side of the road. Beyond the ditch, the hill dropped into a canyon, dark, silent, and deep.

Damn. She'd just had the car serviced and the tires replaced—there went that hard-earned money. She pulled out her cell phone to call roadside service.

"Carol, there are more."

Carol turned her head and froze. Her mother sat in the seat next to her, her face young and smooth, like the pictures Carol had of her propped on the dresser. Lian Juan had been Carol's age, twenty-eight, when she'd died.

"Mama?"

Carol had dreamed of her mother before, but usually in remote, vague visions. In the dreams her mother was always far away and waving, or waiting for Carol somewhere, like at a BART station or on the deck of a ferry. Carol would run to meet her, but by the time she reached the spot, her mother would be gone.

She'd never had such a vivid dream of her mother. Lian wore a white shirt, the seat belt a black slash across it. She gave Carol a scared look from her almond-shaped eyes.

"More are coming, Carol. You must drive away. Hurry."

"The car's stuck."

"Hurry. Please."

Tears wet her mother's face, and Carol reached out and touched them.

She jerked away in shock. Instead of an insubstantial dream, she felt warm flesh, the damp of tears, her mother's breath on her fingers.

"Mama." She sobbed the word. Carol yanked off her own seat belt and flung her arms around her mother. "Mama, I miss you so much."

Lian held her close, and Carol heard the steady beat of the other woman's heart. "More boulders are coming, Carol. You have to stop them."

"How can I stop them?"

"You have to get out of the car and do it."

Carol held her mother harder. Not even in dreams had she been able to feel the warmth of her mother's body, to hear the voice she so faintly remembered from childhood.

"Please, Mama, stay with me."

Her mother gasped as a boulder struck the hood of the car. "Carol, hurry!"

Carol dashed tears from her eyes and saw a huge pile of boulders at the top of the hill poised to fall on them. Moonlight gleamed on their surfaces, making them almost glow.

Carol wondered why she dreamed this. Was she reliving the car accident? She'd never known exactly what happened, only that she and her parents had been driving back to San Francisco from Monterey. She couldn't remember any of it, and Ming Ue had never told her the specifics of the crash.

Had they been on this dark stretch of highway with boulders raining down from above? Had the Order of the Black Lotus decided this was how her mother the Dragon Master would meet her death?

Not this time. Carol slammed open the car door and got out, her high-heeled shoes sinking into mud. She kicked off the shoes and climbed stocking-footed out of the ditch onto the road.

From inside the car, her mother watched worriedly as Carol raised her hands toward the boulders. "Stop," Carol told them.

As if on cue, the rocks started to fall. Carol flattened her palms, and the first boulder bounced away as though hitting a hidden shield.

The next boulder did the same, and the next, each flying clear to plummet into the canyon below. Carol felt the strain in her wrists and arms, the jolt as they smashed against the shield.

The boulders came faster, two and three at a time. Sweat trickled down Carol's back, and her arms began to shake.

The rocks were black and jagged, like the hillside, crumbling and breaking as they struck Carol's shield. Debris rained on her face, cutting her flesh, but she braced her feet apart and held her hands firmly.

Triumph surged inside her as each bolder deflected away. This time her mother wouldn't die. This time they would survive and go home to Ming Ue's, and her grandmother would cry to see Lian safe and sound again.

The boulders came faster, harder, each one larger than the last. Carol's hands were raw, her shoulders aching.

"Stop them, Carol," her mother shouted from the car. "Stop them."

Tears flowed down Carol's face to mix with the blood. There were too many, and they came too fast. They poured over her, rolling past to land on the car.

"No," she screamed.

Dirt rained on her face and blinded her. She heard rocks hitting the car, the hood, the trunk, the roof. Glass crumpled with a tearing sound, and her mother cried out.

Carol swung back to the car. She grabbed the door handle to pull her mother out, but the door frame was bent, and the door wouldn't budge.

Her mother banged on the window, screaming, blood streaming down her face.

"Mama," Carol shrieked. "No, don't leave me again."

Carol pulled on the door, and Lian pounded on it from the inside. But the glass wouldn't break, and the boulders kept falling. Her mother was being slowly crushed.

Carol screamed mindless words, beating and beating on the glass. She felt a darkness well up around her, heard laughter, and a whisper: *Come to me.*

Beyond the car, not affected by the boulders, stood a tall man with white hair. He was naked, his hair a ghostly white, with tiny white feathers at his hairline. Leathery wings rose from his shoulder blades and whispered in the night along with his voice. *Follow me, and I will make your dreams come true.*

"Mama," Carol screamed once more, clawing the window. Inside, her mother went still, her white face streaked with blood.

"No," Carol moaned. She balled her fists and banged on the car roof, her hands hurting and bleeding. She screamed once more, loud and long, and found herself beating her pillows in her lamplit bedroom, safe in her apartment.

Strong hands closed on her arms, and she instinctively fought them.

"Carol." Music slid around her. She smelled wind and the night, and she turned to find herself against Seth's hard body.

She held on to him, breathing the scent of musk, wind, and the fabric softener from his T-shirt. He rubbed his hand along her back, fingers strong through her nightgown. She felt his lips in her hair, but she didn't close her eyes to enjoy it. She'd had enough of darkness.

Across the room, someone softly belched.

Carol jerked from Seth to see Axel grab something dark out of the air and raise it to his lips.

"*Ah.*" He wiped his mouth, then turned around and grinned at Carol. "I love a good nightmare."

The fuzziness cleared from Carol's brain, and she realized she was sitting in bed in a torn nightgown with two men in her bedroom. She hoisted a blanket to her chin and glared shakily over it at Axel. "What are you doing here?"

"Eating your nightmare."

"What?"

"I'm a Baku. A Japanese god who eats nightmares." Axel shook his head in mock disbelief. "Didn't your grandmother teach you anything?"

"Sorry, it never came up."

Axel chuckled. "My work here is done. I'll leave you two kids in peace."

He waved once, politely keeping his eyes averted, and disappeared with a pop. Carol gaped in shock, but there had been so many shocks today that Axel vanishing into thin air was a lesser wonder.

"I felt the incubus come," Seth was saying, his voice low in her ear.

"The white-haired thing with wings?" Carol drew a breath, but the horror and grief of the nightmare had dissipated. Axel's antics, whatever he claimed, seemed to have drained the dream of its power.

"I saw my mother die again," she whispered. The immediacy of the shock had receded, leaving her with profound sadness. "I don't know if that's what happened when I was a little girl, or if the boulders were metaphors for things I've had to face."

"Or the other Dragon Master trying to wear you down." Seth stroked her hair. "Even kill you."

"It was only a dream."

"Someone sent the incubus to take you. He could have sent the dream as well."

Carol's heart gave a throb of fear. "Is that possible?"

"Axel destroyed the dream and left wards to guard against others. The Dragon Master can't try again, not here."

Carol glanced at the window and saw a silver mark just above the window frame. Others lingered above the bed and the door. Burned over these were marks of red fire surrounded by black. They weren't really on the wall, she somehow understood, but she could sense the marks pulsing with power.

Carol leaned against Seth, liking how strong his hard body felt. His music in her head was comforting, a chord that told her *I am here; don't worry.*

"Stay with me," she said softly.

She tightened the threads between them as she spoke, her body instinctively commanding him. His eyes went flinty, and his comforting music faded.

She relaxed the pull, deliberately keeping the threads loose. "Please."

She thought he'd refuse. She thought he'd walk away in frigid anger, his dragon ire flaring.

She stopped herself from reaching for him when he stood up, but instead of leaving her, he peeled off his shirt and dropped it to the floor.

Carol let herself get lost in looking at the beauty of him. Red hair dusted his chest and drew to a point above his navel. The waistband of his jeans dipped enticingly low, revealing the ends of the tattoo on his hips.

Seth sat on the bed and touched her face, brushing away tears with his blunt fingers.

Carol felt a stir of heat, but her emotions were still too agitated, the dream too fresh, for sex. She knew she could lose her fears by having Seth make love to her, but she didn't want that—sex to make her forget.

She wanted it to be special. She wanted to have nothing in her mind when they had sex but Seth and his hard body.

She straightened the pillows, and he didn't offer to help, making her realize he'd never used a bed before. "How do you usually sleep?" she asked.

"Curled up."

Carol suddenly imagined his naked body tucked into itself with his head on his bent arm. His smooth skin would gleam, his breath rising and falling with his deep sleep.

"Tonight will you curl up with me?" she asked softly.

For answer, Seth stretched out on the bed. He was already barefoot, having shucked his boots and socks as soon as they'd come home, as though he didn't like not feeling the floor with his feet.

Still in his jeans, he pulled her against him, spooning himself against her back.

Carol pulled the cool sheets over them, feeling his hardness through his jeans and her nightgown. For some reason the sensation was both exciting and reassuring.

"Thank you," she murmured.

He put his warm hand on her abdomen and pressed a kiss to her hair. "Sleep now."

His words, his body, and his warmth released a tension inside her, and Carol relaxed. He was still slowly kneading her belly when she fell asleep.

8

Carol cracked her eyes open to find sunlight streaming through the slats of her designer shutters and her large digital clock reading 8:00 A.M.

"Crap," she muttered.

She turned over and bumped into the warm weight of Seth. He lay facedown beside her, and the covers had slid down to bare his back.

The nightmare and its frightening images were gone, and all she could think of was that an absolutely gorgeous red-haired man lay next to her in her bed.

She rose on her elbow and brushed her fingers over his taut back. She liked his smooth, warm skin, the contained power of his muscles. The jeans cupped the round of his buttocks, and the flame tattoo peeped above the waistband.

He'd been a beautiful dragon, and he was a beautiful man. The universe had decided to stuff that dragon beauty into an ideal human male body, and Carol couldn't find fault with the universe's choice.

He didn't move a muscle, but Carol felt the music in her head change as his dark eyes slowly opened.

"Don't stop," he rumbled, his voice soft with sleep. "I like that."

Encouraged, Carol glided her fingertips across the small of his back, tracing the pattern of the flame.

"I wonder why the tattoo?" she asked, half to herself.

"It's my dragon essence. That's where it's contained when I'm human."

"Like Malcolm's tattoo on his arm." She'd seen it but thought it simply male decoration. "There's so much I don't know about dragons."

"I don't know much about humans," he returned.

Carol traced the edges of the flame again, but it felt no different than a tattoo on normal skin—not that she was in the habit of touching men's tattoos. This was her first.

She trailed her fingers up his spine, enjoying the firm feel of his back and shoulder blades. His tousled hair was like rough silk, warm with sleep.

He lay still and watched her. His irises were a little wider than a human's, darkness swallowing the white. She could drown in his eyes. She touched his face, feeling the burn of whiskers.

He didn't move until she lifted her hand away, and then he rose on his elbows. His body was warm, and his chest bore creases where the sheet had marked him.

"Now I want to touch you."

His low voice rippled warmth through her, which burned hotter when he tugged at the sleeve of her nightgown. "Take this off."

"You're pushy for someone who claims he's my slave."

"Now. I want to see you."

The room grew brighter by the minute as Pacific sunshine streamed in through her half-open shutters. Carol had never taken off her clothes for a man in broad daylight—her encounters had always been of the nighttime variety. She wasn't ashamed of her body, because she worked to keep herself in good shape, but that didn't mean she was anxious to throw off her clothes under a man's scrutiny.

Now without hesitation, she slipped the nightgown over her head and dropped it on the floor. She wore nothing underneath.

Seth's look was like a caress. "Lie down," he said. "On your stomach."

Carol lay facedown, cradling her pillow under her chest.

He brushed his fingertips over her buttocks. "You're so soft," he murmured.

She turned her head on the pillow and watched him trace each cheek of her backside, then draw his fingers along her hips. She gasped when he bent down and followed the same path with his tongue.

Seth's breath warmed her back as he licked all the way up her spine to the base of her neck. He let her hair flow through his fingers then nuzzled it.

His body heated hers as his tongue found places she'd never known could feel so erotic. His fingers were surprisingly callused—perhaps the magic that shaped him had kept the roughness that came from living on desert rock.

He moved his hands and lips under her hair, down her neck. He worked his way to her buttocks again, stroking and kneading.

He nibbled her skin, and she let out a low moan when his tongue flicked across where he'd bitten. "What are you doing?"

"Do humans not use their teeth on each other?" he murmured into her skin.

"They do—I guess. No one's ever used them on me. Do dragons?"

"A mother nips her young to discipline them or to reassure them. And a dragon may nip his mate."

"Do you have a mate?"

"Not yet."

He lifted her foot and licked the arch. Her fingers curled into her pillow, and she squeezed her eyes shut.

No man had ever touched her like this—so thoroughly, so *playfully*. He knelt behind her and lowered his head to lick the backs of her ankles, making her gasp and squirm.

"Do you not like that?" he asked.

She could barely breathe. "Of course I like it."

He licked his way up to the backs of her knees. "I like the way you taste."

"Good," she said weakly.

When he reached her thighs, the tickling, squirmy sensation inside her gave way to something darker. Her opening tightened, and she suddenly wanted to press herself hard against the sheets.

He licked her buttocks again, then his hot breath danced on her spine. As he moved up her back this time, he slid carefully on top of her, his chest on her back. He lifted her hair, kissing her neck to her ear.

She turned her head, and his lips met hers, but he kept the kiss brief. One swirl of his tongue, then he was moving back down to her buttocks.

"Turn over," he said.

Carol was sweating, but she rolled over, torn between shyness and excitement. She spread her legs a little, amazed at her own boldness but at the same time wanting him to see her. If she was the first human woman he'd ever looked at, she wanted him to like what he saw.

Seth studied her with his head tilted, dragonlike. He let his dark gaze rove over her, occasionally reaching out to touch—a flick across her tight nipple, the backs of his fingers down her arm, his palm across her belly.

He drew a light finger through the curls between her

legs, his gaze moving there. "You're very hot," he said. "And wet."

"That's because you're touching me. Driving me insane."

"Why?" He sounded genuinely curious, but she noticed he didn't stop swirling his fingertip.

"You're making me want you."

"To mate with me?"

"Yes, to mate with you, if that's what you want to call it."

He lifted his finger away, but only to lean down and lick between her breasts. "You taste salty."

"That's normal."

"I like it." He led with his tongue to her nipple and swirled around it. "You like *this*."

"*Yes*."

He circled the nipple again, then tentatively tugged it with his teeth. When she groaned, he sucked it into his mouth.

He pleasured her perfectly. She loved how his black lashes curled against his cheek as his eyes closed, loved how his mouth worked as he suckled and nibbled.

He moved lower, swiping a kiss at her navel as he went. When he moved his tongue over the damp curls between her legs, she dragged in a raw breath.

"Seth, oh, God."

This time he didn't ask if she liked it or didn't. He simply danced his tongue over her.

Carol had never been much for oral sex, regarding it as a much more intimate act than sex itself, and she'd never been comfortable with that level of intimacy.

She quickly changed her mind as Seth licked and teased her, pressing her legs apart so he could find more and more of her.

Carol stretched out her arms, biting her lip to stifle her groans. Seth slid his hands under her buttocks and lifted her, licking her over and over as though he couldn't get enough.

He raised his head, his eyes dark as midnight. "I want more."

"Are you trying to kill me?"

"Am I hurting you?"

"I was joking." She reached for him. "Please, Seth."

She wasn't sure what she was asking for, but he seemed to understand. He lowered himself again and used his teeth and tongue to pleasure her in ways she'd never known were possible. When he licked from her clit to her opening and jabbed his tongue inside, she screamed.

He started to raise his head, but she locked her hand around his neck, holding him fast. He got the idea and continued to lick and suck, moving from her sheath to clit and back again.

Dark fire burned her every limb. Her world focused on Seth's mouth, his beautiful mouth which pleasured her as she'd never been pleasured before. Not one man in her life—and she could count the men she'd been to bed with on one hand—had made her feel like *this*.

She screamed again, her orgasm taking her over. She felt her body gyrating, out of control, and never in her life had Carol been out of control.

Seth held her with firm hands and kept torturing her with his mouth. She was still gasping when he rose over her again.

"I want you," he growled.

"Fine with me."

She heard the buzz of his zipper, then he pushed and kicked his jeans down his legs. He raised up on his hands and knees, his cock hanging heavy and hard between his legs.

He positioned himself on top of her and moved unerringly to her opening. He slid smoothly inside, all the way, until he lay face-to-face with her, his dark eyes fixed on her.

He filled her so full she thought she wouldn't be able to take it, but she wanted to take him. She lifted her hips, encouraging more.

It was a beautiful feeling. He stretched her, and she spread her legs wider, loving his hardness deep inside her.

His eyes half closed as he kissed her face. "I don't know what to do."

"You're doing fine. Believe me."

"I want to *thrust*. But I don't want to hurt you."

"I don't think it will hurt." But he was big. It might.

Seth closed his eyes as though he couldn't hear her anymore. He balled his fists on the sheets beside her and moved his hips the slightest bit.

Carol's head went back on the pillows. "Like that," she whispered. "Just like that."

He opened his eyes as his body took over, and he focused on her face, watching her as he moved. She saw him grow more used to it, relaxing into the rhythm.

The room hummed with the noises of sex, his hoarse breathing, her soft moans, the gentle slap of skin meeting skin.

"Seth," she whispered, simply wanting to hear his name.

The music that was his true name swelled and danced in her head. The threads that bound them together glowed and meshed in perfect alignment until she swore that both of them sparkled with fire.

Seth's climax took him by surprise. His eyes widened, and he shouted her name, and at the same time his music swelled in a rousing crescendo. Their music melded in a cacophony of sound and lights, and Carol felt her skin burning.

Seth drove himself into her a few more times, the muscles

of his arms tight. Another spark of fire jumped from him to her, so searing hot that Carol screamed.

At the sound Seth backed out of her fast, but he fell heavily beside her, his arm around her and his mouth on hers.

And then everything went still. The digital clock hummed faintly by her bedside, traffic hissed gently on the street below, and somewhere in another apartment, a phone was ringing.

Seth lay nose to nose with her, his eyes half closed but holding a look of wonder. "Is it always so strong?"

"Sex?" she murmured. "No. But then, that was my first time with a dragon."

They lay in stillness for a few moments, absorbing what had just happened. Carol felt good, stretched, happy.

"What was that burning feeling?" she asked. "I feel it a tiny bit when you kiss me, but that time it was intense."

"My dragon fire."

"Which is what?"

"A fire dragon's power. A little of it entered you."

"It didn't hurt. It was more like . . ." She trailed off. "I don't know. Not pain, but intense."

"I controlled it. If it entered you completely, it would burn you up."

Carol smiled shakily. "One way of ridding yourself of a pesky Dragon Master."

"I have no wish to hurt you."

"But you'd be free."

He shrugged, his broad shoulders moving.

He was telling her, essentially, that he could have killed her as they coupled. The thought should terrify her, but Carol felt too numb and contented right now to contemplate it. She wondered how close he'd come to losing control, and whether he could while she bound him.

"I should go to work," she said.

"Why?"

A good question. There were a million reasons why—every day at every restaurant, a hundred things could go wrong. For everything that went wrong, a customer could turn to the competition.

She still couldn't move. "It's what I always do."

"It's safe here. Dangerous out there."

Carol felt safe. Seth was wrapped protectively around her and so was the music in her head, which hadn't receded since they'd stopped.

The wards Axel and Seth had drawn shimmered over the windows. Though she'd never seen such things before, they gave her a feeling of safety, just like she'd felt with Ming Ue and Shaiming when she'd been a child.

"I have a business to run," she said without much conviction.

Seth's hand drifted to her breast, and she closed her eyes to savor the feeling. When Seth kissed her neck, his hardness nudged her, and any appeal her office held died a swift death.

She reached for her phone and punched the number, smiling when Francesca cried, "Carol, did you know it's nine thirty?"

"Close the office and take the day off," Carol answered. "In fact, take the rest of the week off. We'll start again bright and early on Monday morning."

Francesca went silent. Carol pictured her with her dark brows drawn behind her red glasses. "Are you feeling all right?"

"Perfectly fine. Has anyone tried to come and see me this morning?"

"There was one man, yes. He didn't stay—in fact he didn't even come in, just stared at me through the door. He wasn't on your schedule. Did you want to see him?" Francesca's tone held reproach that Carol had started scheduling things without telling her.

Carol felt a qualm of worry. "What did he look like? Was he one of the investors from yesterday?"

"No. He had long white hair, but he wasn't an old man. He wore a business suit, looked professional enough. I gestured for him to come in, but he just stood there with his hand on the handle. When a security guard came by, he turned around and hurried away."

Carol sat up. "Don't speak to him if you see him again. Take some time off—as much as you need. Why don't you go visit your sister?"

Francesca's voice changed. "That would be nice." Her sister lived in a little town on the northern California coast with five children, all of whom Francesca adored. The town was also sufficiently remote that Francesca might be spared the danger that was stalking Carol.

"Are you sure you're all right?" Francesca repeated. "There isn't something you're not telling me?"

"I have some family business to take care of, and there's no reason for you to wait around for me to get finished. Let's close the office, and I'll see you on Monday."

"All right, I'll lock up and go. Thank you."

Carol hung up the phone.

"An incubus?" Seth asked. He'd obviously heard the entire conversation.

"He didn't go in."

"Because I put my mark on the office," Seth said. "So did Zhen."

"Like those?" Carol pointed to the still glowing symbols above her windows.

"Very similar. No demons will enter."

"Is that why I feel so safe?"

He kissed her fingers. "It's my task to keep you safe."

"Because I hold you with your true name?"

Seth nodded. Carol suddenly wanted it to be more than

that, his choice, but she had no idea how to give that power back to him.

"Lie back," Seth said.

"Why?"

"I want to touch you again." He ran his hand across her abdomen as she lowered herself back to the pillows. "I enjoy the way you feel."

"It's not bad from my side either."

"Do you like touching me?"

In answer, Carol drew her fingers down his chest. Her touch caught on his male nipple, which firmed and tightened under her fingertip.

"I like that," he said.

"Good." She turned her head and licked the warm areola, and he made a noise of pleasure when she caught the nub in her teeth.

"I like how you smell," he said. "And how you taste and how you feel. I want to savor you."

She loved his words, and at the same time wished he wouldn't say them. She wanted this to be real, and nothing in the last two days had been real at all.

Seth grasped her wrist and drew her hand down his chest again. She didn't resist, liking the warm dampness of his skin and the brush of curled hair. She explored his navel, which made him smile, then drew her hand down to his still very erect penis.

His face changed when she touched it, his smile dying.

She knew from feeling him inside her that he was large, but *large* was an understatement. She could barely fit her hand around him.

The shaft was smooth and soft but held the hardness of an excited man. Carol let her thumb drift over the tip, and he gave another gasp.

She'd never performed oral sex but learned the theory

from a college roommate who'd enjoyed comparing the "tackle" of every man she went out with. Seth certainly had the best tackle Carol had ever seen, and even her roommate, jaded at age twenty-one, would have been impressed.

She leaned down and licked the tiny slit on his tip, then closed her mouth over him.

The cock leapt between her lips. She almost lost him, but she swirled her tongue around the tip and drew him back inside her mouth.

His taste was strange, salty and warm, his skin slightly rough on the underside. Her tongue seemed more sensitive to the differences of him than her fingers had been, and she enjoyed the exploration.

Seth growled softly, and he shifted as though he couldn't keep still. He parted his legs, letting her get closer, and she closed her hand around the smooth, hard balls that hung between his thighs.

All the while, she worked her mouth on him like he'd done on her. She suckled him and nibbled him, liking how it made him move his hips.

She felt him grow harder and harder, if that was possible. She didn't stop to wonder; she simply went on, enjoying the taste of this man who'd invaded her life.

His fingers bit down on her shoulders. With a louder growl, he pulled her up and pushed her into the pillows. He parted her legs and slid hard into her before she could say a word.

He made love to her fast and vigorously, sweat dripping from his body to mingle with hers. She lost control very quickly, crying out as he pumped into her.

Her climax came soon this time, and she felt almost a bite of disappointment that it was over. Seth shouted her name as his seed shot into her the second time, then he collapsed onto her, kissing her and tumbling her sweat-damp hair.

9

When Carol woke, it was well past noon. Seth slept hard next to her, his large body sprawled across most of her bed. He was facedown again, cheek pillowed on one arm, his body fully naked in the sunlight.

Carol slid from the small slice of bed still left to her and reached for her white silk dressing gown with the dragons on it. She'd never paid much attention to the design before, but each of the red dragons on the silk sleeves had night black eyes.

Carol blew out her breath and booted up her computer on the desk across the room. Malcolm had implied that Carol should back off the problem of the other Dragon Master and the Order, letting him and Lisa take care of it while she hid in her apartment with Seth.

But it was Carol's life in shards around her feet, Carol who had a newfound power that scared her to death. She wanted to find this Dragon Master and figure out what to do about him.

She settled herself in front of the screen and brought up San Francisco County's searchable map of properties. Finding the warehouse was fairly simple since she knew the cross streets, and within seconds she had the tax parcel number and the mailing address of the property owner.

The site didn't give out the owner's name, but that was easy enough for Carol to find out. The address was of a business on Sacramento Street, and she happened to know that the business was owned by one Daniel Lok. It was handy to have a grandmother who knew everyone in Chinatown.

Her cousin Lumi knew everyone on the shady side of Chinatown. He'd been caught up in some bad things in his high school days, but fortunately had gotten away from it. Lumi even claimed that Axel, whom he'd known for a long time, was responsible for him going straight. Carol had developed a soft spot for Axel ever since Lumi had told her this.

Carol brought the phone to the desk and punched in the number of Lumi's bicycle shop. He was there and put her on hold while he finished with a customer.

"Daniel Lok?" he said incredulously when she explained what she needed. "You don't want to have anything to do with Danny Lok."

"It's not by choice. He . . ." She broke off, wondering how to explain. "What do you know about incubi?"

"Incubi? Geez, Carol, what are you into? They're nasty bad, and you don't want to go near them. Not even with dragons or Axel with you. It's hard enough to keep Grandmother out of trouble. I don't want to have to worry about you, too."

"I thought you'd be happy I finally believed in dragons."

"Sure," Lumi said. "Wonderful."

"Just find out what you can."

Lumi sighed heavily. "I'll do some investigating and e-mail you a list of properties he owns. But you have to promise me you won't do anything stupid, like talk to Danny Lok."

"I don't need to talk to him. I'm looking for someone, and the last place we saw him was in the warehouse I told you about."

"The Dragon Master. Grandmother told me."

"So will you help me find him?"

"Not if it means you getting anywhere near Danny Lok. Half the drug dealers in San Francisco report to him, and he's got his fingers in prostitution rings, extortion, and murder. He's dangerous and evil."

"I wasn't planning to ask him to a party. I just want to know what buildings he owns so I can find out if the Dragon Master is in any of them."

"Don't worry. I'll find the info. But seriously, be careful. You're my favorite cousin, and I don't want to attend your funeral anytime soon."

"I'm your only cousin."

"Another good point. I don't want to lose you."

Carol hesitated, feeling his fear loud and clear. "I don't want you putting yourself in any danger either."

"Ha. This shop is so heavily marked with dragon that even some customers won't come in. That, and my girlfriend is a witch who likes to practice warding on my store and apartment. I can't move for candles and incense sticks."

He sounded happy, so Carol simply chuckled with him and hung up.

She looked back at Seth, who'd moved in his sleep only enough to cradle his head on his arm. Carol printed out the information she needed, turned off the computer, and returned to the bed.

Seth reached out in his sleep as she snuggled against

him, enclosing her in a warm nest. She let herself enjoy it, but the back of her mind niggled with worry.

The tie to Carol had strengthened. Seth felt its pull like a chain of diamonds as Carol led him to one of her restaurants for lunch.

The sensations of her skin against his body, his hands, his lips had awakened something needy inside him. He wanted to touch her all the time now.

He looked at the sun shining on her hair as they walked down the steep hill. She wore a blouse open just enough to let him peek at what he'd touched, and a skirt that revealed her slim, strong legs. A raincoat went over it all, because this human city was cold, but she let it flap open so he could enjoy what lay beneath.

She'd bound him with his name, and now she bound him with her body. She'd promised to free him, but he didn't think he'd ever be free now.

Seth sat across from Carol in a booth that had been hastily readied for them, his hands on the table as he watched her eat. His meal lay untouched in front of him, chopsticks neatly placed to one side of his plate.

"The chef will be unhappy if you don't at least try a bite," she pointed out.

Seth didn't reach for the food, lumps of meat in a strange-smelling sauce. "Your power has grown since yesterday."

"Do you think so?"

"The bond between us is stronger now."

Color flushed her cheeks, making her more beautiful than ever. "You're right. I feel it. *I* feel stronger."

"But you still can't unbind me."

Carol closed her eyes, and he felt her trying to untangle the thought threads between them. Nothing changed. "I don't seem to have any control over that."

"The Dragon Master in you knows what it wants. It's not giving you a choice."

She glanced at the diners around them, leaned forward, and lowered her voice. "This morning—that was *my* choice."

Seth remembered waking up later and seeing her come out of her bathroom, dressed, damp, and sweet-smelling. She'd smiled, told him she was hungry, and that she had found out some things.

He'd sensed her increased power then, and he sensed it now. "Was it?"

"I'm hoping it was yours, too."

"I thought so. Now I don't know."

Carol sat back, hurt in her voice. "You think I compelled you to do it?"

Her eyes were moist, and Seth watched her blink, trying to master herself.

"Witches and mages use dragons," he said. "They crave their power and bind it to enhance their own. They can drain the dragon until he dies."

"And you think that's what I'm doing?"

He looked at her in silence for a moment. "Not you—not Carol. You don't know what to do with a dragon's power. But the Dragon Master in you does. It called me to keep me from the other Dragon Master, but you couldn't release me after that. I think you hold me for some purpose."

"Maybe to protect myself from the other Dragon Master." She straightened her lacquered chopsticks on their square holder. "You've been very protective of me."

"I can't help it."

"I'm not used to a man protecting me. I've always been self-reliant." She reached across the table and clasped one of his unmoving hands.

Seth felt her loneliness, and he added a soothing note to his music. "You like to stride forward with determination."

"I suppose that's not very attractive. Men want women to be soft and sexy."

"I find you soft." His blood warmed as he rubbed his thumb over the back of her hand. "You are very soft, and you taste like flowers."

Her eyes darkened. "Did you eat many flowers as a dragon?"

"I liked to nibble on them and taste their nectar."

Carol shifted in her seat, but before she could answer, someone stopped beside the table.

A thin, gray-haired Asian man wearing a well-tailored suit stood at the end of the booth, waiting patiently for Carol's attention. He looked ordinary, except that his eyes were wells of coldness. Two younger and larger men flanked him, their eyes also flat and hard.

"Carol Juan," the man said in a calm voice.

"Yes?"

The dragon in Seth tensed. He got no aura of *otherness* from the man—he was human through and through—but the whiff of evil surrounding him was unmistakable.

"I have not yet had the pleasure of your acquaintance," the man said in a low, dry voice. "I am Daniel Lok."

Carol stiffened. "Mr. Lok. What can I do for you? I'm afraid the restaurant is a little full right now, but if you see the hostess, she'll put you on a waiting list."

His tone went frosty. "You have been inquiring into my business, Ms. Juan, searching for information on my properties. May I ask why?"

Seth couldn't stop the growls in his throat, but he stayed still, knowing a move would bring Lok's guards to the ready.

"I often look into properties around San Francisco," Carol said. "I am always thinking about opening more restaurants."

"None of my real estate is for sale."

"But it's always good to keep an eye open. I see a table clearing in the corner, Mr. Lok, if you want lunch. I recommend the lo mein noodles—the chef has an amazing recipe."

Lok's features tightened in displeasure. "I didn't come here for food. I came as a courtesy, to give you a personal warning. Next time, I will not be so polite."

Seth rose, unfolding his big body to tower over Lok and his bodyguards.

Lok looked Seth up and down, his brows quirking in interest. "So this is the prize worth having."

He was talking to himself, but Carol gave Lok a look that said he'd confirmed her suspicions.

"Why is the Dragon Master hiding?" she asked. "What is he afraid of?"

Lok gave her a pitying look. "You have no idea what is happening here, do you? Give up the power to people who know how to use it."

Seth sensed Carol's puzzlement through their threads, but the look she gave Lok was cool. "I don't think so."

"Have you tamed him?" Lok asked. "Will you sic him on me?"

"I will if you don't turn around and leave my restaurant."

Brave Carol. She didn't even back away when Lok rested his hands flat on the table and leaned down to her. "The Dragon Master is obsessed with magic and dragons. I'm obsessed with more ordinary things, like restaurant owners who don't pay their fair share. I will soon have control of your little empire, and you will pay homage to me." He reached out and slid a finger down Carol's cheek.

Touching her was Lok's mistake. Seth had been prepared to let him go.

His growl turned into a snarl of red fury. He grabbed Lok around the middle and raised him from his feet, crunching the man's bones under his big hands. Lok screamed.

The bodyguards dragged thick black weapons from under

their coats and pointed them at Seth. Customers shouted and dove for the floor.

"Seth," Carol screamed, and the weapons went off.

But Seth wasn't there. He'd become a string of flame rising overhead, his clothes crumpling to the floor. The small missiles aimed at him hit the cream-colored wall behind the booth with a shower of plaster.

Lok was on the carpet, gasping for breath, holding his ribs. Seth hovered above him, his fire touching the ceiling without burning it. The bodyguards moved their pistols to Carol.

Seth put his fire between Carol and the bodyguards, and the bullets went wide again, striking the walls around them.

He felt something inside Carol change. The fury that had been kindling since she'd told him in rainy Union Square that her mother had been tortured to death welled in her until it exploded.

The bond between them seared with incandescent brightness. Seth felt the energy in her as it swelled, then burst out of her in a wave of darkness.

The bodyguards' weapons flew from their hands and disintegrated in midair. While the two men stared in astonishment, Seth honed the magic of his dragon fire and dove straight at them.

They ran. Seth soared after them, and the bodyguards ran faster. Their clothes caught on fire as they dashed out into the sunlight, swearing.

Danny Lok was on his knees, his face white, his arms around his ribs. "You are finished, Carol Juan," he rasped. "You will not reach home tonight, and your grandmother will be dead by tomorrow. Your little restaurants will be—"

He never finished. Seth was on him, his fire forming itself into a dragon shape, his mouth gaping.

"Seth," Carol shouted. *Don't kill him.*

Seth raged. His dragon self wanted to strip his enemy's

flesh from his bones and consume him. But Carol compelled him, and he had to obey.

Seth snapped his jaws closed inches from Lok's face. Lok gasped once, went pasty white, then fell back to the carpet and lay very still.

Seth's form solidified for an instant into a true dragon, then winked back into fire. He circled Carol once, his power harsh and hot, then he streamed out the open door into the rain and cold.

10

Carol sat with her head in her hands in the manager's office. She couldn't move, couldn't think, and the cool-headed manager kept trying to make her drink tea.

Daniel Lok was dead. The paramedics and fire department had shown up in record time and pronounced him dead of a heart attack.

Carol had no story to tell the police, and they thought she was too numb and shaken to talk. They suggested a trip to the hospital where she could recover from the trauma, but she didn't want to go.

The explanation circulating through the restaurant was that Lok and his two bodyguards had entered the place, and the bodyguards had shot at Carol. There had been a small explosion and a fire—maybe Lok had come here to plant a firebomb and it had gone off too soon. The fire had burned the two bodyguards and given Lok a heart attack.

No one mentioned Seth or dragons. Carol had gathered

up Seth's discarded clothes and hidden them before the police got there.

Seth hadn't returned. She still felt his bond to her, the threads singing and shining between them, but he was flying free over the bay, the dragon in him rejoicing.

The police took statements, and the manager kept bringing cups of tea and telling Carol that she'd get right on having the bullet-ridden wall of the main dining room repaired.

Carol barely heard her. Her body sang and hummed with the Dragon Master power, her ability to command darkness and dragon fire.

She'd been a hair shy of telling Seth to kill all three men—human beings, no matter how bad they'd been. She had that in herself, a power like Lok had, to decide the fate of others.

She tried to feel justified about Lok's death. The man had lived by terrorizing others, and it was only fitting that he'd died of fright himself. But she felt sick.

"Lisa is here," the manager said in her low voice. She was a mirror image of Carol, a pale woman as calm as water. *Used to be a mirror image,* Carol thought darkly. Carol's calm had deserted her and hadn't returned.

"Lisa?" she repeated.

Silver dragon, something in Carol hissed. *The power of the fire dragon is great, but the silver dragon would be legion.*

Carol gasped and pressed her hands to her head. "No. I can't see her."

"She's worried about you. You should let her take you home."

"Tell her to go. Tell her not to come near me."

The manager looked as though she agreed with the paramedics. "Are you sure you don't want to go to the hospital? You're still in shock. They can give you medication."

Carol shook her head. "Tell Lisa to send Axel to take me home. Only Axel, no one else."

The manager looked doubtful, but made her exit. Carol was the boss.

Carol closed her eyes and tried to still the clanging in her head. She wished she knew where Seth was, but she deliberately halted the music of his name. If he returned now, who knew what she, the Dragon Master, would make him do?

She pressed her hands to her temples and waited with small patience for Axel to arrive and take her home.

Seth flew. He shot high above the clouds that had moved in to cover the city, sun dazzling on a blanket of white. He was fire, but his dragon body flickered in and out as he moved over the vast ocean.

Once upon a time, dragons had been able to easily exist in this world in their dragon forms, a fact Seth well knew. But as centuries passed, humans had lost their belief in magic and dragons. Because of this, the universe stuffed dragons into a form humans could handle, dragon natures transforming into a device or tattoo on the dragon's body.

But occasionally, in private and in the presence of those who believed without doubt, a dragon could form into his true self. Malcolm had told Seth that he and Caleb sometimes flew over the ocean, taking care not to be seen. At least Malcolm took care, the black dragon had added in a dry voice. Caleb was a show-off.

Seth had the advantage of his fire. He could become flame anytime he wished, not bound by corporeal frames like the black and golden dragons.

His dragon came alive now, his hide flickering and dancing in the sunlight. Flying here was not as good as slip-sliding through Dragonspace, but it felt wonderful to stretch his wings and glide over the updrafts from the ocean below.

He felt a slight tug of his true-name bond to Carol, but it had loosened. He was still tethered to her, but she was letting the tether play a long way out. She was giving him a taste of freedom.

The dragon in him wanted to laugh and simply *fly*. The human that Seth had become dipped his wing to make him head back to the city. He knew Carol hadn't been physically hurt by the encounter, but he wanted to touch her, hold her, and assure himself that she was all right.

He soared over the clouds, his dragon form dissolving into a string of fire as San Francisco came into view. There was beauty in the city spreading on the rugged, rocky coastline, the tops of the huge red bridge that led to it poking through the clouds.

He knew where Carol was without having to search for her aura. She'd gone home.

His bond pulled him unerringly to the tall, ornate house on Russian Hill, and he became a stream of fire so fine he could fit between the molecules of glass in her window. He landed on his feet in the middle of her living room, his body solidifying with a rush.

Carol sat on the sofa, her stocking-feet tucked under her, her head on a pillow. Axel stood up when he saw Seth, his usual good-natured grin absent.

"I got her here, but she's upset," Axel said. "She's not used to death."

Carol raised her head, her eyes pools of fear. "Seth, don't come near me. Go to Lisa—have her send you back to Dragonspace."

"You know I can't. Not while you hold me."

"Why not? I won't call you. I'll leave you alone." Her voice held a note of panic.

"The bond would hurt me. I'd always be pulled to you, and I'd search for any way to get back to you."

Her face fell, and she dropped her head back to the pillow. "Seth, I'm so sorry."

Seth turned to the ever-handy box of clothes and chose another pair of jeans. "I prefer bondage to you than to the other Dragon Master."

Axel nodded. "Carol *is* prettier."

"I agree."

"It's not funny," Carol said. She reached for a tissue on the table next to her and wiped her eyes. "I felt the *thing* inside me come alive. I wanted Seth to kill them all—I wanted to command it, like Seth was an attack dog. It was horrible."

"I wanted to kill him," Seth said, pulling on the jeans over his bare legs. "He almost did kill you." He thought of the weapons trained on Carol, the dull explosions as death flew straight at her. "I'm not sorry."

"I'm not sorry you saved my life either. That's not what I meant."

Axel broke in. "You were threatened, and the mage inside you responded to the threat. You used the weapon you had most handy, which was Seth."

"Is that what I do? Use dragons as my personal arsenal?"

Axel sighed and sat down on the couch. "Carol, sweetie, it's a bitch being a magical creature. You can do powerful things, and you wonder if you have a right to. The fact that you wonder is good. It means you're compassionate and aren't about to destroy the entire city just to prove you can." He paused. "If you do decide to destroy the city, will you leave my favorite deli on Van Ness alone? They have great pastrami."

"Please stop joking about this. I'm scared."

"You need me to joke. Isn't that why you asked me to bring you home?"

"No, I asked because Malcolm is right. If I'm a Dragon

Master, that means I control dragons. What if I decide to take over Lisa, Caleb, and Malcolm? What if I want to use them as weapons? What if I get them hurt or killed?"

"Dragons are pretty tough."

"*Axel.*"

Seth folded himself to sit on his heels beside the sofa. He put his hand on Carol's cold fingers. "He's not wrong. Dragons are very strong, and we recover swiftly."

"So it's all right if I use you? You didn't feel what was inside me. It scares the crap out of me. Because . . ." She trailed off, swallowing hard.

Seth stroked her midnight hair, as always loving the satin feel of it. "I'm not unhappy to fight for you."

Axel watched him with a speculative look in his brown eyes. "Neither am I. And I'm not bound to you, Carol."

Carol didn't answer. Seth saw that she'd given up arguing, not because she agreed but because she was too tired to make them understand.

Seth continued to stroke her hair, even leaned his cheek against it. Axel got off the couch, shoving his hands into the pockets of his leather coat.

"I'll leave you two alone, then."

Carol sat up swiftly. "I don't think you should go."

"You need to work things out. I'm not far if you really need me—just call for a Baku, and there I'll be."

Axel winked, gave a fluttering-finger wave, and vanished. A rush of air filled the space he'd been with an audible pop.

Carol shivered and lay back down again. "I *wish* he wouldn't do that."

Carol buried her face in the couch pillow and tried to shut out the clamor in her head. She heard Seth's music mixed with her own, plus the jangling of the Dragon Master within her. She thought with black humor that she ought to rent a concert hall and give a performance.

"You shouldn't stay," she said.

"Yes, I should."

Seth's warm touch drifted across her skin. It felt so good, so comforting, but the magic in her wouldn't let her enjoy it. The Dragon Master within was whirling in triumph at having caught such a fine specimen of fire dragon.

"Axel is the only one I can trust myself around," she said. "He's not a dragon."

"He has a true name, though." Seth's voice was warm and deep. "All living beings do—his is just more unusual."

"Terrific." The worry bit deeper into her gut. "Maybe none of my friends is safe from me."

Seth said nothing. His dragon strength flowed through his thought threads, singing through her aura.

"It scares me, Seth," she whispered. "I realize now I've always been this way. People thought I was driven and motivated and all those things they say about you when you're an obsessed overachiever, but it was this inside me." She put her hand on her breastbone. "This need to use anyone and anything to succeed. I don't like it."

Seth slid his hand through her hair again, saying nothing.

"I was afraid of the Dragon Master when I saw him in that warehouse," she went on. "Now I'm afraid of me."

Seth still didn't answer, and she knew there were no answers.

He wrapped his arms around her and pulled her against his bare, solid chest. The red curls there tickled her cheek, and his heart beat strong beneath her ear.

"You should hate me," she said. "Maybe deep down inside you do, but you can't tell me."

"No, Carol. If I hated you, I could make it known in many ways. I'm a dragon, with a dragon's temper. I could make your life hell."

"You mean it isn't hell already?"

"Not really. I could fight you, trash your house, terrorize your friends, fly free until you jerked me back. I couldn't hurt you or get away, but I could make sure you hated every minute of having me on a leash."

"So why don't you?"

"Because of this."

He cupped his hands around her face and slanted his mouth across hers. The now familiar spark leapt between them, kicking in her adrenaline and pouring energy back into her body.

With energy came a hunger. She needed this dragon and his fire, wanted to drag everything he was into her.

Seth jumped as she bit his bottom lip, then he kissed her back, his lips bruising hers. She grabbed his wrists, kissing him as she slid off the couch onto him. She used her weight to press him to the carpet, and he didn't fight her as they both went down.

She remembered her visions of him with chains around his wrists, the sly smile he'd given her over his shoulder. She raised his thick arms above his head, pinning them as she went on kissing him.

She let go of his wrist only to grab the waistband of his jeans and twist the button open. The zipper went next, and his hardness welled out between the parted fabric.

Seth's entire body went rigid. Carol felt him shift from a man who'd been indulging her to the dragon that could make her life hell if he wanted. He growled and snared *her* wrists in a bruising grip.

She'd never wrestled with a man before. Her lovemaking encounters had all been sedate, two people mutually deciding what tame thing they'd do before they got into bed and did them, no surprises.

Seth rolled her over onto her back, his weight on top of her, and shoved his knee between her legs. He pinned her arms above her head like she'd done with him, playing, but also deadly serious.

"Tell me to stop," he said. "You can tell me to do whatever you want, so command me to stop."

"I don't want you to stop."

"Be very sure." He leaned to her, his eyes dark, this beautiful, wild creature in her power.

"I'm sure," she whispered.

His teeth scraped the skin at the hollow of her throat, then he jerked her shirt open to her waist. Carol tried to reach between them to touch him, but he grabbed her wrists and pinned her hands again. "No."

She struggled, but he wasn't about to let go. He licked across her cheekbones, tasting her eyelids and the hollows of her temples.

His hot tongue, rough on her skin, was one of the most erotic things she'd ever felt. She chased his mouth with her own, but he moved quickly, never letting him catch her.

Down he licked to the valley between her breasts, then he pulled at her bra with his teeth. "Off."

"You'll have to let me up."

He rolled away from her. The loss of his weight and warmth was hard to take, but she sat up and tugged off her shirt. She reached around and unhooked her bra, then he pulled it off her before she could.

She expected him to cup her breasts, maybe lean to suckle them, but he pushed her back to the carpet. He licked her again, not spending any more time on her nipples than the rest of her, then he nudged her to roll over onto her front.

The carpet prickled her stomach, an odd contrast to his hot tongue flicking over her shoulders and down her spine. He licked to the waistband of her skirt then she felt the buttons loosen and the fabric slide down and off her legs. She wore thigh-high stockings underneath, and Seth spent time wriggling his tongue beneath the lacy elastic bands.

"Why do you wear so many clothes?" he hissed as he pulled at her panties.

"So when it's windy, I don't give the city of San Francisco a thrill."

"I want these off."

Carol started to tell him he'd have to let her up again, but he solved the problem by breaking the waistband elastic and tearing the panties in half. Elastic still gripped her thighs, but Seth spread her legs, the panties no longer hampering him.

He lowered his weight on top of her. His jeans were gone, and nothing lay between his hardness and the flesh of her buttocks.

"Seth," she said, curling her hands into the carpet.

He parted her folds, which were scalding and wet, and next she felt the huge blunt tip of him slide inside.

"I can't," she whimpered.

"Command me to stop." His hand was heavy on her back, then his teeth grazed her ear. "Make me do what you will."

She went silent, pressing her lips together to stem her words. She knew damn well she wanted him to take her, hard, right there on her ultraexpensive Oriental carpet.

He must have decided her silence was a go-ahead, because he nipped her ear again and pressed himself fully inside her.

Carol heard the music swell at the same time he slid all the way in, spreading her. He was so big, and in this position, every inch of him pushed at her.

When he began to pump, she closed her eyes, trying to find the control that had dominated her life. Seth's fire was destroying it, breaking her control into a million glittering pieces that flickered away before she could catch them.

She found herself screaming incoherently into the carpet. Seth balled his fists next to her and drove into her in silence.

Carol felt like she was coming apart, but Seth didn't stop. He rode her fast, driving into her so furiously that her body inched across the floor. He pressed one hand on her back to steady her.

"Do you like me doing this?" he growled. "Do you want to command me to do more?"

"Seth, I can't . . ." She trailed off as climax built up in her, and she shouted, twisting on his hard piston of a cock.

The room began to shake. Seth gasped as his own climax hit him, then his seed shot into her, scalding her as much as his fire.

He fell down on her, breathing hard, as the cupboards in her kitchen started to rattle. Plaster trickled from the ceiling in a fine rain, sticking to Seth's wet skin.

It took a moment for Carol to realize that the rolling and shaking of the room had nothing to do with them. She tried to sit up, but Seth was still inside her, his body pinning her.

"Earthquake," she said, and he nodded. Seth had her on her feet in a heartbeat and began pushing her toward the front door.

"No." She grabbed him and towed him to the doorway of the bedroom. "We stand here."

Seth was naked, sweating, his penis still thick and heavy. Carol held on to the door frame, facing him in black thigh-high stockings and nothing else. She started to laugh.

"What is funny?" he asked.

"If we're buried and they find us like this, they'll know what a racy life Carol Juan really had."

"We won't die here," Seth said with conviction.

"You can turn into fire and fly away. Why don't you?"

His stare burned. "If I go, you go."

The building gave an extra hard shake. Across the room, her heavy bookcase teetered forward and crashed to the floor. The cupboards in the kitchen jerked open, spilling their contents.

And then it was over. Outside, car alarms were going off, people were shouting, calling to each other, and sirens began to wail.

Inside the apartment, all was stillness. Carol laid her head on Seth's chest and exhaled in relief.

The Dragon Master turned in his tight prison as the earthquake stopped, but the thick magical walls still held.

He'd thought this time it would crack for certain, but the rolling ceased and the glass remained unbroken.

The incubi were dead, though, beams from the ceiling having fallen on the three that guarded him. They had disintegrated into a pool of green ooze, which stank even through the thick glass wall.

The human called Danny Lok was dead, too, killed by Carol and her fire dragon. One of the human hirelings had returned to tell the Order what had happened. He'd stood in front of Sying's column, his olive face covered in sweat, his dark eyes wide, and told them of the fire.

Idiots. The fire dragon's power wasn't simply flame—any dragon had the power to burn. Seth hadn't used a tenth of his power; the weak human Lok had died of fright and frailness.

It hurt Sying that Seth's exquisite power had been denied him, but at the same time he felt a frisson of pride. Carol Juan was his descendant, after all.

The Order had killed Carol's mother before she'd been properly trained. That was a shame. Lian Juan had been a woman of much potential, and she could have taught Carol the ways of her power.

The fire dragon was a weapon that the Dragon Master had wielded before, and he longed to wield it again. If he could fuse with him, he could escape his prison, destroy the evil, and keep it from the hands of the Order.

But Carol controlled the fire dragon instead, and Sying couldn't reach her. The frustration of that was bitterness in his mouth.

The fire dragon's power would consume her. She needed him, Sying, to help her. He had to make her understand that.

Come to me, he whispered, searching for the fire dragon with his thought threads. *Bring Carol with you, and we will slay our enemies together.*

His call reached nothing.

The Dragon Master sighed and drew his hand away from the glasslike wall. The Order would succeed in destroying Carol and the fire dragon together, and if that happened, there would be no hope for Sying.

He rested his head on the glass and let tears slide down his face.

11

"I brought you the list of buildings that Danny Lok owned," Lumi said, pushing a sheaf of papers at Carol.

They'd met up at Ming Ue's as dusk fell, after Seth had helped Carol restore her apartment.

Seth realized as he and Carol walked down from Russian Hill to Chinatown that her apartment had gotten off lightly. Stores on Powell had wares and debris all over the floor, owners trying to gather everything up and secure the doors. Electricity was off for many blocks, and cars and buses filled roads, unmoving.

Most people were walking, trying to get into stores to buy up fresh water, worried but not in a panic. The earthquake, Carol informed him, hadn't been a big one. Things would return to normal soon.

Ming Ue had thrown open the doors of her little restaurant, letting neighborhood people or stranded tourists come to eat and drink for free. The old woman had given Carol a half-belligerent, half-anxious look when she related this, but Carol only nodded absently and said it was a good idea.

"Are you feeling all right?" Ming Ue asked her.

Carol didn't bother to respond. While Shaiming and a few waitresses filled tables with little plates of dumplings and carried empty dishes back to the kitchen, Lumi handed Carol the list of places that Daniel Lok had owned.

Seth looked over Carol's shoulder at the neat paper that showed about twenty different addresses. "Now that he's dead, who will take over his territory?" he asked.

"He has family." Lumi leaned his elbow on the table. He was tall and rawboned, and wore blue jeans and a shirt with IRON MAIDEN printed on it. "Nephews and nieces, some of them not too keen that Uncle Danny was a criminal. But now that he's gone, his rivals are going to come out of the woodwork and claim his territories. We might have a gang war on our hands."

The music of Carol's thoughts changed to a tarnished clamor. "That's not what I meant to do."

"Carol, he had a heart attack," Lumi said. "Besides, he was a very, very bad guy."

"And now more bad guys are going to fight over what he left," Carol said. "I don't think the Asian community of San Francisco wants to be fought over right now."

"So stop them," Ming Ue cut in.

Carol turned a startled face to her. "What?"

"If you don't want the Tongs to take over Chinatown or destroy it while they're fighting each other, stop them. You have the power. You have a fire dragon. Protect us."

Carol looked at Seth. "Could you do that? This place and mine are protected by dragon marks. Could you put them over every shop in Chinatown?"

Ming Ue answered for him. "The power of a dragon mark lessens if it's spread around too much. That's what

Malcolm says anyway. Witch marks can be put everywhere, but they're not as strong as dragon marks. But you can do it yourself, Carol. You command dragons. You can use their power to stop Danny Lok's rivals."

"You have a lot of faith in me."

"It's not faith. It's certainty."

Carol gave her an impatient look. "What would you like me to do first, find the Dragon Master and defeat him or save Chinatown from organized crime?"

"You must do both. You have the means."

"Grandmother . . ."

Ming Ue firmed her mouth. "You have Seth to look over these places for the Dragon Master. You must let him while you see Zhen to learn your powers. Then you and Seth can mark the shops of our people."

"As easy as that, is it?"

"She's right," Seth broke in quietly. "Finding the Dragon Master is not as important as you being strong enough to face him when we do."

Carol deflated. "You might be right, but I don't want you going anywhere near him. What if he tries snaring you again?"

The music in Seth's head shimmered. "My bond to you is tight now. He won't be able to break it."

"How can you know that? When we were in Union Square, you almost disappeared."

"Because your hold on me hadn't fully formed. Now we are so twined that no one else can call me."

"Are you sure?" Lumi asked. "Last year Malcolm got bound with his true name by two people at the same time. He said it almost ripped him apart."

"Malcolm is a black dragon, an ordinary dragon," Seth explained. "I'm a fire dragon."

Lumi gave him a wry look. "I so don't want to be in the

room when you call Malcolm an ordinary dragon. Or maybe I do." He chuckled.

"The fire dragon is something different from the others," Ming Ue said. "I feel it."

Carol bit her lip as she turned to Seth. "Are you sure?"

He squeezed her hand. "I will ask Malcolm to assist me, and you will have Axel protect you while I'm gone."

"You worked this all out nicely."

"With Lok dead, it's logical that others will move into his territories," Seth said. "Dragons do the same. If the next man finds the Dragon Master, he will use him or be destroyed by him. Better I find the Dragon Master before that happens."

"And if you find him, then what?"

"You kill him." Seth stood up while Carol gaped at him. "So you must grow strong while you can."

Carol got out of her chair, her brown eyes filled with worry. "Damn, this just gets worse."

Seth leaned down and kissed her, closing his eyes to savor her taste.

"I'll locate him," he said. "Not fight him. Not yet."

"While you wait for me to take my Dragon Master lessons?"

Seth brushed his tongue over her lips. "When you are ready, nothing will be able to stop you."

She had such a beautiful face, oval and slender, her almond-shaped eyes deepest brown. Her full red lips made him want to kiss her again, and he touched her mouth with his fingertip before he made himself take up the lists from the table and depart.

Malcolm wasn't waiting in the middle of Union Square as Seth had asked Lumi to tell him to be. Saba was.

"Malcolm went to Dragonspace," the witch said before Seth could ask. "He said he had to look something up in his Archive."

"The Dragon Archive?"

"It's an impressive place," she said, dark eyes amused.

Seth snorted. "Only black dragons crave knowledge for its own sake."

"So what do fire dragons crave?"

"To be left alone."

Saba put her hands on her hips and cocked her head at him. Like Carol, she had black hair and brown eyes, though her eyes were more rounded, and her hair was cropped short. She was also shorter than Carol and curvier, and she wore a cropped white top and blue jeans instead of the blouses and skirts Carol favored.

"You don't seem to want to leave Carol alone. You're sleeping with her, aren't you?"

Seth warmed, thinking of Carol writhing under him on the carpet. "I've mated with her, yes. And enjoyed it."

Saba started to laugh, then shook her head. "Dragons."

"What about dragons?"

"Lisa would know what I meant. Now, how about we go look for the Dragon Master?"

"I wanted Malcolm's help."

"You've got me instead. Before you say I can't possibly, let me tell you, I do one hell of a locator spell."

"I don't think those will work on the Dragon Master," Seth said. "Besides, I have these."

Saba took the lists, looking at the addresses with a grimace. "Most of these are on the south side of town. Figures. I don't want to take too long over this—my daughter is at Lisa's, but with incubi and gangs roaming around . . ."

Seth fully understood. "I welcome your help."

"A polite dragon?" Saba said with a grin. "That makes a change."

"You have come to learn from me?" Zhen wrapped his wrinkled hands over his cane. He looked tired and tense, but he gestured Carol to a chair with a shaking hand.

"I came because I'm afraid." Carol sat down stiffly as he shuffled to the hot plate in his tiny back room and prepared tea. "It's coming too easily to me. I wanted to kill Danny Lok, and then he was dead."

Zhen nodded as he poured hot water out of an ancient kettle into an equally ancient iron teapot.

"The power comes not from your fear but from your anger."

Carol remembered her rage. "His bodyguards shot up my restaurant. Of course I was angry."

"Most people would be afraid. They would scream and duck as I heard everyone else did but you and Seth."

"For some reason, I knew I didn't need to. It was like Seth was a part of me. Like I could swing my arm down, and he'd swoop the exact same way." She moved her arm in demonstration. "I don't want to be able to do that."

"Your tie to him is very strong."

"That doesn't mean I should use him as some kind of weapon. He's a person—well, a living being anyway. That's not right."

Zhen sat down and poured fragrant oolong tea into a delicate cup he placed in front of her. "You are a Dragon Master. That means you master dragons. Dragons to you *are* weapons, extensions of your power. In ancient times, the Dragon Masters were kept by the emperors, so they could harness the power of dragons. That was when dragons easily came and went between this world and Dragonspace."

Carol's interest stirred. "Why didn't everyone have a Dragon Master, if dragons were so sought after?"

Zhen lifted his handleless cup of tea. He still seemed on edge, but he answered readily. "Because there were only one or two Dragon Masters alive at a time. It runs in families, but not always from one generation to the next. Ming Ue has some of the power, which is why dragons like her so much, but your mother was one of the powerful ones. And the last few days have proved you more powerful still." He gave her a significant look over his cup.

Carol sighed and sipped tea, letting the soothing taste relax her somewhat.

"I don't want this, but I've realized today that it's always been inside me. All my life, I've gone for what I wanted without hesitation. I never doubted, never stopped, never asked what others wanted. My business was my life, and I saw no reason to stop when I was so good at it, though I told myself I was doing it to repay Ming Ue and Shaiming." She drank more of the tea. "But that was the Dragon Master, craving power, wasn't it?"

"Yes, it was. Power is neutral, Li Mei. It is neither good nor evil. It is what you do with it that makes it one or the other."

"So me wanting Danny Lok dead was all me? Thanks, I feel so much better."

"You were defending yourself and your territory and everyone within your protection. You acted instinctively—he had come prepared to kill you if necessary. And in the end, you stopped Seth from killing him."

"I suppose that's true." The tea was good. She lifted the teapot and poured more into her cup. "We never know what we'll do when it comes down to it, do we?"

"Now that you do know, you can decide what you will do, how you will use your power."

She sighed. "I'm not sure about that. It wells up inside

me like a black bubble, and it comes out before I want it to. I'm afraid of hurting people, like Grandmother or Lumi."

"You do have the potential for destruction, Li Mei. And you have to face it. You are very dangerous."

"It's funny—as a businesswoman, I always wanted to be thought dangerous. But not to my friends and family."

"Then let me teach you to control it."

"That's why I'm here." She looked into her cup. "This is excellent tea, Mr. Zhen."

He looked modest. "Thank you. I blend it myself—a recipe passed down through my family."

"Do you still have family?" She'd never really thought about the Junk Man being married and having children.

"I did, once. They are all gone. Now it is only me."

Her heart twisted. "I'm sorry."

"Do not feel sorrow for me. I have many friends, and I am blessed. I go to your grandmother's for mahjong every Thursday and enjoy it very much."

Zhen and Ming Ue had been playing mahjong for years. The click of mahjong tiles on the table figured in Carol's earliest and most comforting memories. Ming Ue, Zhen, and Shaiming had played with Lisa's grandmother, and the quiet Shaiming had often won the pot.

"Would you like to play now?"

Carol raised her brows. "I thought you were going to teach me to control my powers."

Zhen smiled, his face folding into wrinkles. "But a game of mahjong will be just the thing to clear the mind."

"We need four people." Carol leaned back in her chair. "And I'm tired. It's been a bad day."

"You are tired because I put a mild sedative in the tea."

Carol blinked at him, then realized that her limbs were limp and relaxed. "What did you do that for?"

"It will be easier for you to focus if you are not, as Americans say, stressed. The sedative will take the edge off your panic, and enable you to do the exercises without fear."

"You might have warned me."

"Then you would not have drunk the tea. There is no need to fear me. You could kill me with the flick of your finger, and I could not harm you. Not that I would." He rose, reaching above the table to pull down a worn box heaped with mahjong tiles. "I have asked your grandmother and Shaiming to join us."

"Grandmother will never leave the restaurant . . ."

She broke off as Ming Ue hobbled through the curtains that separated the back room from Zhen's store. Shaiming was right behind her, helping Ming Ue to the table to sit next to Carol.

"We ran out of food," Ming Ue announced. "So I closed up. It's seven anyway, and we never have much of a dinner crowd."

Carol's restaurant management instincts kicked in. "Grandmother, if we're out of food, we have to stock for tomorrow."

"Sit down, my girl. No one will be surprised if we don't open tomorrow. We'll take the day to fix the damage and restock. I'm sure everyone will remember how generous was Ming Ue's Dim Sum house and we'll have a crowd. That's how you build customer base, Li Mei. Kindness and loyalty. Never mind what they taught you at that lofty school."

Carol sat back, her argument evaporating. Ming Ue was right, and the tea had made Carol gloriously relaxed. "Have you heard from Seth?" she asked.

"Not yet," Ming Ue said, settling herself. Zhen took the chair opposite Carol, and Shaiming sat on Carol's right. "He'll call when he has something to report. Or Malcolm will. Or they'll come to us—dragons never much trust cell phones."

Carol remembered Seth crushing her phone in his strong fingers. She hadn't rushed to replace it. "True."

"I don't blame them," Zhen said. "Shall we build?"

Carol automatically helped turn the tiles facedown and shuffle them. Ming Ue had taught Carol and her cousin Lumi how to play mahjong long ago, and the four had often whiled away a winter's night in a quiet game.

They built a square of tiles two high, all four of them working in silence. Carol let the mundane task soothe her, losing herself in the cool of the tiles under her fingers, the quiet click that brought back so many memories of childhood.

"That is exactly right," Zhen said across from her. "Focus on what you are doing, nothing else."

The tea helped. Carol wasn't exactly sleepy, but the edges of her world had smoothed. She felt calmer and more relaxed than she had in a long time.

They finished constructing the wall and selected tiles. Carol looked at her hand and saw that she'd drawn many dragons. Black and red dragons writhed on the ivory-colored surfaces as she stood the tiles up on the table.

Black and red, she thought. *Malcolm and Seth.* The other color of dragon in Zhen's mahjong set was green, but when Carol turned one over, it shimmered and became deepest gold. *Caleb.*

"When the Dragon Masters worked for the Han emperors," Zhen said, "the emperor would use ink to draw the dragon he wanted to command, then the Dragon Master would sing its name. Once the dragon had done his bidding, the Dragon Master released it. Much later they used mahjong tiles. Look at the dragons, Li Mei, and learn them. You can call them anytime you want, or you can just look at them."

"Will it hurt them?"

"No, child. Learn them and understand them and let

them go. Be separate from them. You call, but they don't become a part of you."

Carol studied the black dragon tile. The lines of its body twisted and moved before her eyes, then settled again into an outline of a snarling black dragon with silver eyes.

Malcolm, she whispered inside her head, and then, just like that, she knew his true name.

The notes of it danced on the edge of her hearing, and she focused on them until they became clear.

She felt Malcolm's sudden fury, dim and far away. His mind was dark and ancient, holding an amazing array of calculations and analytical thought, his intelligence cold enough to form icicles. She also felt the newness of his human emotions, foremost his love for Saba and his baby daughter.

He snarled at her. *No.*

He fought so furiously that Carol's instinct was to close her grip, to hold him down.

"You don't have to," Zhen said. "Know his name and him, but step away."

Carol unclenched her hand. The coiled band around Malcolm loosened, and she studied the tile, stilling her mind.

You are my friend, she said softly. *I'd never hurt you.*

Malcolm snarled again, though with less ferocity. *I'll never bow down to you.*

I'll never ask you to. Promise.

Then go away. I'm busy trying to figure out how to save your ass.

Get back to me on that, will you?

Malcolm didn't answer, only blew out his breath in a dragon *whuff*. Carol turned her black dragon tiles facedown, one by one, and let go.

Caleb answered her call more quickly. *Don't mages have anything better to do than bother dragons who are minding their own business?*

I'm practicing, Carol answered.

Do I look like a guinea pig? Go pester Malcolm.

I did already. Carol sang Caleb's name, its golden chimes amazingly beautiful and wrapped in warrior strength. She sensed silver threads within the gold, his love for Lisa.

Caleb said grumpily, *I'm so impressed.*

He was easier to release. Carol turned his tiles face-down, breathing a farewell. She felt Caleb's surprise when she unwound him from her, then he was gone.

Seth next.

Because she already had his name infused in her thoughts, she barely had to reach for him. She sang one note, and his fire flowed around her like molten wire.

He was searching for the Dragon Master. She sensed Saba through him, the witch's purple aura hovering in the background. Malcolm wasn't with them. He'd been far, far away, in Dragonspace.

Carol. Seth's word was a whisper, almost tender.

Have you found him? she asked.

Not yet.

Carol drew the threads of his name out like a song, loving every pitch, every nuance. She studied what she held, and then, as she had with Caleb and Malcolm, tried to let it go.

She turned over the tiles, but instead of the blank ivory backs, she found the red dragon etched there, too. Before she could stop it, the name tightened around Seth and began to pull.

He resisted. The Dragon Master in her laughed and pulled harder.

She felt Seth come to her, the fire between them like a tightrope. His outline appeared in the curtains of the doorway, his face dark with rage.

"Not yet," he growled.

Come to me. Carol pulled at him, and he drifted across

the floor until he solidified beside her. Zhen and Ming Ue looked distressed, and Shaiming blinked.

"Not yet," Seth repeated, more forcefully. He smelled like wind and water like he always did. "You aren't ready for it yet."

I want the power of the fire dragon.

It will kill you. Let me go.

"He is right, Li Mei," Zhen said, springing to his feet. "You must not take him until you can control your power."

"I don't understand. I'm trying to let him go, but I want to draw him into me instead."

"You must resist," Zhen said in agitation. "You must be very strong to withstand the combined power of the Dragon Master and the fire dragon."

"I'm trying. I don't know how to let go."

"Send him back to where he was. Send him back now."

"I can't. I want to take . . ."

Carol closed her hand around Seth's sinewy forearm. A shock jolted through her, similar to what she felt when they made love, then sudden power so raw she thought her fingers would sear off.

Zhen looked scared to death. "Send him away, Li Mei. Anywhere. Now."

Seth began to dissolve into flame, not the usual string of fire he liked to become, but fire that outlined his human body. His eyes filled with deep, intense pain.

"Now, *now!*" Zhen shrieked.

Go. The power inside Carol gave Seth a strong push, and he suddenly dissolved and was gone.

12

Seth flew free again, arrowing over the city and the glittering Bay Bridge that linked it to the inland cities. Beyond that, a few hundred miles east, he felt mountains, sharp and tall like those of his own home.

If he was free, he'd go there and see them, if he didn't simply tear back to Dragonspace.

Carol had nearly commanded him to give her his dragon fire, and Zhen had been right to stop her. She wasn't ready to handle his power. The first night he'd met her, when he'd been enraged that she'd called him forth and bound him to her, he might have let his fire kill her and be done.

He stopped the thought—*no.* He remembered the softness of Carol's body under his when he'd pinned her against the car, the startled look in her eyes, the scent of her that still drove him crazy. He'd never have hurt her, and he didn't want to hurt her now.

He flew back to the place where he'd vanished from Saba, the first of Danny Lok's addresses he and Saba had stopped to check. He didn't see Saba's car there, which meant she'd sensibly left instead of trying to investigate on her own.

Seth streamed into the empty building before he solidified, to find himself in another dark and cold place. The earthquake damage had been a little more severe in this part of town, likely because the buildings were run-down, many of them abandoned.

Seth looked about the small, empty building and wrinkled his nose. A dark cloying odor permeated the room, something that spoke of more than disuse or decay.

Seth silently sent a tendril of flame above him to light his way and began to explore. In a corner he found a wooden trapdoor set in the floor, with enough broken slats to let through a draft of fetid air.

When he reached down and pried the door up, the stink hit him hard. Holding his breath, he propped open the door and sent his flame down into the darkness.

The sickly sweet smell of death had wrapped around the musty smell of damp. Seth peered into the hole for a long time, then made himself test the wooden stairs.

They seemed stable enough, and he started down, ready to turn to flame if they gave way. At the bottom he found a rubble-strewn basement.

This earthquake or a previous one had cracked the brick walls, and in one corner was a pile of dirt, bricks, and beams. In front of it were damp green smudges that glittered under his flame, all that was left of incubi.

"He was here, then," Seth whispered.

He wondered, as he crouched near the three stains, whether the earthquake had killed the incubi or Lok's hirelings had. There was no way of knowing that or whether they'd been the enhanced incubi or the usual brainless variety.

Help me.

The voice rasped in the air around him, cold and desperate and terrifying.

Seth stood up in a hurry. He'd heard the voice before, recognized the black aura that went with it, groping toward him with sticky threads. But the threads were thin, weak, and broke off as soon as Seth stepped away from them.

Carol, he whispered.

Her answer came loud and clear. *Seth? Where are you?*

Ask Saba. He slid aside one bit of rubble and stood looking down with hands on hips. *I think I've found the Dragon Master.*

Carol hurried out of the Junk Man's shop over the protests of Zhen and Ming Ue.

"I have to go," she said. "If he's found the other Dragon Master, he can't face him alone."

Only Shaiming seemed to understand. Her quiet cousin nodded to her and said in his soft voice, "Go to him, Li Mei."

Carol wasn't foolish enough to try to drive with the limb-relaxing sedative Zhen had given her. She called Axel, who popped in out of nowhere at the front of the store.

"Will you stop that?" she snapped at him. "What if someone saw you?"

"People see what they want to see," Axel said amiably. "Where are we off to?"

Carol gave him the address Saba had related. Saba had wanted to go with them, but Carol wouldn't let her. If the Dragon Master was there, along with the Dragon Master's henchmen, Saba would be in too much danger.

Axel popped out again and returned in a few minutes at the wheel of Carol's own car. In the shop doorway, Zhen watched in distress as Carol slid into the passenger seat, but he didn't try to stop her.

Axel roared off, narrowly missing a car in the tight alley. He bounced them toward Union Square, then down again to Market Street, nearly bottoming out on the intersections.

"Would you be careful?" Carol held on to a strap and watched white-faced as he cut in front of a cable car.

"I love driving in San Francisco," Axel said, grinning widely. "Like in a *Dirty Harry* movie."

"This isn't a movie," she shouted as they slammed through another intersection and dove down the next hill.

"No, I mean, I was *in* one of the *Dirty Harry* movies. I drove one of the stunt cars. Those were good times."

Carol gritted her teeth and directed him down to the small warehouses Saba had told her about. Axel got them there without wrecking the car, and Carol crawled out, the adrenaline rush of the drive canceling out the effects of the sedative.

Seth was nowhere in sight, but the door to the warehouse was wide-open. Axel stopped her before she dashed inside, and firmly led the way, Carol close on his heels.

"Whew," Axel said, holding his nose. "What died in here?"

"Incubi," Seth rumbled.

He stepped onto the floor from an opening in the corner, his way lit by an orange flame that danced over his head. "Three of them. I think other things are dead down there as well—rats and other vermin."

Carol's heart throbbed with relief upon seeing Seth's tall, upright body. He'd dressed again in the jeans and long raincoat he'd worn to Ming Ue's.

"And the Dragon Master?" Axel asked. "Is he dead, too?"

"No."

With that cryptic comment, Seth descended into the hole again and Axel followed.

"Oh, no, you don't," Axel said when Carol started behind him. "Let us be the superheroes, and you be the sidekick. You stay up here and don't come down unless we say it's all right. And even then, be suspicious."

Carol chafed with impatience, though she had to admit she didn't want to descend into that horrible stink. She waited in the cold, pulling her coat closer about her, trying not to worry.

She occupied herself musing that this had been one of Danny Lok's properties. She wondered what he'd used it for—it had been emptied some time ago.

It was creepy up here anyway. Through the open door, she saw the gray light of the winter day and her gleaming black car incongruous in the empty parking lot. A target of opportunity if she ever saw one.

She was almost relieved when Seth called up the stairs, "Carol, please come down."

She stepped to the trapdoor. "Are you sure? Axel told me to be suspicious."

Seth wrapped his thoughts warmly around her. "Be careful, but come."

Nothing dire happened as she descended. Seth and Axel waited for her near the pile of rubble, which they'd cleared part of. Carol gasped.

In the middle of the rubble lay the column of glass that she and Seth had seen in the warehouse a few streets south of here. It lay on its side, stretching wall to wall as though each end had been attached to the bricks.

In the middle of the column was the figure of the man

they'd seen before. His hands were pressed to the glass, and he was whispering.

Help me.

"The Dragon Master," Seth said quietly.

As soon as they uncovered him, Seth felt the other Dragon Master *tap-tapping* at his thoughts. *Free me. Please.*

Seth sensed the tendrils again reaching for him, tiny snakes trying to twine around his brain. They met with the fiery tendrils of Carol's thoughts and backed away.

"He's in there?" Carol asked, trying to peer through the thick glass.

"Something is." Axel cupped his hands around it. They could see the outline of a human body, but it was very faint.

Help me.

Carol stood up suddenly. "Are you hearing that?"

Seth nodded, but Axel looked puzzled. "Is he trying to talk to you?"

"He wants us to free him." Seth pushed his hands into his pockets, trying to shut out the desperate voice. Sying couldn't still be alive—that was impossible.

"He sounds scared," Carol said, resting her hand on the glass. "I wonder what happened."

Seth wondered as well. He'd never found out the fate of Sying the Dragon Master; Seth had only awakened free. He felt a tiny trickle of evil from him now, though not as sharp as when they'd seen him in the larger warehouse yesterday.

Carol studied the column with a mixture of fear and interest. "If we leave him here, what happens? Will more incubi come to serve the Dragon Master, or will they abandon him?"

"Who the hell knows?" Axel said. "If we make the building fall on him, will he die?"

Seth eyed the thick column. It looked like glass, but it

was likely something held together by a magical field. "I don't think so. He'd be buried here until someone else dug him out."

Carol shivered. "That would be horrible."

Axel put his hands on his hips. "What do we do with him, then? It's not like he'll fit in Carol's car."

"I don't know," Carol answered. "I'm trying to decide if he's more of a danger if we leave him or hide him somewhere."

"The ocean," Seth said.

"Sorry?"

"I could carry him over your ocean and drop him in. He would be difficult to reach there."

He felt a shudder from the column, and a twinge of horror, but the deep ocean might still the voice.

"Could the incubi find him and bring him up?" Carol asked him. "I don't know anything about them—can they swim?"

"They are creatures of air and fire," Seth answered. "They don't like water, but in this human world, you have solved the problem of such things."

"Like boats and scuba." Axel barked a laugh. "An incubus in scuba gear. I'd love to see that."

Carol gave him an impatient look. "What I mean is, are we solving the problem by getting rid of him, or simply staving it off? How long before the incubi or the Order of the Black Lotus find him and make him powerful again?"

Seth had a solution, but he wasn't sure Carol would like it. A fire dragon's power could destroy the column and also the man inside.

Axel watched him, his dark eyes glittering. He'd guessed what Seth wanted to do.

"Carol," the Baku said. "Why don't we stroll out to your car?"

"Why?" she asked sharply.

"It stinks in here, and you need the air."

Carol looked from him to Seth. "I'm not stupid. You and Seth want to destroy this, don't you?"

Seth sent his threads to soothe her and found her brittle and resistant. "It's the best way."

"How dangerous is that? Is there a chance you'll be hurt, or killed, or enslaved in the process?"

Seth couldn't lie to her, because she'd know instantly through their bond. "There is a chance, yes."

"Then forget it."

"Carol," Axel said in a reasonable voice. "Look at it this way: If Seth kills the big, bad Dragon Master, there's no more need for you to hold him. You can let Seth go, he can return to Dragonspace, everyone's happy."

Her music darkened, and she drew a tense breath. "It's not that simple. Even if I wanted to let Seth go, I don't know how. And what's to say we won't be hunted down by enraged incubi or the Order? How will that be safer?" She broke off and looked at the column. "Besides, he's asking for our help."

Axel shook his head. "You're a sweet woman, but misguided sometimes."

"The male solution to everything is to kill it," she said. "A woman's strength is her ability to step back and think about it first. We know there are more solutions to problems than just one."

"Oh, very nice," Axel snorted. "Well, Ms. Businesswoman of the Year, what does your ability to think about it tell us?"

Carol gave him a withering look. "I don't know yet." She stopped. "Yes, I do. Seth, can you put a mark on this place? You know, like the ones on my apartment?" She traced her finger in the air.

"Keep him here, you mean?" Seth asked. "And keep others away from him?"

"Sure. If we need to store him somewhere, why not here?"

She looked excited, her eyes sparkling. Axel regarded her skeptically. "What if this Danny Lok's relatives want the building for something, or decide to tear it down next week?"

"That's easy," Carol said. "I'll buy it."

Axel ran his gaze over the ruined basement. "Buy it? It's kind of a dump."

"A good investment. You never know when an area will be gentrified. Or I can use it to warehouse goods for my restaurants, or turn it into an Asian grocery store or something. Many possibilities."

Axel eyed Seth and shook his head. Carol surveyed the room without dismay, having clearly decided what she wanted to do.

Without speaking, Seth turned to the walls around the Dragon Master and began to mark them. The symbols he traced flared out with a touch of fire, then settled into quiet shimmers.

Axel shook his head one more time but joined him, overlaying dragon magic with his strange purple-hued Baku magic. Axel didn't have to physically touch the walls to mark them—he simply looked at them and muttered under his breath.

"I can see those," Carol whispered in delight.

Axel chuckled. "Welcome to my world."

"Shouldn't we stand him upright?" Carol motioned to the column that still lay on the floor.

Seth had no interest in making the Dragon Master comfortable and no interest in touching the column with his dragon magic. It was massive, and he had no idea whether such a magical thing could be moved at all.

"Best to leave it alone." Axel voiced Seth's thoughts.

Carol opened her mouth to continue, but the roar of a

car engine came to them from above. "Crap," Carol said, and started up the stairs.

Seth grabbed her before she'd reached the third one. "No. Listen."

Doors slammed and footsteps sounded in the warehouse above.

"Time to depart," Axel said. He looked at Carol.

"I can get her out," Seth said. "But not through solid walls. I need to be upstairs with the door open."

Carol's warm body rested against him, her hair temptingly brushing his nose. She looked back up at him, putting her lips in reach. "Why don't we see who it is, first? It might be my grandmother and Shaiming worried about us. They weren't happy with me leaving."

"The aura is wrong," Seth said in her ear.

"Incubi? Can they drive?"

"It's human, not magical. At least, not much magical."

"How about if I go check it out?" Axel said. "I'm pretty scary."

Seth snaked his arm around Carol, ready to surround her with his flame and carry her away. He moved aside to let Axel pass.

"Oops, too late," Axel said.

Men came pouring down the stairs. They were human and dressed like Danny Lok and his bodyguards. All of them had hard faces and dark eyes, and one had helped shoot up the restaurant.

"Hi," Axel said. "Did you come to join the party?"

The first two on the stairs hesitated a split second, then came on down. They carried weapons, though they held them in neutral positions.

One man pushed his way to the front. He was larger and heavier than Danny Lok had been, and possessed a dark magic that made Seth's skin crawl. He stopped, feeling the marks that Axel and Seth had placed over the room.

"The Dragon Master is ours," the man said in clear English.

"Finders, keepers," Carol said. She was shaking, but her voice came out steady.

"You have no idea what you've gotten into, girl. Surrender to us and give us the fire dragon. You don't know how to use his power without killing yourself."

"And I should give him to you, why?"

"You don't have a choice."

"No, I have a fire dragon. And a Dragon Master. Why do you want them so much? Are you with the Black Lotus gang?"

"The Order of the Black Lotus has inherited the right to the Dragon Master. He is ours."

"You inherited him?" Carol asked in surprise.

"My ancestors imprisoned him, and passed on the task of keeping him. Which is why you will give him to us."

Imprisoned. Seth blinked in shock. The Order hadn't killed the Dragon Master for disobeying them after all. They'd imprisoned him in magic so thick it had broken the bond between the Dragon Master and his dragons.

Which was why this Dragon Master had reached out for Seth of all the fire dragons he could have—he'd already known Seth's name.

Seth tightened his grip around Carol's waist and whispered into her ear. "Be ready."

He felt Carol tense, sensed her Dragon Master power pressing around his mind. She looked back at him, her eyes full of fear, not of the men, but of herself.

"Get me out of here. *Please.*"

Seth looked at the Baku. "Axel."

"I'll do what I can," he said cheerfully.

He disappeared with a puff of air and reappeared at the top of the stairs. "Catch me if you can." He popped out again, startling the men gathered there.

The leader didn't pay attention, keeping his cold eyes on Seth and Carol. Shouting sounded above, indicating that Axel was enjoying himself.

Carol pressed her hand on top of Seth's, and he sensed her trying to tap into his dragon fire. "No," he whispered.

She kept pulling at him, likely not even realizing it. Seth jerked his arm from around her and pushed her against the wall. The spark died, but she spun around his thoughts, looking for a weakness.

Seth hissed, letting his body flow into his string of fire. He flew up the stairs, startling the leader and the two men who'd stayed with him. While they focused on him, he sent a string of flame up to Axel, snarling at him in dragon to get Carol and go.

Axel popped into existence again right behind Carol, and she gave a startled scream. He wrapped his arms around her and said, "Hope this works."

"Wait, you hope . . ." Carol began, then she and Axel were gone.

Seth whizzed around the men of the Black Lotus, who simply stared at him, realizing their weapons were useless. The leader snaked a tendril of magic to Seth, trying to entwine it in his fire.

Seth attempted to solidify into his dragon form and was surprised when it worked. The warehouse was large enough, and these men believed in—and feared—dragons.

The leader's face whitened as Seth dove toward him, reaching out with a talon to snare him. The man slapped back with dark magic, and Seth missed, but he followed up with a stream of real fire. Men screamed and dove to the ground, beating flames out of their clothes.

The leader drew himself up, magic swirling around him like a dark cloak. Seth blew his fire again, then let his body flow once more into pure flame.

Seth brushed fire over all the walls, marking them as

his. The leader cried out in sudden pain as Seth's fire magic wrapped around him like an iron band. He ran for the door, and Seth streaked flame past him before flying outside himself.

Carol's car still sat shining and whole in the parking lot, but the men of the Black Lotus ignored it as they rushed to their own vehicles and fled.

13

Seth found Carol arguing with Axel in her apartment. "I worked hard for that car, Axel. I need it."

"You kids and your obsession with vehicles," Axel growled. "You don't see me with a car."

"I can't pop in and out of wherever I want as handily as you. And what did you mean, *I hope this works*?"

Axel spotted Seth standing in the middle of the room, and he made for the front door. "Fine. I'll go see if I can retrieve your Beemer. I'll leave it in your usual garage, all right?"

He paused in the doorway to give Seth a grin and a thumbs-up, then he was gone.

"You're all right?" Seth asked.

"No." She rose shakily. "That was an experience. I'm not even sure what happened, but suddenly I was here."

"Safely. Good." Seth crossed the room and checked the locks, but Axel had magicked them shut behind him. "I don't want you to stay here."

She gave him a confused look. “I live here. What are you talking about?”

“I want to take you far away from here. There are other cities in this human world still, aren’t there?”

“Plenty, but I don’t want to live in any of them.”

“You’d be safer if you let me take you.” If he could get her to a place where the Order didn’t have a stronghold, he could protect her better.

“What about my grandmother and Shaiming?”

“They can come, too.”

Carol went to him, the flame of her wrapping itself around his senses. He knew she’d try to persuade him to leave her alone, but she didn’t understand that her brown eyes and flowerlike scent made him want to protect her all the more fiercely.

“Seth, our entire lives are here. Ming Ue’s is our home; we can’t simply abandon it. The Order wouldn’t leave it alone if we went.”

“You’re stubborn like a dragon.”

“If I run away, then they win—the Order and the Dragon Master and whoever else wants to kill me. I refuse to let them bully me; I refuse to give up my life for them.”

“At least let me take you to Dragonspace until I can slay everyone in the Order. No one will be able to get to you in my lair in the heart of my territory.”

“What do I do while I’m there? Count rocks?”

Seth fell silent. He knew the only way he’d get her away would be to surround her in his fire and drag her to Lisa’s, so the silver dragon could open the way to Dragonspace.

The idea was tempting, and he didn’t abandon it. Carol held his name, and she could compel him to stop anytime she liked, but if he took her by surprise, he might have a chance.

Carol watched him as though she knew what he was thinking. “Don’t even try.”

Seth made his thought threads innocent, but he couldn't let the idea go. He wanted her safe with a franticness he'd never experienced before.

"Then stay here while I slay your enemies," he said.

"Slay? What's this talk about slaying?"

Seth growled, the dragon in him chafing to fly out and finish them off. "You'd rather wait for them to slay you?"

"They could have killed me in that basement. I have to wonder why they didn't."

"Fear. They weren't sure what a Dragon Master could do, or what you'd make me do."

"No, it didn't feel like that. They were waiting, yes, but not to fight. It's like they wondered what I'd do with the other Dragon Master."

Seth slowed his thoughts, bringing them back from bloodlust. "Why would you want to do anything with the other Dragon Master?"

"I don't know. Interesting, don't you think?"

Seth moved to the other side of the room and looked out the window. The electricity had been restored in this building already, so the air was warm against the cold that seeped through the window glass.

Outside people hurried back and forth, calling out to one another, or stopping to talk in little groups. They were still putting things together after the earthquake, coming together to commiserate. Humans did that sometimes—clumped together for safety and comfort, somewhat like baby dragons did. It's something adult dragons would never do, except fire dragons, and then only with their mates.

He realized that part of the protectiveness he felt for Carol was not of a slave bound to its master, but of a dragon caring for his mate. His thought of tucking her in his lair was exactly what a fire dragon did when the female was ready to have her clutch. The male guarded her against the world while the female curled around her eggs.

Never in his wildest dreams would Seth have thought of a human being as mate. Malcolm had taken a human, but she was a witch; plus Malcolm said that Saba had been given a magical gift from the silver dragon—she could bear Malcolm children in the human way and her life span would increase to match his. Their children, half dragon, would be magical, too.

Carol as a Dragon Master should in theory be able to control the silver dragon herself. No one seemed to understand Carol's magic or its untapped potential, not even the old man Zhen.

"Seth." Carol gasped behind him. "Your tattoo."

Seth looked over his shoulder, but he couldn't see the flame tattoo from that angle. "What about it?"

"It's different. It's bigger."

Seth went into the bathroom and examined his back in the full-length mirror. The flame that outlined his buttocks was thicker and reached higher up his back.

"Why did that happen?" she asked, staring at him in the mirror.

Her face was smudged from the dirty basement, her hair in disarray. She'd changed, too, from the pristine, elegant woman he'd found in the alley behind Ming Ue's two nights ago. She looked stronger, more able to take frightening things in stride, more accepting of the magical and bizarre.

"I don't know," Seth answered her. He reached out and brushed the dirt from her face.

Carol caught sight of her reflection in dismay. "Oh, God, look at me. I'm a mess."

He clasped her hands. "I like you a mess."

"Don't start with the compliments. I don't think I can take it right now."

"I'm a dragon who never wanted to meet a human woman." He touched her chin. "And I can't stay away from you."

"Because I hold your name."

"Maybe that's it." He didn't think so as he leaned to kiss her lips.

"Tell me about dragons," she said softly.

Right now? He wanted to snarl. "Why?"

"I think I need to know more about them. If the other Dragon Master gets free, and I do need to use the powers— I'd feel better if I were prepared, is all."

"Malcolm knows more than I do," he said, touching her lower lip. "Black dragons have a damn library all about dragons."

"So black dragons like information. What do fire dragons like?"

"Solitude. Beauty." Seth thought of the scent of dry air and acacia floating across the vast desert stillness of his home. "Flying, hunting. Peace."

"I'd give you all that back if I could."

"You will."

"You have confidence in me. Zhen tried to teach me how to let you go, using drugged tea and mahjong tiles. I could almost do it." She paused, her gaze going remote. "I had no trouble calling to Malcolm and Caleb and then turning them loose. But you I couldn't. The more I tried to let go, the more I called you to me. That's why you appeared in Zhen's back room. I wanted you so much." She trailed off.

"You want my dragon fire."

The worry and despair in her eyes almost undid him. "What does that mean? Why doesn't your fire burn me, by the way? You're living flame, but you don't burn."

"I can burn if I choose, but I choose not to hurt you."

"But if you did . . ."

"You would burn to a cinder."

Her brows drew together. "So why should I crave your fire? Maybe deep down I really want to get burned?"

He shook his head. "My flame form is not my dragon fire. It's just another form I can take, like the silver dragon can become a string of lights."

"Now I'm really confused."

Seth leaned his bare buttocks against the counter and didn't miss how Carol's gaze moved to regard them in the mirror.

"My dragon fire is my magic," he said. "It's the essence that makes me a fire dragon, and it's more powerful than what any other dragon possesses. The silver dragon can do more with her magic than I can with mine, but my fire is a concentration of pure energy. I could destroy the world with it if I wanted to."

"Oh." Carol's lips parted. "Which explains why the other Dragon Master wants it so much. I wonder if the Order wants him to have it or is trying to keep it away from him."

"My fire is why you woke and called me to you," Seth said.

"And why I don't want to let you go?"

He nodded, feeling the rough ends of his hair on his neck. "You crave my fire and have been trying to draw it into yourself from the first. You aren't strong enough yet, but soon you'll be able to pull it in from me, and I won't be able to stop you."

"What happens then?" She backed up a step, sliding her arms across her abdomen. "What happens when I take your dragon fire, whatever it is? Does that leave you without it?"

"If you were a fire dragon, it would leave me fused with you, bound absolutely. Fire dragons do that when they mate, but we're born with the capacity to endure it. With you . . ." He drew his finger down her cheek, as always reveling in her softness. "It will burn you up from the inside out if you're not ready. It will kill you."

Her eyes widened. "Then I won't do it. I have no desire to burn to a crisp, thank you very much."

"You can't help it. The Dragon Master in you wants to command it, just like the other Dragon Master wants it to get himself free of that column thing. Dragon fire is the whole reason I was sucked here from Dragonspace."

"Are you sure about this?"

"Yes." He'd never been more certain of anything in his life. "You want my fire. A bit of it jumps to you every time we mate."

"I noticed that." She drew a shuddering breath. "I thought it was just a great orgasm."

"I try to keep my fire from you always, but when I mate with you, I lose some of my control." He reached for her across the small bathroom and touched her cool, bare shoulders. "It is intense mating with you, and I am buried in the joy of it."

"But if you ever lost hold of this dragon fire, then I'd be toast? Literally?"

"I would never, ever hurt you." He moved his thumbs over her collarbone. "You wield my true name, which would make me work hard not to harm you, even if I hated you. Something in me always holds back the dragon fire, even if a spark escapes."

"Not the best reassurance you could give me."

"I like mating with you. I like how your body moves under mine, how hot your skin gets, how you taste. My dragon fire craves you, but I won't let you pull it into you. The bond protects you."

She started to push him away, but then her fingers curled on his shoulders and held him in place. She lifted on her tiptoes and brushed a kiss to his lips, then paused as though waiting to see what would happen.

His dragon fire trembled inside him, but Seth quieted it.

"I can't seem to stop wanting you, Seth," she whispered. "I'm not a sexy woman, not the kind that men chase. They think I'm cold and too focused on money. But I'm not, not really. I made money because I had to, because Grandmother and Shaiming would have had nothing if I hadn't. But all everyone sees is overachiever Carol, hard as nails and cold as ice."

"You aren't hard," he said, kissing her very soft and very warm neck. "I am."

She dissolved into laughter. "Seth, damn it, don't do that."

"Don't do what? Want you?"

"Make me laugh while I'm pouring my heart out."

Seth touched her chest, feeling her heart beating swiftly. "It's still in place."

"I can't believe someone like you likes to touch me," she said in wonder. She cupped his cheek. "I never thought I'd let a man get close to me—never thought one would want to. Except you're not a man; you're a dragon."

"A *male* dragon."

He took her hand and guided it to his very erect penis. She grasped him readily, and he closed his eyes in pleasure.

She touched him gently, her fingers exploring as before, as though she found him fascinating. She dipped her hand to his balls and lifted them in her palm.

He couldn't stand it. He lifted her until her face was even with his and let his kiss press her against the cream-colored wall.

When he broke the kiss, she reached for him, her eyes half-closed. He kissed her again, drawing her lower lip between his teeth.

She stroked his face, her soft body moving against his hard one, his staff thick between them. "Axel will be back soon."

Seth didn't care about Axel. He dipped his head and nibbled down her neck, slowly easing her to stand on her feet again. "Let me feel you," he whispered.

"Aren't you feeling me already?"

"All of you. Why are you always in clothes?"

"I was going to ask you why you're always out of them."

Seth opened the buttons of her shirt. "They're annoying. I can change faster if they aren't in the way." He pushed the shirt from her shoulders and tugged at her bra. "At least stop wearing this."

"How about if I quit wearing underwear altogether?"

He sensed she was joking, but he remained serious. "That would be best. Then if I want to do this . . ." He slid her skirt up her thighs, finding the bare skin of her legs and the barrier of her panties. "It would be easier."

"I couldn't possibly go to board meetings without my underwear."

"Why not?"

She pretended to contemplate. "I suppose if my investors knew I was pantyless, they might be less disparaging about my profit-and-loss statements. Most of them are men and try to look down my blouse anyway."

Seth pinned her to the wall again. "If they ever do again, tell them you are *mine*."

"I don't think it would be easy explaining my dragon boyfriend."

Seth kissed her, letting the heat of her mouth dissolve his tension. He wanted all of her. The touching and kissing only satisfied him so much.

He left off his teasing and leaned over her. "I can't ever have what I want with you."

She gave him a startled look. "What do you want?"

"Everything. I want my life to be all around you, all about you. I don't know why I wish this. You aren't dragon, and this world is like hell to me." He balled his fist on the wall. "*Why?*"

"I don't know." She didn't move, but he felt the rapid rise and fall of her chest. "I wish I wasn't so tangled up in you. I want you to be able to leave, to not hate me for holding you. And I want to wake up and be Carol again, going to my office and running my restaurants. I don't want to know about dragons or Dragon Masters, or the Order of the Black Lotus. I want my life back."

"I want to fly free again." He unclenched his hand and rubbed his thumb over her chin. "We both want what we can't have."

"If I can figure out how to let you go, I will."

"You don't understand. It doesn't matter if you send me back to Dragonspace. I have touched you, mated with you, watched you while you slept. I won't ever be able to untangle myself from you again."

Her dark eyes flicked to his. "Maybe you say that because you're trapped. Maybe it's the true-name thing making you think you want to stay with me."

"It feels real to me."

"But how will you feel when the bond is broken?"

He shrugged. "What if the bond being broken means I can't stay with you? Maybe the magic that brought me here won't let me stay if it's broken."

"Caleb and Malcolm stay."

"They came under different circumstances and were freed by their mates. Can I stay with the one who enslaved me? Or will the magic not let me?"

"You ask difficult questions," Carol said. "I thought getting my MBA was challenging."

He had no idea what that meant, but he understood the gist. "I don't want it to be difficult."

Life was easy as a dragon—his basic emotions were his need to hunt, anger and protectiveness over his territory, joy in the beauty around him. He'd been content with his life.

Humans were completely different, and even though he was only in this shape temporarily, he was flooded with complicated human thoughts and emotions, wants and needs.

Carol might be right that without the true-name bond he might not want her any longer. He couldn't imagine that now, as furious as he'd been with her when he'd first encountered her.

He hated being trapped, but if he had to be, he couldn't imagine a better woman to be trapped with.

"I should clean up," Carol was saying. She looked sideways at herself in the long mirror, and Seth studied her, too, her mussed hair, open blouse, and smudged face. *Delectable.*

"A shower?" Seth asked. He wouldn't mind being wet with her.

"I need to go back to Zhen's and tell them what happened. I want to continue with my training, too, so I don't do something stupid. When we were in the basement, I wanted to tell you to strike again. I could feel it, and it was physical pain to hold it back."

"I don't want you to feel pain."

"Neither do I. That's why I need Zhen."

Seth reached into the tiled shower stall and turned on the water. It gushed out, hot and clear, and the room soon filled with steam.

"That's lucky," Carol said. "I worried that the water would go bad or be shut off indefinitely. Looks like it's fixed."

He didn't follow what she was babbling about, and he didn't care. He pulled off her blouse and started working on her skirt.

Carol tried to back away, but the wall stopped her. "I meant you should find something to wear while I shower and change. I'll be out in a minute."

Seth opened the skirt wide and let it drop down her legs. "That wouldn't be as much fun as washing with you." He scooped his arm around her backside, lifted her off her feet, and set her under the stream of water.

Carol gasped in dismay at the bra and panties still on her. "I haven't finished undressing."

"You should finish, then. Malcolm told me humans washed their clothes anyway."

"Not at the same time as themselves."

"Hmm. Seems like a waste."

Carol unhooked her bra and slid her panties off, dropping them to the bathroom floor with a wet splat. She had to lean against the tile wall and bend over to slide her stockings, equally sopping, from her legs.

Seth folded his arms and enjoyed the view. Carol was tall for a woman, her limbs slender but not bone-thin like her cousin Lumi's. She had soft curves, her waist nipping in above the swell of her hips.

Her wet hair flowed from her forehead in a sable wave to her shoulders. Her breasts were full, the tips dark red, and a twist of black hair peeked from between her legs.

Beautiful.

Seth stepped into the shower with her and closed the glass door.

14

Carol admitted that Seth decorated the shower far better than her designer tiles and etched glass doors ever could. Water beaded on his shoulders and arms and darkened the red hair on his chest.

He leaned his head back and let the stream wet his hair, pushing it back from his forehead as he'd watched her do. Droplets clung to his lashes, cheekbones, and parted lips.

The universe had known what it was doing, Carol reflected. His arms were sculpted with muscle, showing nature's perfect design that no gym had any hand in.

Seth was tall enough that Carol just fit under his chin. She couldn't resist leaning her body to his, wrapping her arms around the solid male she knew she was falling in love with.

Carol didn't fall in love. She didn't have time for it. She'd seen her friends in college fall in love and abandon their dreams and goals to marry. She'd also seen them divorce a few years later, with one or more children to take care of and no money with which to do it.

Even Lisa had tangled herself in a bad relationship that had nearly drained her dry before she'd come home to work at Ming Ue's. She'd only found happiness with Caleb, and he was a dragon.

Carol had made it plain that she was about career and drive, not love, marriage, and babies. It worked—men steered clear.

Perhaps it was the fact that she, Lisa, and Saba were magical women, she thought as she soaked up Seth's warmth. As magical women, they could only look for happiness with magical men—dragons in this case.

Not that she thought her situation would end in happiness. Zhen would train her well enough that she'd learn how to let Seth go, and then he'd go.

The throb of pain in her heart surprised her. She tightened her arms around him, realizing she didn't want to let him go.

Seth kissed her again, holding her face in his hands while he tasted her lips. He kissed his way down her throat and began licking her there, chasing water droplets with his tongue.

He liked to lick her, as though she were an exotic taste he couldn't get enough of. She didn't mind his hot tongue on her body, and she turned her head so he could taste more.

He flicked his tongue down her chest and sank to his knees. Carol rested her hands on his shoulders and gritted her teeth as he plied his tongue to her navel, then trailed heated kisses to the tuft of hair between her legs.

Seth ran his hands up the backs of her thighs and leaned in to delve his tongue into her. He was getting practiced at it.

Carol gripped his shoulders, watching her nails slightly

indent his skin. At the tiny pain, he licked faster, his tongue an amazing implement of pleasure. He opened his mouth and fastened it to her clit, then he suckled.

Carol cried out in delight. All kinds of wild sensations tingled through her, darkness, bright fire, and dizziness.

"I love it," she heard herself saying. "I love it, Seth."

He ignored her to keep playing. His grip tightened on her legs, not about to let go while he tortured her.

Nothing mattered. She didn't care that an ancient Asian gang was trying to kill her, that there was another Dragon Master trapped in a warehouse basement in SoMa, that she had the power to command dragons.

All that mattered was Seth kneeling at her feet and his magical tongue. She rose on her toes, wanting to thrust herself at him as hard as she could. She was glad he was so strong, because he took her gyrations without flinching.

He drove her crazy. He pleasured her until she spiraled into darkness and cried out as she came. She didn't even blush at the thought of her neighbors hearing.

She pressed Seth into her, wanting him to go on and on. He did for a few minutes, then he rose, his face drawn with longing, and dragged her up to him.

His kiss tasted of her juices coupled with the spice of his mouth. His hands were bruising, his lips just as punishing.

She wanted his fire. It wasn't only the Dragon Master in her craving power; she wanted *Seth*, all of him.

She fanned her hands out on his back and dug her fingers in, then she opened her mouth and called to his fire.

It came quickly at first, a hot spark that dove into her and lit her body all the way to her toes. She groaned with it, and Seth echoed her, as heartfelt as he did in climax.

Another spark, and her body was hot as flame.

Seth jerked his mouth away, his eyes fully black, no white showing. "No."

"I want it. Let me have you."

"No!"

Seth shoved her away and stumbled out of the shower, putting as much space between her and himself as he could in the small room.

Carol fell back against the wall, the tiles freezing against her hot skin. "Seth."

He gazed at her in anguish, his stiff penis lifting at a right angle from his body. "Stay away from me."

She could make him do what she wanted. All she had to do was wrap his name around her mind and command him.

The Dragon Master in her started to do it. She sang the notes of his name, each symbol burning the air. Seth slammed his arm against his stomach and doubled over, but he couldn't stop himself taking a step toward her.

She felt his pain, but the Dragon Master didn't care. The fire dragon belonged to *her*, and she could do with him what she willed. Right now, she willed him to finish what he'd started, to take her over the edge again and again, to pleasure her as much as she demanded.

Seth took another step. He looked up at her, his eyes black wells of rage and anguish.

"It will kill you," he rasped. "Don't make me."

But she was strong; she was a Dragon Master; she was Carol who didn't take shit from anybody and had built her businesses from nothing by being smarter than the men around her.

She kept pulling. Seth gasped for breath, then he reared up, tears of blood welling from his eyes. "*No.*"

He burst into flame, the fire like an orange-red translucent shield across her bathroom. He streamed down under the crack in the door and flowed away.

Carol the Dragon Master growled low in her throat. She latched onto his name in fury and started to drag him back.

Seth, in his male body once more, slammed against the

bathroom door from the outside. She heard the crack of his head against the wood, then his grunt of pain.

The small sound slapped Carol to her senses. She gasped and jerked the shower water from hot to cold, uttering a cry at the abrupt chill.

She flung his name away from her, her hands coming up to make the movement through empty air. *Go,* she screamed in her head. *Please, go.*

The water turned ice-cold, and Carol shuddered. She snapped off the water and grabbed for a towel at the same time the door opened.

Steam roiled through the room and Seth stood in the middle of it, naked and dripping. "Are you all right?" he asked in a low voice.

"I told you to go."

He stood there stubbornly, not moving.

Carol pressed the towel close around her, her hands shaking. "I wanted to hurt you and keep hurting you until you did my bidding. You can't stay here if I'm going to do that."

"I told you, you can command me wherever I am—in Dragonspace or far away in your world."

"Damn it." Carol pounded the marble counter with her fists. "I don't want this *thing* in me dictating what I do. I want to get rid of it."

"You can't. It's what you are."

Carol closed her eyes, balling her sore hands. In her life, she'd had to be the calm, cool one, making tough decisions and sacrifices so that the family would survive.

Ming Ue and Shaiming lived by nostalgia, telling stories about the old days and playing mahjong and talking about magic and dragons. Carol had shut out the enticing world of stories and dreams to make it in the real world.

Carol had made it by ignoring her emotions, by being smart but also listening to her instincts. She'd gotten through school and past her first steps in the world of big business by marching to her own music, having her own plan, and not letting anyone stop her. And she'd done it.

I can do the same with this, she thought. She could knuckle down and face it, apply the same cool work ethic she'd applied to growing her small restaurant into something great.

"I'll call Zhen," she said carefully. "I'll go back and resume his training, and if he wants me to play forty-five games of mahjong to master myself, I'll do it. I don't care what it takes. I'll beat this thing, and then you won't have to look so afraid of me."

She opened her eyes and found herself talking to empty steam.

"Seth?" She hurried out of the bathroom, clenching the towel. Seth was dressing in the living room.

The afternoon had waned into night, and the room was dark except for the streetlights wavering in the windows. She watched Seth fasten the jeans over his bare backside and pull on another shirt, this one a much-washed camouflage-patterned T-shirt.

"Did you hear? I said I'd go back to Zhen and get a hold of this thing. Then I can let you go, and we'll both be safe."

His skeptical look stopped her. "You can't change what you are," he repeated.

"I know. I can't change that I'm Chinese either, no matter how many people think *Juan* is a Spanish name. I've learned to not try to pretend my ancestry away in order to fit in. I can do the same with this."

He only straightened the shirt on his body and found another pair of shoes that Axel had left for him. "You are right to go back to Zhen."

"Where are you going?"

"To look into a few things."

"What things?"

Seth shrugged, and Carol's throat tightened. She'd told him to stay away from her, hadn't she? "Be careful," she said.

"I will try to stay out of danger."

He came to her and turned her face up to his. He smelled of the shower and his own clean scent, of the lovemaking they'd stopped so abruptly.

He kissed her, and the hunger in her reached for the spark.

Seth stepped away, his eyes haunted, then he unlocked the door and walked out without looking back.

Seth sent a trickle of his dragon fire into the locks to do them up from the outside, then he walked down the stairs and out of the building.

His heart beat hard from the interrupted encounter. Carol had stopped herself—his lady was strong—but for how long? Sooner or later, she wouldn't be able to resist the pull of his fire, and then she'd pay the price. Perhaps if she mastered the magic in her, like she said she would, she might be able to take his fire without consequence, but for now, it was best he stayed apart from her.

He walked into the night that was filled with people still cleaning up after the earthquake. Things were slowly returning to normal: lights on in the houses, cars sliding up and down the street instead of clogging it. Seth made for the park across the street and the man he'd seen waiting for him from Carol's apartment window.

Malcolm wore his usual black raincoat, and his silver eyes were pale smudges in the darkness.

"What do you want?" Seth asked him irritably.

Malcolm raised his brows. "I'm trying to help you, but if you'd prefer I left you alone, fine."

Seth waved it away, not yet having mastered the human technique of apology. "You went to the Dragon Archive."

"I did. I had my assistant, Metz, do some research on Dragon Masters, and by the time I got there, he'd turned up some interesting material."

"What interesting material?"

Malcolm peered at him. "What's the matter with you? Has something happened?"

Seth stroked a hand through his wet hair, feeling the bite of winter wind. "Can we go somewhere warm to talk, or do we have to skulk in the dark?"

Malcolm frowned, his dragon irritation evident in his black and silver thought threads. He led the way out of the park and down a street until they came to a small, noisy place filled with people and smelling of alcohol.

All the tables were filled, but somehow people melted out of Malcolm's way, and the two dragons sat at a table in the corner. Seth tasted the foaming drink a tight-skirted girl set in front of him and liked its tangy bite.

"Beer," Malcolm grunted. "You get used to it."

Seth took another sip and waited for Malcolm to get to his point.

"This Dragon Master we're facing is called Sying, and he's two thousand years old."

Seth had already suspected that. He waited for Malcolm to continue.

"Two thousand years ago, during the Han dynasty, a Dragon Master called Sying was imprisoned in a column of magic that looks like glass. The Order of the Black Lotus performed the spell."

Seth thought of the column on its side under the rubble, Sying's faint pleas for help. "Why?"

"Apparently, because he wouldn't do the Order's bidding. They wanted their god to be made manifest. They wanted the Dragon Master, using his powers and that of dragons, to accomplish this task."

Seth didn't answer. Memories came flooding back to him.

Malcolm gave him a hard look. "This Dragon Master, Sying, had the ability to command five dragons at once: three goldens, a black dragon, and a fire dragon." He sat back, watchful.

"Yes," Seth answered. He remembered the three snarling, always fighting golden dragons miserable in their captivity. The black dragon had been coldly arrogant, keeping himself away from the others. Seth had pointedly ignored them.

Seth had been special anyway, kept apart, the subject of speculation by the other dragons.

"You?" Malcolm asked with brows raised.

Seth nodded. "I don't remember everything. I know Sying tried to kill or banish the Order's demon-god once he'd summoned it. I thought they'd killed Sying, because I woke up free one day."

"Apparently, they imprisoned him instead. And now this Sying has called you back. For what purpose?"

Black dragons had to have a logical answer for everything. "He begged me to free him. Isn't that enough?"

"Not where the Order of the Black Lotus is concerned. Why hasn't Sying summoned you before? It's been, what, two thousand years?"

"Maybe he couldn't. Maybe he just now got his power back."

"Could be. I'd like to ask him. Also, I'd like to know how he managed to get rid of the Order's demon-god." Malcolm gave Seth another pointed look.

"Whatever the spell was, the memory of my part in it has been blurred. That might have been part of the spell, or maybe the Dragon Master commanded us to forget." Seth took another sip of the beer. "Does the Archive say what happened to the other dragons?"

Malcolm gave him a grim nod. "The Order feared that the dragons would band together and try to free the Dragon Master. So they killed the dragons."

Seth froze, his glass halfway to his mouth. "Killed them?" He set the glass down again. "Dragons are hard to kill."

"Banded together, the Order had that power. They got to the dragons before they could find their way back to Dragonspace. All except the elusive fire dragon, who got away in a burst of flame."

As a dragon, Seth would have felt no remorse. Every dragon took care of himself, and that was the way of things.

But now, he thought of the strength of those four grumbling dragons, their magic, their powerful bodies stretched out in the sunshine. They'd been feared and revered, and then slaughtered like animals. His anger rose.

"The Order has survived," Malcolm continued. "They've passed down its secrets until this day."

"And they've kept track of the Dragon Master."

"It was one of their society's missions—to keep watch on the imprisoned Dragon Master, to make sure he didn't escape. They also kept watch on one other person: the Dragon Master's assistant."

Still thinking of the horrific deaths of the other dragons, all those centuries ago, Seth barely heard him. "Assistant?"

"Every Dragon Master has a faithful second who watches out for their physical welfare. In ancient times, they made sure the Dragon Master was given enough to eat and was looked after so he could spend his time communing with his dragons. The position was inherited, passing from one generation to the next, the same way inclusion in the Order of the Black Lotus is passed down."

Seth had barely paid attention to the humans surrounding the Dragon Master. He hadn't cared.

"Zhen," he said now with conviction.

"Yes, the one called the Junk Man. He's stayed close to Ming Ue and her family, ready to serve the next Dragon Master. The Order seems to know him well."

Seth itched to grip the old man between his fingers and ask him some pointed questions. "Why does the Order still want to kill Carol? They have the Dragon Master imprisoned, their god is gone, and it happened a long time ago. Is their need for revenge that strong?"

"The Order only wants one thing: power. I mentioned that prominent businessmen make up its ranks. It's no accident that they're all wealthy and powerful. Their inherited magic and their demon-god's lingering magic help them."

Seth's anger burned inside like a slow furnace. "How many are in this Order?"

"In San Francisco? Fifty-two. Many of them are Asian business leaders or outright mobsters like Danny Lok. The Order was pretty much obliterated in China in the early twentieth century, although a few linger in Taiwan. The largest concentration is now in California, although many branches no longer believe in mages, dragons, and Dragon Masters. Some look at it as a quaint old title passed down by their grandfathers."

"Fools," Seth said.

"Humans have grown forgetful and interested in mundane life. Magic and philosophy have been subsumed by the need for food, clothing, and the latest computer games."

Pompous black dragons. "I think I'll pay the Dragon Master a visit. Come with me."

Malcolm gave him a speculative look. "What about Carol?"

"I don't want Carol there. She's too vulnerable, and she's safer in her apartment behind my marks."

Malcolm signaled to the waitress and paid her for the drinks. "What are you planning to do?"

"I'm not sure yet." Seth walked out onto the chill street

and waited for Malcolm to catch up. Malcolm led him down the hill to a building from which he retrieved the small car Saba had used to take Seth to the warehouse earlier that day.

In near silence, they wound through the streets, Malcolm following Seth's directions. The street in front of the small warehouse was empty, this part of the city very dark, although Seth had no doubt that the Order was keeping watch on the building.

Malcolm parked the car, then wove strong magic over it before he left it to follow Seth inside. The stink of the place had dimmed slightly—incubi decomposed to dust and vanished relatively quickly. The walls glowed with the marks Seth and Axel had put on them.

The basement stairs had been smashed. Seth lowered himself by his hands through the opening and then dropped, and Malcolm followed suit.

The column lay untouched where Seth and Axel had unburied it. Seth felt a flicker of power from inside, a small taint of evil overlaid with fear and desperation.

He put his hands on the column. The dragon in him sensed the powerful magic holding the Dragon Master inside, but the magic or spell or whatever it was felt like thick, cool glass.

Malcolm followed more slowly, studying the column with a frown. "What are you going to do?"

"Free the Dragon Master," Seth said. "And then use him to help me hunt down and kill the Order of the Black Lotus."

15

Carol wrapped her silk dressing gown around her as she hurried through the living room. Someone was pounding on the front door, and she heard Zhen's thin voice through it.

"Please, Li Mei, I must speak with you urgently."

Carol unlocked the door and yanked it open, ignoring her downstairs neighbor peering up through the ornate staircase. Her neighbors weren't used to dusty old Chinese men banging on doors and calling out in the middle of the night.

Carol pulled Zhen inside and shut the door. "What's the matter?"

"Where is the fire dragon? Is he here? Please say he is here."

"He isn't. He went out." She waved her hand toward the window. "He didn't say where."

Zhen looked frantic. "Call him. Bring him back."

"I don't want to. I tell him I don't want to enslave him, and then I keep yanking him around by his name."

"That doesn't matter. If he's gone to the other Dragon Master, he must be stopped."

Carol felt a qualm of disquiet. "Why do you think he's gone to the other Dragon Master?"

"Saba told Ming Ue that Malcolm learned much about the Dragon Master, and he was seeking Seth. If he has told Seth . . ."

"Told Seth what?"

Tears ran down his wrinkled cheeks. "All of this is my fault."

"How is this your fault?" Carol began. "Never mind. Stay right here while I get dressed."

She left Zhen wringing his hands and hurried into the bedroom to pull on jeans and a sweatshirt.

Zhen hadn't moved by the time she returned. He was crying in small sobs, hugging himself.

Carol tugged his sleeve and got him to follow her. She grabbed her spare set of keys and headed out of the building and around the corner to where she garaged her car, hoping Axel had returned it there.

He had, and a cursory examination showed no scratches or damage. Zhen hung back, but Carol urged him into the car and started it up.

She didn't want to call to Seth, but Zhen was so distressed, and she needed to know where he was. She reached out tentatively, trying to keep the musical syllables in her head gentle.

Seth, where are you?

She got a growl for an answer. She carefully tugged at the threads between them and got another growl.

Please answer me.

Stay home, he flashed. *You are safe there.*

Too late. I'm on my way to where we left the Dragon Master. Unless you say different, I'm assuming you're there.

Don't come!

Zhen is worried, Carol sent doggedly. *He wants me to stop you, whatever you're doing.*

Zhen betrayed you, Seth snapped, then went silent.

She glanced at Zhen next to her, who was chewing his lip, looking small and incongruous in her large leather seat.

"What does he mean?" Carol asked. Zhen looked confused, and Carol repeated Seth's words, still not used to conducting conversations inside her head. "Seth says you betrayed me. What did he mean?"

Zhen's eyes became wells of pain. "The night your mother first called a dragon—so easily, and then she let it go just as easily—I reported it to the Order of the Black Lotus."

Carol hit her breaks and pulled over to the side of the street, earning her honks and foul language from the drivers behind her. She turned to Zhen, her hands locked on the steering wheel.

"You told them?"

"You don't understand. They watch me all the time. They have watched all my life. I have to tell them what they want to know."

Carol felt empty, drained of everything. "Zhen," she whispered.

"I did not know they would kill her. They said they wanted to recruit her, have her pledge her powers to help them. They said they'd teach her how to use them. Her magic terrified her. I thought they could help her."

Carol drew a breath that hurt. "So what really happened that night?"

"They caused a landslide that shoved the car off the road. The car flipped over and caught fire. A few members of the Order pulled your mother out. They told her to join them, that they could help her save your father. She was terrified, and she refused. They beat her. It was horrible."

Carol still felt nothing, the news too powerful to take in.

"Why didn't she defend herself? If she was a Dragon Master, why didn't she call a dragon?"

"She didn't know how to control what she had, and she was too afraid of what the dragons or her own magic might do to you."

So Carol's mother had let men beat her to death, not wanting to draw a weapon that might mean harm to her husband and child.

"You were there," Carol said, her voice icy calm.

"The members of the Order brought me with them. I tried to stop them, but my power, it is so small. They forgot about me, left me behind after they beat Lian. I pulled you out of the car and sat next to your mother while she was dying. She begged me to hide you. The car was burned to nothing by the time the police got there, and I told them you had died in the flames. You were so tiny, and I was certain the Order would never know that you had survived. I took you to Ming Ue. She healed you and took care of you."

"And the Order never found out? They'd have heard that Ming Ue and Shaiming were raising a child."

"They didn't care. I never told the Order you had lived, and you showed no sign of having the power. They watched Ming Ue, yes, but as long as you weren't a threat, they left you alone. Many of those men from the Order then are old now or dead themselves."

Carol stared out the front window, trying to banish the pictures in her mind of the car fire, of her mother rasping her last words, of Zhen cradling her mother in his lap.

"You told them about me when Seth came to me," Carol said with certainty.

Ming Ue had probably rushed excitedly to Zhen the night Seth had first appeared with the good news that Carol could call a dragon. She'd have crowed about it, so proud of her family's abilities.

Zhen bowed his head. "They sensed the call. They came

to me and made me tell them. That is why I hurried to your office the next morning and hid myself until you came in. I wanted to warn you and keep you from entering the room with the demons they had sent to capture you. I was so afraid you would get there before I could, but thank all the gods, for the first time in your life, you were late."

Yes, she had been late, something she never allowed herself to do. But she'd just spent a sleepless night coming to grips with the fact that the very naked male who'd appeared in her apartment had been a *dragon*.

Carol drew a breath, put the car in gear, and slowly pulled out into traffic. Zhen hunkered into a lump of misery and didn't speak as she drove carefully through the streets.

"Why is it so important we stop Seth?" she asked, amazed at how steady her voice was. "Is the Order coming to attack him, too?"

"You must believe me when I say that you must not help the Dragon Master. Your dragon must not let him out."

She swung around a corner and down a hill, heading for the south end of town. "Why not? Is he that dangerous?"

The wrinkles at the corners of Zhen's mouth turned straight down. "I am the caretaker of the Dragon Master. This task has been passed down to me through the ages, and I take it very seriously. But there are things more important than keeping the Dragon Master safe. The Dragon Master himself knows this."

Carol glanced at him, but he'd gone back to pressing his mouth shut, in the stubborn look she knew well from living with Ming Ue.

They were almost to their destination anyway. Carol pulled over to park next to Malcolm's car and cut the engine.

Seth's music jangled in her head, loud and cacophonous. He was enraged and determined, and she felt his fire building.

Seth.

Damn it, get away from here.

She sensed Malcolm with him, the silver threads of his aura troubled but watchful. She hurried inside, Zhen at her heels, her body tingling with the power of the dragon marks swirling through the building.

Carol stopped at the trapdoor, the firelight from below showing that the staircase had been destroyed.

"Seth?" she shouted down.

"You must not free the Dragon Master," Zhen called. "You must not."

Seth glanced up at them. He was naked, firelight gleaming off his body. Malcolm stood apart from him, still clothed, silver threads shimmering around him with just contained power.

"Malcolm, help me down," she called.

Malcolm ignored her, and she muttered a few swear words. She knew she'd never be able to climb down herself, and she'd be foolish to jump. She stayed put, chafing in frustration.

"You must command him, Li Mei. Make him stop."

"Tell us why," Carol said sharply. "Will the Dragon Master be strong enough to enslave Malcolm and take Seth from me? I won't let him."

"That isn't why. I didn't tell you the whole story."

Seth turned to flame. He burned white-hot, hotter than she'd ever felt him. Malcolm took a step back, screwing up his face at the brightness.

Seth's heat reached her like the blast from a furnace as he slowly snaked himself around the column. He was trying to melt it like putting flame to real glass, except this was magical flame and magical glass.

She didn't really want him to free the Dragon Master, but Zhen was nearly hyperventilating in distress.

"Tell me now," Carol said in a loud voice. "What did you leave out?"

"The Dragon Master isn't the only one imprisoned in there. The demon-god is, too. Sying didn't kill the god; he trapped him, and this was his punishment—to spend eternity with him. If you free the Dragon Master, you'll let out a demon-god of destruction, too."

Zhen was sobbing, winding his hands over and over themselves.

"Seth," Carol yelled. "Stop!"

She sent the command straight through the flame.

She felt Seth snarl his rage, and he lashed back at her, like an animal instinctively striking. Carol softened her pull, caressing the notes of his name, begging him to stop.

The flame unwound from the column and poured into the body of Seth, who stood panting, gleaming with sweat, in front of the undamaged column. The flame tattoo on his back, which seared red then changed to deepest black, had doubled again in size.

Outside, Carol and Seth faced each other. He'd dressed again, but his face was dark as thunder. The Dragon Master in Carol was still singing his name.

"Let me go," he said.

"You can't free him."

"I know. I heard Zhen."

The old man and Malcolm stood a little way away, Malcolm having said he'd take responsibility for getting Zhen home. Black dragons had healing powers, Ming Ue claimed, and perhaps Malcolm was soothing Zhen's panic.

"I'm exhausted," Carol said. "Can we go home now?"

"Have Malcolm escort you. You are safe there, and not here."

"And what will you be doing?"

"Destroying the Order of the Black Lotus. I can do it without the Dragon Master's help."

"You can't."

His dark eyes flashed as he tilted his head to study her. "Why not? They murdered your mother and want to murder you. No doubt they're watching as we speak, but can't come closer because of the dragon marks. If I get rid of the Order, end of problem."

The Dragon Master in her laughed with glee and urged her to let him get to it.

"That would make us as bad as they are," she said.

"This is the way of dragons, Carol. We have an enemy, we slay them. No gloating, no torture, no drawing it out. We kill them. We move on."

"Maybe, but . . ."

"Perhaps you'd like to invite them to dine at your restaurant while you talk nicely to them? You can convince them to be your friends, perhaps."

"That's not what I mean."

"There is no other way to deal with this," Seth said in a hard voice. "They're dragon killers, and I can't let that pass."

Carol's throat tightened. This was more evidence Seth wasn't human—he was an animal in human shape, with an animal's ideas of justice and retribution.

On the other hand, her own complicated human thoughts gave her no answer. The Order wanted her, likely to join their ranks and use her powers like they'd wanted her mother to do. Perhaps they'd wanted her mother to open the trap and let out the other Dragon Master and their demon-god. They'd killed her when she refused. Men like that would stop at nothing.

She wanted them to die for that, but she tried to stuff her anger and grief into something useful and controlled. The Order wanted to use her powers—well, she'd think of a way to use the Order. Let them be the means of their own destruction.

"Can we think about this? Axel's a god. I'd like to have his input."

Seth gave her a disparaging look, and she realized she was trying to face this like she faced a board meeting. *We have a god problem, Axel. You're the god expert—what's your view?*

"Please?" she said. "Damn it, Seth, I'm scared, and I don't want them to win, but there has to be a better way than wholesale slaughter. It would come back on me, too. I'd be an accessory to murder—no, accessory to a bloodbath."

"Your ways are not my ways."

"Obviously."

"They are weak." He looked as arrogant as he had the night in the alley when he'd first found her. "But I must obey you, because you hold my name."

Carol eased back, letting the notes slide from her mind. "I'm sorry."

"You can't help your instincts," he said, bitterness in his dark eyes. "And I can't help mine."

He opened her car door and held it for her, not budging an inch until she got in and closed it. She held her breath until he folded himself into the passenger seat beside her, half expecting him to turn to flame and fly off into the night.

When he didn't, she let out her breath and pulled out into the street.

The last thing she saw as she drove away was Zhen and Malcolm standing together, the tall dragon-man and the small mystic bathed in red from her taillights.

Inside the spelled column, Sying despaired. The dragon fire had almost reached him—he'd been so close to touching it.

Then he felt the presence of the other Dragon Master, the girl Carol, his descendant and heir.

She'd called the fire dragon away. She'd taken him away before, and she took him now. She didn't want the Dragon Master free, didn't want to free the evil that resided there with him.

He couldn't blame her.

But Sying had wanted to feel air on his cheeks once more, to see the sky and the stars, to smell the wind. Even if the evil with him crushed him and everything the next instant, he wanted it with all his strength.

The fire dragon's magic vanished. He, Carol, and the black dragon had left him alone again.

They didn't note what he did: that the extreme flame of the fire dragon had left, in the bottom of the column, one tiny crack.

Seth sat quietly in the living room while Carol moved restlessly around her apartment. She pretended to do things like sort papers on her desk or arrange food in her cupboards, but she was avoiding Seth.

He'd told her she should hole up here until they talked to Axel and decided what to do, and she hadn't taken the suggestion well. She was confused and frightened, both of herself and of him; he could see that in the way she moved.

On her next rush past, he caught her arm and pulled her down to him.

Carol resisted, but Seth's physical strength far outmatched hers. She glared at him as she sank to his lap.

"Why is your tattoo larger?" she asked abruptly. "It's gotten bigger again. I saw that in the warehouse."

"The dragon fire," he said, unconcerned. "In Dragonspace, my flame can be vast. Maybe I'm able to use more and more of my fire here so the mark of my dragon essence has to grow."

Her eyes narrowed. "Do you know that for certain?"

"No, but I know you like neat explanations."

"I wish . . ." She broke off and shook her head. "No, it wouldn't have worked."

"You wish what?"

"I was going to say that I wished you were a normal man. But none of this would have happened if you were a real human man. I'd probably have never noticed you, or you, me."

Seth let the music of his dragon thoughts touch her in a light caress. "I'm glad I'm not a normal man, then."

"I'd be too busy running my business and seeing you as competition." Her eyes softened, despite the roiling emotions he felt inside her. "I'd have missed so much."

Seth caressed her abdomen, feeling his hunger for her. He wanted to follow his desires to their conclusion, but there was too much crackling between them.

"Tomorrow, I will fetch Zhen here, and he will give you more lessons."

Carol hesitated, a flicker of anger in her gaze. "You told me Zhen betrayed me, and he did."

His anger rose again at the old man for endangering her, but Zhen was a weak mage, easily coerced by the stronger mages in the Order.

"I know, but he can also teach you."

"Can we trust him not to turn around and tell the Order everything I do? My grandmother might help, but I can't trust that she won't simply relate everything to Zhen." She deflated. "Besides, if I see Zhen again, I might do something terrible to him. He caused so much tragedy."

"The Order did, and the Dragon Master, and their evil god." He went silent, putting his words in order. "They will continue to come for you, Carol. And I think the only way

I will be free of this bond and able to return to Dragonspace is if we release the god and kill him. I think that's what I was brought here to do."

"How can you kill a god?"

"Disable him, then, or push him back into whatever hell he came from. You wanted to ask Axel—he'd likely know." He exhaled. "I have been thinking of this much, which is why I went to release the Dragon Master. I thought I had to kill *him* to free myself, but now the task has become harder."

"Zhen was right, though. If you'd let him out tonight, you'd have died. You're a dragon, but that thing in there is a demon-god." She shuddered. "I'm glad we got there in time."

Carol's distress came to him through her thought threads, and Seth slid his arm around her waist. "I am pleased as well."

"You didn't look pleased at the time." She frowned, and he didn't tell her that she looked beautiful when she frowned.

"I've had time to think since then," he said.

"So what do we do? Malcolm learned the Dragon Master's history from his Archive, you said. Maybe there's a book in there called *Defeating an Evil God and Living Happily Ever After*."

"He didn't mention it."

"I was joking. I do that when I'm scared."

Seth wrapped both arms around her. "We don't need Malcolm and his Dragon Archive. I think I know what we must do."

He looked at her, her face so close to his, her scent filling him, her warmth the finest thing in his world. "I will fill you with my dragon fire, and we'll defeat the demon."

16

"Your dragon fire," Carol repeated, her eyes widening. "The same dragon fire you told me can burn me to a crisp?"

"The same." He said the words unhappily. He knew in his heart that it was the solution to their dilemma, but he still knew there was a danger that Carol could die. "I'm right that you're not ready to take it now. We must make you ready."

"Without Zhen and his mahjong games."

Seth didn't know what she meant about games, but he understood her gist. "We'll have to try. If you won't let me send you somewhere safe, we'll have to face the enemy and defeat it."

"We can't just bury the column and hope the Order forgets about it?"

"Do you really think that would work?" He knew she didn't—she was grasping at straws. "The Order will tend it as they have all these centuries. And they'll continue to try to trap you. Even if you escape them, they'd come after your descendants and will do so as long as they can."

"I know." Carol sighed. "I told you before I was willing to master this. So what do I have to do to suck down your fire without dying?"

"You have to learn to *not* take it."

She looked surprised. "To keep it out, you mean?"

"To learn to take it a small bit at a time, to learn to prevent yourself from absorbing it all at once."

"Like I tried to do in the shower."

"Exactly. Your power wanted it too much. You must learn to control it."

She looked worried but determined. "How do we start?"

For answer, he slid his hands under the warm fleece of her sweatshirt and dragged it off over her head. He smiled as he caught the globes of her breasts in his hands—she'd stopped wearing the lacy thing that bound them.

"Oh, of course," she said, her eyes half closing. "I should have known we'd have to be naked."

"It's easier that way."

It truly was easier for him to handle his dragon fire without hampering clothes, though he admitted any chance to see Carol's body was a welcome one.

"Take off your pants and sit on the floor," he said.

Her brows quirked. "Oh, yes?"

He started to rise, which made her scramble off his lap. Seth peeled off his own clothes and sat cross-legged on the carpet.

Carol stared down at him for a few moments, a delectable sight with her small breasts bare and her jeans dipping to reveal her navel. Humans liked to capture images and display them in their homes, and Seth thought the image of Carol standing half bare above him would be perfect.

Carol snapped her gaze away from him and skimmed off her jeans, underwear, and stockings. Even better.

She tucked her hair behind her ears and lowered herself to the carpet, crossing her legs under her. "Now what?" she said. "I already feel what's in me craving the fire."

"Take my hands."

Carol tentatively laced her fingers through his, and he raised their hands between them. She bit her lip, nervous, but he saw the twist of hair tucked enticingly between her legs glitter with moisture.

"Close your eyes," Seth said. "Imagine a sphere in your mind. Focus on it—what color it is, how big it is? Keep watching it."

Carol closed her eyes; her face at first took on a look of interest, then it relaxed as she began to meditate. Seth held his breath and eased a very tiny spark of his fire into her hands.

She jumped, but didn't open her eyes.

"Keep looking at the sphere," he said softly. "Only look."

Carol's chest rose with a deep breath. Seth glided another spark into her. She made a soft noise, the same kind she made when he caressed her, and her skin began to shine with sweat.

Sying had been strong, Seth remembered. Carol was stronger, but Sying's experience had already been great when he'd trapped Seth the first time, and he'd easily controlled Seth's fire.

Carol's strength was raw and new, the power in her hungry for his.

Seth let another tiny spark in. Carol made a noise of pleasure, her face softening. "I like that."

With Sying it hadn't been sexual. Sying had been cold in his power, keeping everyone at a distance and wielding the dragons like a puppet master. Seth had hated him.

With Carol the connection was already so much deeper.

"More," she whispered. She rocked back and forth a little. "Give me more."

"No."

Her slick hands tightened on his. "I need it."

He shook with the need to obey her, but he forced himself to still.

"Remember what happened in the shower," he said. "Savor this much, then let it go."

He felt her tense, the notes of his name tightening, then she slowly and deliberately eased back.

Seth let out his breath. Carol's fingers continued to bite into his, but she held herself still.

His own fire wanted to slide into her, filling every space it could, but he restricted it. One taste, that was all.

Carol opened her eyes and smiled at him. Their fire twined together, and the bond between them sang notes through his head.

I want her.

The longing had nothing to do with his fire. Carol was a brave, beautiful woman, and he didn't care that she held his name or that they had to prepare against danger.

Keeping hold of her hands, he pushed her down to the carpet and lay on top of her, liking how she smiled in response. He held her hands above her head and nuzzled her cheek.

Her smile deepened. "I should also have known the process would involve lovemaking."

"It doesn't," Seth murmured. "I just want to."

She turned her head to catch his lips. "So I don't need to have sex with you to take your fire? That's handy to know."

"In battle, it would be inconvenient."

She laughed softly, jiggling in the finest way. "True."

"Spread for me." Seth worked his hand between her legs, rubbing her already moist opening.

Carol moved her legs apart, and Seth slid his needy cock between them.

"You're beautiful," he said. *I love you,* he wanted to say.

He still wasn't sure whether the intense feeling winding around him was real or the result of his enslavement. He couldn't be certain of anything until the bond went away, and then who knew what he might feel? Fire dragons didn't feel. They lived, hunted, survived.

Intense emotions washed over him now, but he had no way of knowing if they'd last. He closed his eyes, savoring them as long as he could.

Days passed. Carol didn't leave her apartment, and she didn't want to. She found that being holed up here with Seth was the closest thing to bliss she'd ever found.

She knew that outside, the world was moving on. San Francisco cleaned up from the earthquake and the smaller aftershocks and went on as it always did. She phoned Francesca at her sister's, assured her everything was all right, and told her to extend her vacation. Francesca seemed relieved that Carol was staying put and safe.

Lumi reported that Danny Lok's properties were quietly being taken over by people in the Order of the Black Lotus. Any outside crime lords who tried to muscle into his territory were turning up dead.

The small warehouse in SoMa, on the other hand, was untouched. Malcolm was watching it, and though the Order kept it under observation, they never went on the property. The dragon magic and Axel's marks kept them far away.

Carol did feel safe inside the walls of her apartment, the symbols Axel and Seth had left comforting rather than confining. She ordered food to be delivered from her local grocery store and the small Asian food store attached to one of her restaurants, though she was never really hungry after her sessions with Seth.

Every day, she took a tiny bit more fire from him, and

every day, she held it, looked at it, played with it, and let the fire return. She felt stronger, more energetic, but also more content.

Seth, on the other hand, consumed the meals she brought in with increasing gusto. Using his dragon fire made him hungry, more restless, more volatile, and their lovemaking turned from sessions of pleasure to wild rides.

They lay in bed at the end of the fifth day, Carol drowsing in the sunshine that peeked through clouds above the city. Seth slept hard next to her, his naked body shining with sweat. He breathed heavily, having collapsed after his last, loud climax.

She lifted her hand, studying the sparkle of fire on her skin. She knew that in the last few days, she'd kept some of Seth's fire instead of releasing it, and that was why she felt energized while he ate ravenously and slept deeply.

I'm stealing part of him, she thought. *This isn't right.*

It's yours for the taking, the Dragon Master in her whispered. *He belongs to you.*

She shut out the voice. Since his arrival, Seth had shown her a world she'd never known. She'd lived in San Francisco all her life, and knew its streets and neighborhoods like she knew her own face in the mirror.

But she'd never known what a magical place it was. Now she saw dragon marks shimmering on Ming Ue's walls and Lumi's store, and evil lurking beneath the surface. She found it terrifying and astonishing at the same time.

The veil lifting from her eyes wasn't the only astonishing thing. Seth was also. He'd kissed her and touched her and made her understand what passion was for the first time.

Carol knew now that the men she'd dated in the past hadn't been able reach her because she hadn't let them. No wonder her life had been cold and lonely—she'd shut everyone out. If any man had made signs he wanted to get close, she'd pushed him aside all the harder, pretending to herself that she had too much work to do to keep up a relationship. She hadn't done this consciously, but she'd done it.

She looked at Seth again, his hard, naked body glistening in the sun, a beautiful man who touched her as though he'd never before felt anything so fascinating. He focused on *her*, not on meetings or the people he had to call or the annoying incidents in the office today.

When Carol was with Seth, she knew no one existed for him but her.

The phone beside the bed rang, and Carol reached for it. Seth didn't even stir.

"Carol, I'm worried." Ming Ue's voice came over the phone loud and clear.

"About me? I'm fine."

"About Zhen."

Carol stilled. She didn't want to talk about Zhen.

"Why are you worried, Grandmother?"

"Because no one has seen him for days. His shop is shut, and he doesn't answer his phone or the door."

Carol felt a prickle of unease. "Malcolm drove him home on Saturday night, didn't he?"

"I saw him on Sunday. We had dinner and played mahjong, and he seemed very worried and upset. I haven't seen him since. Shaiming used his key to go check on him, but Zhen wasn't there."

The prickle of unease grew to full-blown worry. Had Zhen run off to the Order, or had they done something to him?

"Grandmother, there's something I need to tell you about Zhen. You're not going to like it."

"Tell me later. Can you ask Seth to go look for him? He can fly around as that flame like he does. I'm going to ask Lisa, too."

"What about the police?"

Ming Ue scoffed. "The police are useless. Dragons, now, they do a thorough job and understand how to *hurry*."

"We're coming over there, Grandmother."

"Don't be silly; just send Seth. No need for you to leave where you're safe."

"There's as much dragon magic in Ming Ue's as there is here, and I need to talk to you."

Ming Ue sighed. "Suit yourself. But tell Seth, and tell him now."

Ming Ue slammed down the phone with her usual vigor, leaving Carol holding a silent instrument. She replaced it on the cradle and turned to shake Seth awake.

Later, as she parked in the alley, and she and Seth ducked into Ming Ue's restaurant, Carol felt the weight of interwoven dragon magic over the place as she never had before. Golden and black dragon magic leapt at her senses, and the Dragon Master in her wanted to lap it up.

Ming Ue didn't even greet them. "Why is *he* here?" she asked, glaring at Seth. She made shooing motions. "Go out there and find Zhen. What are you waiting for?"

"*Grandmother.*"

Seth regarded Ming Ue mildly, his arrogant dragon ire dampened for the small woman. "She is right, Carol. We must find him."

"I don't want you going alone."

Seth brushed his hand along her arm, sending a tingle of his fire through her. "I will search and come back."

"At least take Caleb or something." Carol thought she'd feel better if the bulky, snarky man were with Seth.

"He can follow if he wants. I will tell you what I find."

He turned and walked out, his tall body enticing in a tight T-shirt and jeans. When the door closed behind him, Carol rose, suddenly not wanting him out of her sight.

She'd been with him nonstop for five days, but she'd

never once wished him elsewhere. She wanted to open the door and call him back to her.

"Let him do what he is good at doing," Ming Ue said behind her. "And we will talk about Zhen."

Carol turned back reluctantly, not sure she wanted a chat over a cup of tea. Ming Ue dragged out a chair and pointed to it. "Sit."

Carol obeyed, wondering how it was that Ming Ue could still make her feel like she was six years old. "I don't know quite how to say this."

"About Zhen?" Ming Ue sat down across from her and reached for the teapot. "About how he is a slave to the Order of the Black Lotus? He told me on Sunday when we played mahjong. He confessed all."

Carol's eyes widened as Ming Ue continued pouring tea without looking up. "What did you say to him?"

"I was horrified, naturally. I also know that the Order is ancient and evil. It would take someone of much more power than Zhen to resist them."

"You forgave him?"

"I did not say that. I am very angry. He caused the death of my daughter. But I also know he had no choice, and it was my fault as well. I was the one who told Zhen that Lian had learned to call a dragon. I must learn to live with that."

"You're still worried about him."

"Of course I am. We have been friends for decades. If the Order has taken him, they might kill him or otherwise punish him. And if anyone is going to harm Zhen over what he's done, it will be *me*."

17

Seth flew over the city, scanning its streets for the distinctive aura of one old mystic. The dragon in him hadn't much compassion to spare on Zhen, but the man was special to Carol and Ming Ue, and Seth would find him for them if he could.

He was tired. Training Carol to take his fire had been more of a strain on him than he'd thought it would be, but she was becoming good at it.

Part of him could flow into her now and enjoy all of her body inside and out. The mating when they did this was exquisite. It made him feel more alive than he ever had, but it also zapped him of strength, and he slept for hours afterward.

He had to be careful, or he'd drain himself and delight in the ebb too much.

Zhen could be anywhere in this city of so many souls. He might have tried to go to the Dragon Master and been taken by the Order. Or he might be holed up with the

Dragon Master, instinctively returning to help the man he'd been bred to serve.

Seth angled there across the city, seeing the small, dilapidated warehouse rushing up at him in the cold sunlight.

He smelled the incubi before he landed. They surrounded the building that housed the Dragon Master, watching with dark eyes, their leathery wings hanging limp to their heels.

No human being was in sight, the street deserted. No cars thumped by on the cross street behind him. Chill wind and fog drifted in from the bay, blotting out the sunshine.

The incubi could have nothing to do with Zhen, or this could be a trap waiting to spring. If it was a trap, Seth thought as he hovered above the incubi, they could have baited it better.

He morphed to his human self and faced them, not minding that they surrounded him. Seth still had the dragon strength to wipe out a contingency of incubi.

"Where is the old man?" Seth asked them. "If you know, tell me before I kill you. If you don't know, I'll just kill you."

No response. The incubi studied him with black voids of eyes, soulless beings, but these had the flicker of intelligence that had bothered him before.

He stopped when all twelve of them suddenly got down on their knees and bowed their heads. One of them looked up, keeping his submissive posture.

"We serve the new Dragon Master called Carol," he hissed. "We will be her slaves and help her rid the world of the demon-god."

Seth knew better than to let down his guard and believe him wholeheartedly. "Why would you care about the demon-god?"

"Because he will gather his power by consuming other demons. The Order has the old man. They want to use him to trap the Dragon Master called Carol Juan so she will release the demon-god. We will take you to him."

Ming Ue's restaurant went silent as a tall Asian man walked in the front door. Something oppressive blanketed the room, and the other diners sensed it.

Carol recognized him though she'd never met him: Benedict Fai, a Chinese businessman originally from Hawaii, who had a heavy presence in banks and mortgage companies. He often appeared in newspaper write-ups about large charity events, and his wife was a well-known philanthropist to the homeless and the displaced.

Two weeks ago, Carol wouldn't have noticed the darkness surrounding him, but today, it flared at her like a neon sign. He looked uncomfortable, obviously bothered by the dragon marks.

"Can I help you?" Ming Ue asked primly.

"I came to talk to Ms. Juan. Will she see me?"

Fai stripped off his leather gloves and shoved them into the pocket of his thick woolen coat. The words were cast in polite tones, but he obviously expected Carol to say, "Yes, of course."

Carol knew the game. She'd never played it as Dragon Master to demon worshipper, but she'd done it often enough in the business world.

She motioned for Fai to sit down. "I have a few minutes to spare. Perhaps you would like a cup of tea?"

"That would be fine."

Ming Ue thumped over to them. "He's not drinking a drop of tea out of one of my cups. We'd have to throw it away."

Carol personally agreed, but she kept her thoughts to herself. "We'll have to do without the tea."

"It makes no difference. You know who I am?"

"Mr. Fai, isn't it?" Carol asked, keeping her voice neutral. "I also know now that you are in the Order of the Black Lotus."

"I have that honor." He shrugged out of his coat to reveal a black cashmere business suit beneath. Carol speculated that the cost of the suit could have funded several of his wife's soup kitchens for a month.

Fai noted her assessment and inclined his head. "I am a wealthy man and enjoy a wealthy man's trappings. I've come to talk to you about the Order and tell you a little about it."

"An organization of organized crime?" she asked, quirking her brows.

Fai looked pained. "Please do not lump me into the same category as men like Daniel Lok. Lok was a criminal, a lowlife, and his cronies are no better. But yes, they are also in the Order. It's inherited, you see, stretching back generations to the original Order. Much like you being a Dragon Master is inherited."

"And this should turn my sympathies to you?"

"Of course not. I am here because I want to put a face to the Order for you—one other than a crime lord's. There are many like me—businessmen with wives and families, who inherited the position through no fault of our own."

"There's more to it than that," Carol said. "Evil leaves a taint, and the threads of it are all over you. I know you feel the dragon marks, which are created to keep such evil out."

"Yes, well, the magic in me is very small, which is why I was able to cross the threshold."

"Which is why they sent you," Carol corrected him.

"Which is why I volunteered." He placed his hands on the table, revealing well-groomed nails, a large wedding ring on his left hand, and a diamond-studded band on his right middle finger. "Our organization is not a collection of black hats, men sitting around a table rubbing their hands and contemplating mindless evil."

"Just men thinking about extortion and murder."

He raised his hands, showing palms free of calluses. "Again, please don't lump me with the likes of Daniel Lok. You have heard of me, I know, and not only about my work to help the downtrodden of this city. While many mortgage companies are diving into bankruptcy, mine have remained running sensibly and steadily. I have children to raise and a wife I love, and I have no wish for greed to destroy me. I am in the Order because I was born to it, and I use its power for good."

Carol couldn't restrain her anger any longer. She felt a dark tendril of Dragon Master magic snake out of her. "Murdering my mother was using its power for good?"

"I knew nothing about that," Fai said quickly. "I hadn't inherited my power then. It was twenty-five years ago. But the Order has always maintained that killing Lian Juan was a mistake."

Ming Ue exploded. "A *mistake*? The cold-blooded murder of my daughter was a mistake?"

Fai winced. "What happened between Dragon Masters and the Order in ancient times should remain ancient history, in my opinion. Nowadays, there isn't much use for good versus evil, is there? Not that I consider Dragon Masters *good*, myself. They have a power of destruction much like the Order has. But the demon-god is trapped, and the power he once gave the Order has waned. I used what powers I was given to build my business and help others, like you have."

Carol tasted bile in her throat. "Your opinions on right and wrong don't mean much in the face of my mother's murder."

He sighed. "I know that. I do regret her death, believe me. If I thought you would accept compensation, I would offer it to you, but I know you won't."

"Why did you really come here, Mr. Fai?" Carol said in a hard voice.

"To honestly extend an olive branch. Feuds are bad for business, and as I said, I have a family. My daughters are eleven and thirteen. They're doing so well, and my thirteen-year-old is a soloist in her school choir this year. She's so excited."

"Which of them will inherit your place in the Order?" Carol asked curiously.

"Neither. It only passes to the males of the family. My brother is next if anything happens to me, and then his son."

Carol rolled her eyes. "Oh, of course."

Fai made an apologetic gesture. "The Order was created in the days before women were acknowledged to have intelligence. The powers the demon-god gave us have not changed with the times, I'm afraid."

His silky smooth voice grated on Carol's nerves. "Why are you still in the Order if you think its ways are outdated and you don't want to be associated with crime lords?"

"Not my choice," Fai said. "The power was bestowed on me at my father's deathbed twenty years ago. He told me all the secrets of the Order, the power filled me, and it's never left me. I was twenty-five at the time. I've never been able to get rid of it, no matter how much I try, and I decided to turn the power to good. I've been very lucky, I admit."

Carol studied him, a successful, handsome man in his forties, well dressed and quietly confident. He no doubt had a very expensive car and perhaps a driver waiting for him outside.

"Does your wife know?" she asked. "And your daughters?"

"No. It's not something I want them to know about. I

married for love, Ms. Juan. I didn't need a society woman with her daddy's money to help me—I had my own success. We've had a happy marriage, and me having this power hasn't marred it."

"And if she did know that you were the consort of a demon-god, what would she say?"

Fai barked a laugh. "I'm not a consort of anyone. My ancestor was given this power, and I inherited it. I know my wife very well—we were high-school sweethearts. She would think as I do, that I should use this power, no matter how dubious its origin, for good."

Carol had no doubt he told the truth. Likely his wife hadn't an inkling of what the Order of the Black Lotus was about. She doubted the woman would believe the story even if she did know it. Dark Orders and demon-gods and Dragon Masters didn't exist in the world of most ordinary human beings.

"I still wonder what your purpose was in coming to see me," Carol said. "*Extend the olive branch,* you said. You want us to work together, but why do you? What exactly are we supposed to be doing together?"

Fai's dark eyes glittered. "Keep a bloodbath from happening, Ms. Juan. The Order doesn't want you dead, you see. Danny Lok went after you without the Order's sanction—he was a loose cannon."

"A bloodbath?" Carol repeated, her skin prickling.

"Some of them want you to help them open the trap and let the demon-god out again. I personally would be grateful if you'd keep him *in.* The fire dragon is a wild card in all this. He could be a weapon of great destruction, both to the demon-god and to the Order. I am here to ask that you send him back to dragon-land or wherever you conjured him from before things get out of hand. The members of the Order who want the demon-god freed also want to use you and the fire dragon to smite their enemies."

"*Smite?*" Carol would have laughed if the situation weren't so dangerous.

"An old-fashioned term for an old-fashioned problem. As you can see, not every member of the Order sees eye to eye."

"Where is Zhen?" Carol asked abruptly. She knew Fai could fence with her for hours without him committing to anything. He was good at the game.

"Ah. That is the other thing I came to see you about."

Carol waited, and Ming Ue leaned on her cane and glared at him.

"Some members of the Order have Zhen. A simplistic trap to make you come forward, leverage to make you release their demon-god if necessary. As I said, I would not like it if you did this."

"Where is he?" Carol repeated.

"I can take you if you like. I believe your fire dragon has already gone searching? If so, that's a bad thing, because if trapping the old man didn't work, they are perfectly prepared to capture your fire dragon."

Seth followed the incubi as they flew between reality and darkness, traveling on threads of thoughts and dreams. Seth in his fire form could mimic the way they slipped through, but it was very different from slip-streaming through Dragonspace. In Dragonspace it was a joy—when he emerged with the incubi, he felt unclean.

They led him not to another seedy warehouse but to a lush house on a high hill with panoramic views of the city and ocean beyond. All but one disappeared, and he led Seth into the shadows of darkening fog.

There were five men inside the house. Seth placed the aura of each one, including the faint, terrified one that must be Zhen's.

"Kill them," the incubus whispered, his breath foul. "Kill them here, and then I will take you to more."

Incubi had one-track minds. The house had been demon-marked, which would make it difficult for Seth to get in but not impossible. The men were in the front of the house, so Seth stepped quietly to the unlighted back door.

High shrubs and the gathering darkness hid him from any curious passersby as he whispered his fire into the locks. The door opened a crack, showing him a dark, empty kitchen.

A car swung up the drive, its headlights dying before they could sweep light over the house. Seth sidestepped off the back porch and hid in the shadows.

The car was Carol's, and Carol got out of it. With her was a tall man in a long coat who carried the same dark aura as the men inside the house.

In fury Seth sent a fiery thread to her, his music harsh and angry. Touching her mind told him she was afraid but also determined. *I'm all right,* she whispered.

There are four men inside with Zhen, he sent back. *Get back in your car and drive away.*

This isn't what it seems, came her thought, and then she went silent.

Seth swore under his breath as Carol and the other man, oblivious to their exchange, approached the front door. The man knocked politely.

Seth changed to fire and swarmed in through the open back door, solidifying in a cavernous living room behind the men who had turned to face the front hall. Zhen was upstairs, but Seth would have to pass the men of the Order to reach the stairs, and right now he was more worried about Carol.

"Mr. Fai," the man who'd opened the front door said. "What a pleasant surprise."

"I've brought the Dragon Master." The man took off his

coat and gloves and hung the coat on a hook of an ornate coatrack. Carol kept her raincoat firmly buttoned.

The man who'd opened the door, the same one who'd confronted them at the small warehouse, chuckled. "I didn't think you deigned to associate with us, Mr. Fai."

"Not generally, no," Fai answered calmly. "But I heard of your scheme to capture the Dragon Master, and I thought I'd bring her to you."

"I won't argue." The man's gaze swept over her. "She's very pretty."

"I hear you want me to help you free your god," Carol said coldly. "I think it's a bad idea."

The dark man gave Fai a puzzled look. Fai shook his head. "I said I brought her. I never said she'd capitulate to your demands."

"She needs to, or the old mystic dies."

"How very dramatic," Carol said.

Her voice was steady and icy, but her uneasiness screamed at Seth through the bond. She was poised to run, but she wasn't sure what the Dragon Master in her would do if they chased her or caught her.

Seth pointed silently at the ceiling, feeling Zhen's aura in the room above.

"Zhen," Carol shouted up the stairs. "Are you all right? Can you come down?"

Seth heard a shuffling above then a door creak open. After a long time, Zhen's voice came from the top of the stairs.

"Leave me here, Li Mei."

"Don't be heroic," Carol snapped. "I'm taking you home."

"I am not heroic; I am ashamed. I was a coward, and it will be justice if I am the first thing the demon-god consumes."

Seth felt Carol's growing impatience. "We'll talk about

it later. Right now, you need to come down here, because I'm not doing anything these people want until I see that you're all right."

There was another hesitation, then more shuffling, and Zhen made his slow way down the stairs.

Seth sensed the trap spring. From the warding marks on the house came the dark threads of a spell. Sticky blackness oozed through the air, twining its way toward Carol.

The man she'd come in with, Fai, looked startled, then grabbed his coat and bolted out the front door. Zhen froze on the stairs, sucking in his breath.

Seth wasn't certain what the spell would do, but he sensed Carol's power weakening even before the threads reached her. He turned to fire and sailed across the room, landing behind her.

None of the men looked surprised to see him. They simply watched, smug looks on their faces, while the spell flowed through the room.

"Seth," Carol said, her eyes wide. *Should we?*

Seth wrapped his arms around her from behind and pressed his face to her shoulder. He felt her relax to him, then his fire flowed into her.

The exercises they'd done served her well. Seth closed his eyes and basked in Carol's warmth as a part of him became part of her.

His fire twined through her, turning the threads between them white-hot. He opened his mouth and pressed his teeth to her neck.

The fire magic swept through the room, popping the dark wards from every door and window. Seth saw through Carol's eyes the inky threads draw back, the men who'd cast them watching worriedly.

Carol raised her hand and let fire flow out of her fingertips. She was taking too much, and Seth couldn't stop her, but the men of the Order cowered and shrank away.

The men in the hall reached for one another, joining hands to increase the spell. Darkness reared toward Carol, but she washed it with fire.

Seth grunted with the impact of it, fire and darkness fighting each other. Pain jarred up and down his spine, but under him, he felt Carol sparkle with fire, heard her laugh.

His head throbbed, and every nerve flared with pain. He tasted blood, felt tears trickle from his eyes. She was reaching into him and taking the essence of him, draining him while he gasped for breath.

The men fell back, terrified. *Idiots*. They had no idea what they'd awakened, provoking a Dragon Master to wield a fire dragon's power, but Seth knew all too well.

He'd tried to hold back from Carol, fearing he'd hurt her, but he now realized the danger to himself. He was sweating and shaking, barely containing his agony.

When the fire rushed back into him, he cried out with it. The men of the Order were breathing hard, expressions of fear and pain on their faces, every single ward and dark magic thread in the house gone.

"We're leaving," Carol said in a clear voice. "Zhen, come down here."

Seth straightened, but he was clumsy and half fell against Carol.

Carol swung around. "Seth, are you all right?"

She sang with strength, her skin sparkling. She was beautiful and terrible at the same time—a Dragon Master alive with power.

"Seth," she whispered as everything went dark for him. She caught him around his waist as he collapsed.

18

"Help me with him." Carol shouted the words at Fai, who was sitting in the driver's seat like he could start her car by sheer willpower.

Reluctantly, Fai got out and opened the rear door as Carol staggered under Seth's weight down the driveway. Seth was still conscious, but barely. Zhen took hurried half steps behind them, reaching with his wizened arms for the dragon-man who was easily three times his size.

When Carol had seen Seth's face drained of all color, with blood leaking from his mouth, it had terrified her. Blasting away the dark spell of the Order hadn't frightened her half as much as watching Seth crumple and fall.

She got Seth onto the backseat, where he collapsed full length. "Give him your coat," she said to Fai. When he hesitated, she slapped him with the residual of her fire magic, leaving a red crease across his face.

Fai gave her a shocked look, then peeled off his coat and laid it over Seth's inert body.

Zhen crawled into the backseat with Seth and cradled Seth's head on his lap. Fai got into the front passenger seat, uninvited, and sat with his hands folded, saying nothing.

"Give me your cell phone," Carol commanded as she started the car.

Fai silently unhooked it from the holder on his belt and handed it to her. Carol punched her grandmother's number and held the phone away from her ear when Ming Ue answered with her usual shout.

"Hello, this is Ming Ue's."

"Grandmother, you told me that black dragons were healers, right? Will you tell Malcolm to meet me at my apartment? I'm heading there with Seth."

"What's wrong with Seth?" Ming Ue screeched. "Where is Zhen?"

"I have them both. I don't have time to explain. Please call Malcolm."

"I'll send him—don't worry." Ming Ue clicked off the phone, and Carol peeled out of the driveway onto the steep street. It figured that the Order would take a house in Twin Peaks, she thought grumpily. The demon-god's power had manifested much material wealth.

"What about me?" Fai asked her. The wealthy businessman was pale and contrite, a view that the newspapers likely never saw.

"I'll drop you off at a bus stop," Carol growled at him, and zipped on down the hill.

Seth lay across her bed like a dead man. Carol pressed her hands to her lips and studied the pasty pallor of his skin, the bruises under his eyes. She'd piled blankets on him, not liking the cold of his body, and he lay unmoving under them.

Malcolm stood on the other side of the bed, his mouth a

grim line. "I can't do much for him here. I'd have to take him back to Dragonspace, where I can tap into all my healing powers."

"Would it hurt to move him?"

"Probably. On the other hand, it might help him if he could revert to his dragon form."

"And he can only do that in a place where everyone believes in dragons? That seems so fairy-tale-like to me."

"Where do you think fairy tales come from?" Malcolm asked. "They're stories about true things that have gotten twisted around through the centuries."

Carol's heart squeezed in fear. She could still feel some of Seth's fire in her, but she couldn't seem to give it *back* to him. "I just don't want him to die."

"Why not?" Malcolm said with his quiet sarcasm. "You're a Dragon Master; you can call any dragon you want. If you use one up, there's an entire world of them waiting."

Anger welled up inside her, and before she could stop it, she lashed a fiery thread at Malcolm. She caught his silver aura and the first notes of his name and wrapped them tight.

"Do you think I want anything to happen to Seth?" she demanded.

"I think you can't help yourself," Malcolm rasped.

"I don't ever, ever want to hurt him."

"So Seth is safe from you, but black dragons who are trying to help you aren't?"

Carol gave his name one last twist, then let go. "It's the same for me as if it were Saba for you."

Malcolm gave her a quiet nod, the only sign that he'd been in pain a slight sheen of perspiration on his lip. "I did hurt Saba. I almost killed her trying to force her to use her powers to help me. I believed in her. I knew my witch was strong, but she almost died because of me."

"Then you do understand."

"You're saying that you love him."

Carol smoothed Seth's hair back from his forehead. His eyes were open slightly, cracks of black against his pale face.

"I think I am," she said softly. "I've never fallen in love before, so I'm not sure."

Malcolm gave her the ghost of a smile. "Then we have something in common. I had never fallen in love until I met my Saba. Black dragons don't fall in love."

Carol thought of the way Malcolm's voice gentled when he talked about Saba, how his usual cynical expression dissolved when he looked at his daughter, Adara. Her heart gave a painful throb.

"Will you have to take him to Dragonspace?" she asked. "Can Lisa open a way anywhere, or do we have to take him to her apartment?"

Malcolm drew a small velvet bag out of his pocket and opened the drawstring. He poured a handful of amethysts across Seth's chest and pressed Seth's hands over them.

"You can help him right here, you know," Malcolm said. "You hold his true name."

"How can that save him?"

"That's the power of the true name, life and death. The essence of us. You can crush it, or you can nurture it."

"I'm glad you have so much confidence in me."

"You're much like my Saba. You have the power in you, Carol, but you must draw it and *use* it."

"Is there a guidebook?" Carol asked, feeling slightly hysterical. "*How to be a Dragon Master*? You say you have everything in that Archive of yours."

"It's all here." Malcolm reached over and touched her temple. "Put your hands on mine. I'll walk you through it."

Carol drew a breath and placed her hands over Malcolm's. His were warm, but Seth's beneath his were ice-cold.

"Sing his name. Take that music and put it into the stones, and then I'll spread the healing through his body. Ready?"

Carol tried to steady herself, and then realized the effort was futile. She closed her eyes and reached for the fire-hued music of Seth's name.

He grunted when she started, everything in him resisting.

"Keep going," Malcolm said.

When Carol tried to deliberately make her mind repeat the notes, she realized she couldn't find them. She let her thoughts go blank, like she'd learned to when she took his fire, then she quietly reached for the notes again.

His name sang through her mind, a beautiful, powerful melody that twined around her heart.

Seth, I love you. Don't leave me.

"Pour it into the stones," Malcolm said.

Carol pictured the pile of purple stones on Seth's chest and channeled the music into them. The stones resonated, picking up the name and doubling it, tripling it.

Malcolm's hands twitched, and she felt a blade of heat stab from the stones into Seth. Seth moaned.

Carol kept singing his name. She saw without opening her eyes the purple glow expand and cover Seth's chest then his neck and face. It spread down his limbs, bathing him in healing purple fire.

She felt his pain ease, his body reach for the magic. Malcolm muttered something under his breath, a whispered chant in a language she didn't know. The words grew louder as Seth grew stronger.

Suddenly, the crystals burst apart, shards of amethyst exploding into purple fragments. Sharp bits cut Carol's cheek until Malcolm shoved her out of the way.

Seth had opened his eyes. He glared at them weakly, but a flush stained his cheeks.

Carol sat down next to him, brushing the remains of the stones from his chest. "Are you all right?"

"No, I feel like shit."

Malcolm gathered up pieces of amethyst and rolled the larger stones back into his bag. "Snark is a good sign in a dragon."

"What happened?" Seth asked in a weak voice. "I remember you wiping out the spell in the big house on the hill, but nothing after that. Where is the incubus?"

"What incubus?" Malcolm growled.

"The one who led me to the house." Seth wet his lips and told Carol a tale of finding a dozen incubi who knelt to him and pledged their loyalty. "Not that I trust them."

Carol thought of the white-haired incubus who had called to her in her dream. He'd been beautifully handsome and repulsive at the same time.

"They led you to Zhen?"

"They might have led me there so the Order could take me, along with you." Seth squeezed Carol's hand. "What I don't understand is what *you* were doing there, with a member of the Order."

"Mr. Benedict Fai, well-known business leader of San Francisco. I think he wanted me to take his side against the rest of the Order. Why shouldn't he benefit from my anger at them?"

Malcolm's brows rose. "Fai? I've heard about him. I wonder how the city would feel if it were made known he was in the Order with Danny Lok and other criminals?"

"It's tempting to spread the word," Carol said. "But he has two daughters, and the scandal would ruin them. I'm not sure I could do that."

Malcolm shook his head. "Compassion. It can be a mistake."

"I'd like to think it's never a mistake. Fai is just a selfish man who wants everything no matter what the cost. Worshipping their demon-god certainly has benefited members of the Order."

"Not for long," Seth promised. "We can't let the Order release him."

"I agree." Malcolm stood up, shoving the bag of stones into his pocket. "But you're not ready to fight him yet. I'm a healer, and I advise that you rest for a few days before you and Carol attempt sharing any magic again." He gave Carol a pointed look. "Of any kind."

Carol flushed. "Thanks for being here, Malcolm."

"In Dragonspace, I might have let him die."

"That's brutal."

"That's the way of things among dragons. He consorted with a Dragon Master, endangering all of us. He'd have died. Caleb would agree."

"This isn't Dragonspace," Carol pointed out.

"Saba would say the same." Malcolm actually smiled, then he touched her on the shoulder and left the room.

"Black dragons," Seth rumbled from the bed. "Most arrogant bastards in the universe."

"I heard that." Malcolm's voice floated to them, then they heard the front door close behind him.

Carol stretched out on the bed beside Seth, laying her head on his pillow and resting her hand on his chest. "I was so scared."

"You shouldn't have gone in there. I was ready to snatch Zhen and take him back to your grandmother's, and then you came driving up in your car. You should have stayed safe in the restaurant."

"I meant to until Fai came in. I knew right then I could drive up to that house, get Zhen, and walk out again. They were afraid of me. I don't understand why, but they are."

"Because they know you could destroy them. And you

have reason to, because of your mother. Their god is trapped for now, and they can't fight you."

Carol traced his cheek. "Is there any way we can destroy or bind the god without opening the column? You were there when it was made."

"I remember little of it. I think the Dragon Master wiped my mind, so I wouldn't know how it was done. He didn't want it opened again."

Carol traced his cheek. "He needed your dragon fire to make the column."

"That's why I think it will take my dragon fire to unmake it." He kissed her lips, but the caress was weak, betraying his exhaustion. "But I don't think either one of us will survive it."

Carol blinked in shock. Seth could feel the flutter of the fire magic between them and the musical syllables of his name in her head.

"Why do you say that?" she asked.

"If I fill you entirely, I will lose my fire, and then my life. I was afraid of killing you, but I'm certain now that I'm the one who will be drained."

Carol stared at him with wide, dark eyes, her panic welling through their thought threads. "Then we can't do it. Forget about trying to kill the demon-god. It's not worth it."

"The Order gets its power from him," Seth said.

"It's too big a risk." Carol rose up on her knees. "I've built my career understanding risk and reward. We don't know if we can banish or kill the demon-god, and I'm not going to lose you trying."

"We'd have two Dragon Masters and a fire dragon."

"One Dragon Master who was trapped for two thousand years, another Dragon Master who still can't control her powers, and a fire dragon convinced he'll die. I don't like those odds."

"If we do nothing, the Order continues to stalk you. You wouldn't let me kill them all, remember?"

Carol scraped her hand through her hair. "Does everything have to be about violence?"

"In the world of dragons it does."

"Can't we do something else? What about your idea of dropping the column into the ocean?"

He shook his head. "I'm sure now that the Order could retrieve it. They will keep at you until they find some way to make you do their bidding." He paused. "And eventually, they will try to coerce your children if they don't succeed with you. The problem will only be passed down."

A sadness entered her eyes. "I probably will never have children. I doubt I'll get married."

"You might have my children."

Her gaze sharpened. "You're a dragon."

"Yes, but Saba and Malcolm successfully produced offspring. I am human here, and perhaps I can create children the human way."

He sensed her agitation grow. "I thought Saba could only have the children of a dragon because of Lisa's magic. My grandmother told me that—I thought she was crazy at the time."

"I am more magical than a black dragon. Maybe my seed can stay." Seth touched her abdomen, liking the idea of a child of his growing there.

"It's impossible."

"Not so impossible."

Carol went silent. She moved her hand across his on her stomach as though carrying a child was a new and strange idea, one that terrified her more than facing a demon-god did.

"Is this a bad thing?" Seth asked. He'd seen that humans doted on their offspring, but the idea seemed to dismay her.

"No." She said the word vehemently. "It's not a bad thing. But it's all the more reason I don't want anything to happen to you." She took her hand away. "Anyway, we don't know if you can give me children. Nothing's for certain."

Seth sent his threads through her, touching what he'd learned to touch while they shared his fire.

"It is possible," he said softly.

Carol closed her eyes. She liked to do that when faced with new and frightening information, and he waited until she processed it all.

"I can't be a mother," she said. "I never had a mother—I don't know how to be one." She opened her eyes and looked at him. "I don't even know what I have with you."

"You're a Dragon Master. You command the power of dragons."

"And you hate it."

Seth laced his arm behind his head. He was feeling better, Malcolm's cure having restored some of his dragon strength. "I hated when the other Dragon Master held me. It was cruel and degrading and I wanted to kill him."

"And this time?"

His voice softened. "This time, I want to be free and find out whether my need for you is true or part of the bond."

"So you never wanted to go to bed with the other Dragon Master?" she asked with a little smile.

"I was a dragon then, and you are a female. I thought that was the only explanation at first."

He didn't think so anymore, though there was still no certainty. But he knew that he loved to touch her and taste her and feel her body with his. He'd never wanted this with any living creature, and the pull to her was so strong.

"When I figure out how to break the bond, maybe you'll feel nothing," Carol said. "Maybe you'll want to rush back to Dragonspace, or maybe you'll try to kill me so it won't happen again."

If Sying had arrived in his territory after Seth had been freed, Seth would have immediately flamed him to keep from being enslaved again. Perhaps if he ever got free of Carol, he'd regard her with the same hatred.

Seth couldn't envision this, but he couldn't reassure her, or himself, so he said nothing. He brushed her cheek, feeling the fire within her. It had grown.

"I'm not giving up," Carol said with that determination he found so beautiful. "I want to get rid of the Order or take away their power or whatever we can do, but I won't do it at the expense of your life."

Her voice rang with sincerity, and her eyes shone with it. She leaned over and kissed him, brushing her chest enticingly over his, then she got up and started to be efficient, chattering about setting up meetings with Lisa and Axel and ideas for how to proceed.

Seth lay back and watched her, seeing the fire flicker every time she moved. He couldn't tell her what he was thinking: that he'd die for her if it was the only way to keep her safe.

Sying kept his hand over the crack in his prison, loving the feel of real air on his skin. A week had passed as people reckoned time in this era, and the crack had not grown, nor had the demon behind him figured out how to use it.

He was huge, the demon-god, both in his corporeal form and in his spirit form. It was his corporeal form that was trapped in the column, so it was not about to escape through a tiny crack.

The demon-god's magic had seeped out somewhat, though. Sying sensed it snaking from his black thoughts to touch the members of the Order of the Black Lotus. He was giving them power, drawing them back to him.

The Order could not come into the building because of the marks the fire dragon and the strange Japanese god had made, but eventually, they would grow enough in power to be able to breach the marks. Then they'd let out the demon-god, and hell would truly break loose.

Even the incubi the Order had created didn't want this to happen. The poor things scrambled to help the fire dragon, fearing the demon-god might mean their destruction.

Sying had been trapped in corporeal form, too, the magic putting him in a bubble of nonreality, keeping him from aging or dying while the rest of the world moved on. He couldn't escape through the small crack, but when the demon-god slept, he could push his thought threads through.

He caressed the marks of the fire dragon, learning them well. The dragon had given himself a human name: *Seth.*

Sying sensed that Seth was confused, unsure of his very non-dragon attraction to the human woman. Perhaps as a reward for helping him, he'd teach Carol, his however-many-great-granddaughter, how to use Seth's fire.

She was complicated, this Carol. Sying felt her in the marks the dragon had left, her threads inextricably tied now with his. She longed to love, but she didn't know how. She thought in terms of material things—wanting to repay the kindness of her family by making them wealthy.

She had so much to learn, and he itched to teach her.

But first, he had to get out of here and convince Carol that he was worth saving.

He glided his thoughts across the city of San Francisco, unerringly finding his way to the house on the hill also marked by the fire dragon. He slid in under the marks and touched Seth sleeping in the female Dragon Master's bed.

Seth, he whispered, making the word a caress. *Come to me.*

19

When Carol woke, Seth was gone.

He'd been sound asleep when she'd finally come to bed, and she'd left him alone, wanting him to heal. She'd talked to Lisa and Axel on the phone, taking comfort in making plans. Neither of them had been hopeful that Carol's ideas would work, but she felt the need to organize herself.

Seth wasn't in the bathroom or the kitchen, and the apartment felt empty.

"Seth?"

He didn't answer. She pulled at the threads and felt them still binding him to her, but he didn't respond.

Seth? Are you all right?

Yes, came the answer, then silence.

Carol gnawed on her lip. He wanted her to leave him alone, whatever he was doing. If he needed help, wouldn't he say so?

What are you doing?

Busy, he snapped, and then the connection closed again.

She told herself not to be a nag. She let the bond slack a bit, but she felt uneasy.

She showered and dressed, then rummaged on the top shelf of her very organized closet for a mahjong set. She dumped the tiles on the top of her dining room table, turned them all facedown, and shuffled them.

She built the wall as though she were preparing for a game, and drew her tiles.

Most of them again were dragons. She sorted them: four red, four black, and four—silver. She stared at the pieces, fairly certain that the dragons in her mahjong set hadn't been silver before.

She had no idea what kind of sedative Zhen had mixed for her the last time, but she went into her kitchen and brewed herself a pot of oolong tea.

Sipping slowly, she carried the cup of tea back into the living room and laid all her dragon tiles facedown.

One by one, she turned the silver dragon tiles up again. She studied the outlines, focusing on them and concentrating on shutting out everything else around her.

It took a long time. She'd been able to coalesce the black and golden dragons' names in her mind fairly quickly, but the silver was elusive, slipping from her like a fish in a roiling stream.

Carol concentrated, reaching out to close her hand around the slippery flash of silver.

The notes of the silver dragon's name came to her like sparkling wind chimes. They were hideously complex, but rich and vibrant. The sounds spun around in Carol's brain, and she chased after them, feeling both triumphant and dizzy.

Lisa.

She felt a sharp push, the rage of a being thousands of years old but never trapped in her life. Silver-white fire flickered across Carol's mind, burning like a whiplash.

Lisa, it's only me.

Foul expletives poured into her brain as the silver dragon fought for her life. Carol hadn't been aware Lisa even knew those words.

Carol started to laugh, and the Dragon Master in her laughed with her. *I have caught the silver dragon.*

Let me go, damn you!

Through the name, Carol felt Lisa's incredible bond to Caleb and the fierce joy that was Lisa's love for her children. Carol touched the enmeshed threads in envy, but also gladness for her old friend's happiness.

She also sensed a baby dragon, Lisa's daughter, start to cry.

Carol caressed the bond, trying to convey she meant no harm, then she turned the tiles over one at a time and released the silver dragon's name. The Dragon Master in her snarled in disappointment, but she remained firm.

After a few more sips of tea, she peeked at the underside of the tiles she'd just turned facedown, but they were blank. She felt no residual energy from Lisa's anger—she'd truly let her go.

Carol set down the teacup, placed her hands on the table, and drew a breath. She'd grown stronger and more in control. If she hadn't, she'd never have been able to reach the silver dragon, let alone release her.

Her fingers shook as she reached out and turned the red dragon tiles over.

Seth's outline blazed like fire, and the drawing squirmed on the tiles as though trying to break free. It was easy to reach out and sing his name, because she sang it almost continuously now.

Seth responded in a wash of fire, the flame running along the threads between them. They were so bright she was amazed that all of San Francisco didn't see them.

Seth.

She caressed his name and wished with all her strength

that he was with her so she could touch him. What she was about to do scared her, and what frightened her the most was that she'd be left alone.

She'd always thought of herself as alone, but in truth she had Ming Ue and Shaiming, her cousin Lumi, her best friend, Lisa, and now Caleb, Malcolm, Saba, and Axel. Zhen the Junk Man was also part of her world, and had even saved her life, though she'd grown up not knowing that. If not for Zhen, she'd have died in that accident or at the hand of the Order.

But Seth had filled every corner of her existence since he'd come into it. He'd taught her about carnal pleasure, both gentle and wild. He'd taught her that her cold focus on her business blinded her to the colorful side of life, to a world where dragons and magic were real.

Most of all, he'd taught her that she had the capacity to fall in love.

Too bad I had to fall in love with a man who could turn into fire or a dragon, she thought wryly. He'd prefer basking in the middle of a vast desert to hanging out in coffee houses, but she'd be ever grateful to him for teaching her that she had it in her to love.

Seth, she whispered again. *I love you.*

She felt him start, jerked from whatever he was doing.

Before he could send his thoughts to her, she grabbed his name, clenching her fists as though she held it physically, then she let it go.

The dragons on the tiles squirmed and spun, the Dragon Master in her fighting her will. Fire seared into her brain, and she felt Seth's vast surprise.

Then, one by one, the red dragon vanished from the tiles, and she turned them over. *Click, click, click.*

The fourth tile remained in her hand for a long time, and then she made herself slowly turn it facedown on the table. *Click.*

The last notes of Seth's name faded like faint chimes on the wind, and then the music in her head went still for the first time in many days.

The threads between them untangled and drifted away. She tentatively reached for one and found nothing.

Seth was free, and Carol was alone.

She buried her face in her hands and cried.

Seth stood still in wonderment as Carol's voice ceased, as the bright music in his head died. He reached for the threads that had bound them and saw his fire red ones fall empty to the ground.

She'd let him go.

The fire dragon in him roared. The basement of the cold building shook with it, and he felt the other Dragon Master gasp.

Sying was still shut fast inside the column, but he'd managed to penetrate Seth's dreams through the tiny crack in the bottom. He hadn't attempted to snare Seth with his name, being too weak to fight Carol.

Now the Dragon Master tried to pick up Seth's name, but he was still too weak, and Seth easily shook him off.

He was free. This cold world and the humans who crawled its surface no longer bound him. Seth turned instantly to flame, watching the clothes that chafed his skin fall harmlessly to the floor.

He was *dragon*, he was powerful, and he was free again. He owed nothing to Sying the Dragon Master, who'd enslaved him in the first place, nothing to this world. Let the demon-god escape and wreak havoc on them.

Seth thought briefly of the other dragons here—the golden, the black, the silver—bound by their love for their mates, *human* mates. Their own fault. They were dragons, and dragons should be bound to no one.

He circled the confining space, then flowed up out of the hole and out into the morning. He flew high, soaring over the city that had forced him to walk slowly along its streets, tearing through the fog that had clogged his lungs.

He indulged himself in flying over the ocean, changing to pure dragon once he'd gone far enough over the Pacific. The fog broke up offshore, and sunlight glittered on the water far below. If he wanted, he could fly higher than the highest vehicle that humans had invented and not come down for days.

But he came down, because he wanted to go *home*.

In the old days, he'd simply burn a hole between Dragonspace and this world, but that was no longer possible. He needed the silver dragon's magic to do that, or the magic of the witchling called Saba.

He had to make the decision of violating either the black dragon's territory or the golden's in order to return home. He chose the golden's, because while golden dragons could put up a hell of a fight, once it was done, they forgot about it. Black dragons could hold a grudge for eons.

Enjoying the flight, Seth soared in toward the city again, changing to fire when he reached the Golden Gate Bridge. He had a fondness for the bridge now, but he bypassed it to fly over the green smudge of the Presidio and down to the house that bore the shimmer of the gold and silver dragons.

He flew right in through the open balcony door, flinching at the golden dragon wards all over the house. Then he flowed for the last time into his human form.

Caleb and Lisa looked up at him in shock, each of them holding a baby that they were trying to soothe. Both children stared at Seth, their tears ceasing, and the male one suddenly popped into the shape of a tiny golden dragon.

"Send me back," Seth grated to Lisa.

Lisa rose from the couch, followed closely by Caleb.

Lisa pushed both babies into Caleb's arms, but the golden looked no less belligerent.

"Send me back," Seth repeated.

Lisa studied him, her eyes widening. "She freed you."

"Open the way to Dragonspace," Seth said. "I want to go back. I *need* to."

"What about Carol?"

Something stirred deep inside him among the complex human emotions that had taken him over. He pushed it aside. "Let me through before the Dragon Master calls me again." He paused, not sure what was swirling through his mind. "Tell her thank you."

That didn't seem to be what he wanted to say, but he was too keyed up to think it through. He wanted to go home.

Lisa nodded. "All right."

She opened the door that led to her children's bedroom and pointed at the air. The little girl behind her watched carefully as a black tear began to form.

Before it was even a foot wide, Seth flowed into a string of fire and dove through. The gap snicked shut behind him, and he was slip-sliding through the wilds of his home, until desert wind greeted him like the warmth of Carol's arms.

Carol didn't know how long she sat at the table with her head in her hands, but a knock at the door finally roused her. She knew who it was even before she opened it, easily feeling the auras of her friends through the walnut.

Caleb came in first, his scowl dying as soon as he got a look at her face. Lisa set her children on the sofa and her bag on the floor, and came to enfold Carol in a hug. Carol was too raw for more weeping, but she laid her head on her best friend's shoulder.

"He went back to Dragonspace," Lisa said, her hands comforting on Carol's back. "He asked me to let him through."

Carol wiped her eyes. "Thank you for not stopping him."

"He has to make the choice. As you do."

"I did make my choice. I let him go because what he wanted to do would have killed him."

Caleb laid his hand on Carol's shoulder, his touch dragon-warm. He liked to play the irritated warrior, but now his blue eyes held understanding. "He'll come back. I can't think why he wouldn't."

Carol gave a faint laugh. "You're nice to say that, Caleb. But he never wanted to be here in the first place."

"Neither did I," Caleb said. "But when I saw Lisa, I never wanted to leave."

Carol's heart squeezed. "The circumstances were different. It doesn't matter now—he'll either want to see me again or he won't. I took the chance."

She went to the sofa and lifted little Li Na into her arms. She saw the silver dragon aura in the baby, who regarded her with curiosity.

Holding Li Na made Carol remember what Seth had said about giving Carol a child. If she was pregnant, what would she tell her baby about his or her father? *He lives far away in a magical land and can turn into fire.*

But no, she couldn't be. She couldn't even think about it.

"We still have the problem with the Dragon Master and the demon-god," Carol said, pretending to become matter-of-fact. "Seth was right that we can't let the Order free it."

"He was right that we can't let them try to use *you* to free it," Lisa corrected her. "I think Seth wanted to do it himself to spare you."

"The Order will find a way. They can coerce incubi. The spell they used in that house in Twin Peaks was pretty strong."

Lisa and Caleb exchanged a glance, and she sensed the shift in the music they shared. "It's dangerous, Carol," Lisa said. "Let me take care of it, like I offered to before. It's a dragon problem."

"Lisa, I've felt this evil—you haven't. The demon-god is strong, maybe even stronger than you. The Dragon Master needed Seth and four other dragons to conquer it before, and then he only trapped it. I want to see if I can at least talk to this Dragon Master and find out how he did it. He altered Seth's mind, so Seth can't remember. I think that's what Seth was doing before I freed him—trying to communicate with the Dragon Master."

"You're not going down there alone," Lisa said.

"Are all dragons hard of hearing?" Carol snapped. "Dragon *Master*, Lisa. I learned how to call you, so it can be done. Caleb and Malcolm, I scooped up like that." She snapped her fingers.

"Don't rub it in," Caleb snarled.

"Besides, this Dragon Master is related to me in a bizarre way. He might talk to me."

"I can't let you go alone."

Carol gave Lisa a patient look. "Who said anything about going alone? I'll take Axel with me. He's proved he can teleport me out of there, although he should have told me first that he'd never done it before."

"Why?" Caleb asked with a grin. "You wouldn't have let him."

Carol ignored him and bounced Li Na in her arms. "You have children to look after. I don't want you to endanger yourself."

Lisa gave her a steady look, then shook her head. "You were always so much more determined than me. I was a dreamer, and you were a planner. I got my heart broken, and you succeeded where I failed. I've always admired you for that—and envied you."

"Your dreams let you believe in dragons," Carol said. She glanced at Caleb. "And brought you happiness."

Carol felt the music between them again, tender, loving, and full of laughter. A hollowness settled in her chest.

Lisa came to embrace her, making her daughter gurgle. "We'll stay with you a bit if you don't mind and help you plan. It's a chore to lug these two across town, and I could do with a rest." She sat down with a thump and lifted Severin to her lap.

"You'd better give me Li Na," Caleb said, moving toward Carol. "She's been burpy today, and dragons tend to burp on the acidic side." He stopped. "Oops, there she goes. I hope that wasn't your best blouse."

"I feel so used," Axel said.

The next morning, Carol drove with him back down to the warehouse where the Dragon Master waited. It was rush hour, and the roads that led from bridges were clogged with commuters pouring in from Oakland, Berkeley, and places farther south. Hardly anyone was driving on the back roads toward the old abandoned buildings of SoMa.

"Bringing you was the only way I could get Lisa to agree to stay behind," Carol said, navigating the streets. "She likes to rush in."

"Not like you. Quiet, calm Carol, never doing anything dangerous."

"I'm just investigating," she replied. "You're protecting me. If I'd have run down here last night when you were unavailable, *that* would have been impetuous."

"I'm a Baku. Night is my busiest time."

"When do you sleep?"

"I don't need to." Axel patted his tight abs. "This body isn't real, just the one I show so I don't scare anyone. *I* think I'm gorgeous, but most people would fall over gibbering if they saw me. Except kiddies, who think I'm cute. And lady Baku."

"There are lady Baku?" Carol liked that he was rambling as he usually did—it kept her from panicking.

"Sure. There's one in particular I'm thinking of. She's always telling me what an idiot I am." He grinned. "I think she likes me."

"How can you be so powerful and so ridiculous at the same time?"

"Because I got over myself millennia ago. Fighting evil shouldn't make you morose." He showed his pointed teeth in a smile. "It's too much fun."

"If I were a lady Baku, I'd like you, Axel."

"Oh, she flatters me. Something's on your mind, Carol. I mean besides Seth and Dragon Masters and the Order and demon-gods. What's wrong, sweetie?"

Carol hadn't wanted to tell anyone, at least not yet, and not a male friend. But Axel was different, maybe because he was a god so beloved of children. Lumi had told her he'd found himself opening up to Axel for no good reason when he didn't even know the man, and Carol suddenly wanted to do the same.

"I bought a home pregnancy test last night," she said. A lump formed in her throat, and she couldn't continue.

"I see." Axel's bantering tone softened.

Carol's vision blurred with tears. "Those tests aren't one hundred percent accurate, and it might be too soon to know anyway." She'd been telling herself that since she'd checked the test this morning after a sleepless night and found it positive.

"Does Seth know?"

"He thought it was possible, which is why I took the test. I can't really believe it. I'd have insisted on birth control if I'd thought that I could have children with a dragon."

"Honey, I'll bet birth control was the furthest thing from your mind."

"Yes." Carol remembered her wild lovemaking sessions with Seth and flushed. "I never could think very clearly around him."

"You're going to tell him, right?"

She gripped the steering wheel. "That depends. He might try to kill me if he sees me again—I *am* the one who enslaved him, after all. Lisa said he was different when he came to her, very animallike. I've always thought that about him, that he was more dragony than Malcolm or even Caleb."

"Fire dragons are strange beasts—that is true. But I saw the way he looked at you. He cared for you."

"While he was ensnared by his true name," she said. "It wasn't exactly of his own free will."

Axel frowned, started to say something, then broke off and shook his head.

They'd reached their destination, thankfully, and Carol parked her car and switched off the engine. She felt eyes on her back as they entered the building, but Seth's dragon marks still burned brightly on the walls.

Carol stared down into the dark hole of the basement, her skin prickling at the noisome chill. Axel snapped on a flashlight and played it around the room below. The light caught on the ripples of the glasslike column.

"Still there," he grunted.

"It feels different."

Axel gave a terse nod. "You want to go down there? Even though I think you shouldn't?"

"I want to talk to the Dragon Master."

Axel frowned at her. "One itty-bitty thing goes wrong, I take you out of there."

Carol didn't argue. She started to ask how they would climb below when Axel grabbed her wrists and the world jolted. When she blinked, she was standing in the basement next to the column.

She jerked away. "*Please* warn me when you're going to do that."

He smiled his imp's smile. "More fun to surprise you."

Help me. The cry came stronger than before, and Axel's light fell on the outline of the small man pressing his hands to the wall of the column.

Carol couldn't see him well through the opaque glass, but his thoughts drifted to her clearly. The threads that touched her were weak but thick and dark gray.

You are the one called Carol.

Carol put her hand on the glass. "That's me."

You are a powerful Dragon Master. The line has continued well. She felt a trickle of pride.

"It might not have continued at all if it weren't for Zhen," Carol replied.

She surprised herself with her sudden warmth for the old man. She realized now that the Order would have found out about her mother even if Zhen hadn't told them. Lian's power would have screamed to them, like Carol's did now. Zhen couldn't have saved her mother, but by knowing the Order's plans, he'd saved Carol from them twice.

You set the fire dragon free, the Dragon Master whispered. *Why?*

"He was unhappy, and I didn't like enslaving him."

The Dragon Master seemed puzzled. *But we need him. You have the golden and black at your disposal, and even the silver, but the fire dragon is essential.*

"I care about him. I prefer that he stay with me out of choice."

Choice? His words were incredulous. *You are a Dragon Master. Dragons do service to you. They have no choice.*

"Times have changed, Sying. Sying is your name, isn't it?"

It's been a long time since I have heard it on the lips of a girl. Yes, I am Sying, Dragon Master to the emperor called Ho. He sighed. *His family is long gone to dust, his empire vanished.*

"China is still there," Carol said. "My great-grandfather came here from Hong Kong, along with many other Chinese. The country is still there, but a little different." She pondered. "Maybe not so different. People there are just trying to get on with their lives like people anywhere."

Axel cleared his throat. "This is all very interesting, but what about this demon-god thing? We came here to ask about him."

Carol felt Sying fix his attention on Axel in wonder. *This is a lesser god of a foreign nation. Have you ensnared him, Li Mei?*

"No one ensnares a Baku," Axel scoffed. "I feel you trying, so don't even bother."

"He's a friend," Carol said. "And how did you know my nickname?"

I have heard Zhen say it fondly. Sying's touch withdrew, but he regarded Axel in curiosity. *Have you no one in your power then, Li Mei?*

"Not currently. What I need you to tell me is about that demon-god in there with you, and what happens if we let him out. Also what happens if we don't."

He will emerge soon, Sying said. *Look at the base of the column and observe the crack. Through that hole, the demon-god will eventually draw enough power to free himself.*

Axel flashed his light around until they found what he was talking about, a hairline crack that ran under the column. Axel crouched down and pressed his fingers to it.

"Through that?" Axel asked.

That's all he needs.

Carol blew out her breath. "That means we have no choice."

"You have a choice," Axel said, getting to his feet. "You can move to Australia."

"I'm not leaving San Francisco. Why should I? My life is here, and I'm not letting some demon-god push me out. I fought hard for what I have."

"True, but this isn't a business organization trying to topple your empire. It's a *demon*. A very powerful one."

Carol massaged the bridge of her nose, the cold and damp giving her a headache. "I know, but he's trapped, and he'll do anything to escape. I have a feeling Australia won't be far enough away if he does. What we have to concentrate on is what we'll do with him once he's out."

Kill him, Sying said.

"Do you have that kind of power?" Carol asked him. "If you did, he'd be dead already."

You have the power. You are strong. How many dragons can you command now?

"I have no idea. I only had Seth, and that wasn't on purpose. When I practiced calling the others, it was one at a time."

A note of despair entered his voice. *Li Mei, you must summon all the dragons you can. We cannot rid ourselves of this demon-god unless you do. It took five dragons to put him in here.*

"Seth told me he helped you, but he doesn't remember now how he did it."

That is so. This is what you must do, Li Mei. You must take the dragons and concentrate their power with yours to one point, so much so that they forget all about their own wills. It is a power so intense—you will never feel anything like it.

"Almost like hypnotizing them," Axel said. "So they don't know what they're doing."

A very perceptive little god, Sying said. *The dragons were on the whole easy to manipulate, except the fire dragon. He was always willful. I admire you for taming him as much as you did.*

Carol felt a dart of glee that Seth had not been as obedient to Sying as Sying would have liked. Seth had still been wild at heart.

"That's why he remembers some of it, if only vaguely," she realized.

Yes. When you call him again, perhaps between the two of us, we can quell him.

Axel gave the column a look of disgust.

Carol wondered whether, if she had lived in Sying's day and age, she would have been as arrogant and greedy for power over the dragons as he was. Then again, Carol thought, she had already shown such a desire for power, though she had channeled it in a different direction. The staff of her restaurants always scrambled about worriedly when she walked in the door.

"If any dragons help, it will be because they want to," Carol said. "I want to know what we need to do first, so I can explain it to them."

Sying's thoughts were stunned and uncomprehending. Axel chuckled. "She's a New Age kind of Dragon Master. Sensitive and sweet."

Carol frowned at him. "You're not helping. And I've been meaning to ask you—how *would* a person banish or kill a god?"

20

"Not exactly information I want made public," Axel growled. He busied himself playing the flashlight around the column and wouldn't look at her. "I'm a god, too, you know."

"But he's a demon," Carol pointed out. "I thought you weren't."

"It's not the demon part of him that's the same as me; it's the god part." Axel fixed his flashlight on Carol as he spoke, the light blinding her so she couldn't see his face. "I'm not a lightning-and-thunderbolts, destroy-the-world kind of god, and I wouldn't want to be. But I'm still a god, which puts me on a certain plane of existence with different rules from humans and dragons. He's a demon, sure, but he's a demon-*god*, a being of power and destruction which makes him more like me than I'm comfortable with. You see? So I tell you how to get rid of him, I'm giving you a way to get rid of me. You're a powerful Dragon Master—what couldn't you do with that knowledge?"

"You're my friend," Carol said. "I'm grateful to you for all you've done for me and my family and friends. Does that count for anything?"

"But I've seen what the power inside you can do. And what about him?" Axel flicked the light to the column.

"If I'm as powerful as everyone thinks, maybe I can make him forget. I can make everyone forget."

You do have that power, Li Mei, Sying said somewhat wistfully.

"And who will make *you* forget?" Axel asked her.

Carol gave him a smile reserved for recalcitrant investors. "You'll just have to trust me."

Dragonspace was vast and beautiful. Seth absorbed its beauty with all his senses as he soared over open terrain. His territory stretched for leagues in all directions, everything his as far as he could see. Jagged mountains creased the horizon, separating black and gold desert from bright blue sky.

He rode the thermals, wings stretched, his freedom sweet. A hawk split the sky not far from him, a predator like himself, searching the ground for a meal.

Seth had flown almost nonstop since he'd arrived. He caught himself searching for something, but he didn't exactly know what. Dragonspace was vast, beautiful, and *empty*.

It took him a long time to realize that the emptiness was inside himself.

He'd been bound to the one called Carol for ten days as humans calculated time, and he'd grown used to it. He had to expect it would take a while to become unused to it.

He'd never learned her true name. He'd come very close to it, hearing the beginning notes that spun around *Carol* and her nickname, *Li Mei.*

Seth didn't know it now, and he found himself wishing he could at least remember the music of it. Things he'd experienced with her were fading, memories drifting from him like sands stirred by desert winds.

He flew back to his cave hidden behind a slit in a rocky cliff and blew his fire across the bed of gemstones. He had the power to make them come alive—rubies, emeralds, and sapphires, liquid with fire, melding into the mountain and singing in jangling melody.

He hadn't had a chance to show this to Carol.

The dragon in him writhed and twisted over the vibrating stones. She'd been his keeper, tethering him like a beast, winding his name around him like a brutal chain.

And yet her eyes had gone so soft whenever she'd said, "I'll find a way to let you go. I promise."

Her body had been warm and smooth to his human fingers, and he'd liked nothing better than to lick her skin and touch her. She'd been salty and spicy, and he'd never tasted anything better than the honey between her legs.

The sky outside rent, and something invaded his territory with a rush of air.

Seth dove from the ledge and soared across the valley, dipping to scan the two tiny people who stood watching him on the desert floor. One had a strange dark aura that was neither dragon nor human, and one was so bright it was as if she were made of flame.

Dragon Master.

His dragon instinct shouted at him to kill her. All he had to do was swoop down and crush her or flame her alive. She'd be dead in an instant.

She stood looking up at him, not calling, not sending her thoughts to his, not attempting to sing his name. The darker one stood next to her tensely.

Seth landed a few yards from them, his body sending dust and creosote spewing upward. The dark one sneezed.

Seth caught the woman's scent. She smelled like flowers in the rain, always fresh. The sun caught in the black satin of her hair, making it shine.

Seth moved closer and lowered his head to study her. He inhaled, cocking his head, alert for any attempt to snare him.

The woman very slowly reached out and touched the scales below his eyes.

"I don't know if you can understand me," she said, voice unsteady. "But I thought I should inform you that you're going to be a father."

The red dragon blinked the great black eye he'd fixed on Carol and didn't respond. She couldn't even tell if he registered her words.

The Seth she knew had gone, if he ever existed. He might have been the product of his enslavement, a being made human the way Carol wanted him to be.

You can have him again, the Dragon Master inside her whispered. *Call his name, and he's yours.*

As if sensing the voice, the dragon's lips curled back from massive teeth. He raised his head.

"Carol," Axel said.

"Not yet. Please, let me try a little longer."

At the sound of her name, the dragon lowered his head again, sliding sideways to stare at her with one eye.

"He doesn't remember you," Axel said quietly.

Carol's throat tightened. She'd fallen in love with Seth, the man who'd taught her to put aside the details of life and let herself feel joy.

"Offspring," she said, remembering the words Seth and Caleb had used to discuss children. "Mine and yours." She put her hand over her abdomen. "I guess a fire dragon is magical enough to mate with a human woman, because it worked."

His claw stirred on the ground, wings rustling.

"He's not hearing you. We're going."

Tears filled Carol's eyes. She leaned forward and pressed a quick kiss to Seth's scales, then reached for Axel's hand.

Carol.

The word whispered through her mind, but his voice was subdued, as though he weren't certain of the meaning of the name.

"I love you, Seth," Carol said. "I always will."

In a rush, he turned to a string of fire and whooshed around her. Axel jumped back, cursing.

Carol.

She felt herself rising, Seth's fire surrounding her. Axel was still cursing, and suddenly the ground and Axel dropped away, a dragon talon solidifying to hold her.

Seth swooped with her across the valley and straight up the side of a cliff. Turning to fire again, he streamed through a crack in the surface and set her upright in a cave that spun with light. Seth landed beside her in his huge dragon form, his black eyes throwing back spangles from the gems around him.

The dragon bumped Carol with his nose. His music spun in her head, filling her with fierce, joyous notes.

Mate, he said.

Carol heard a sharp, buzzing sound, and a strange creature on batlike wings hurtled in and landed beside her. She just had time to register the lion's head and long snout with teeth when it popped back into the shape of Axel.

Seth snarled and bared his teeth, but Axel shook his head. "Nope, not leaving my friend. I'm her bodyguard."

"He thinks I'm his mate," she said to Axel, stunned.

Axel chuckled. "I want to see you explain this to him."

"I don't have to." Carol touched the magic of the singing stones and reached out to draw a line in the air. "Lisa," she whispered, and then sang the first few notes of the silver dragon's name.

You found him then. Lisa's answer came loud and clear. *Good.*

Seth saw the air part, and then panic took him as pain grabbed his insides and twisted them around. He seared into his string of fire, but found himself dragged without mercy toward the black slit.

He flung a tendril of flame around Carol and pulled her close, his every instinct telling him to protect his mate. Memories flooded him as he felt himself be squashed and compressed into a human shape, felt his fire shift and settle into the tattoo across his hips.

Carol stumbled through the slit with him, landing in her apartment, which was full of dragons. Or at least full of Caleb, Lisa, and two baby dragons zooming around the room, squeaking in excitement.

Axel jumped through the slit just before it hissed shut, and stood panting in the middle of Carol's living room. "Oh, that was fun," he drawled. "Let's do it every day."

"Thank you, Axel," the silver dragon said in her musical voice. "Good to see you again, Seth. Are you all right?"

Seth was far from all right. His body burned, his heart beating so fast that sweat trickled down his back. He felt the flame of Carol near him, but she'd not reached out with his name, hadn't tried to bind him.

But this was his territory; his marks were above the doors, and Carol was *his*.

He looked pointedly at Caleb. "Go."

Caleb retrieved the larger of the two little dragons from the air. "Fire dragons have no sense of gratitude."

Lisa said nothing, only gathered up her daughter and

took Caleb's hand, towing him toward the door. Axel hesitated.

"Want me to stay, Carol?"

Seth didn't want him to stay, but Axel looked worried. Carol shook her head.

"Go on. I'll be fine."

"If you're not fine, you call, all right? I'll be here in an instant."

"I know. Thanks, Axel."

Axel glanced between the two once more, then followed the dragons out.

"Seth . . ."

Carol broke off as Seth snatched her up and ran with her for the bedroom. He tossed her on the bed, then climbed up on it before she could sit up.

He was already hard with wanting, which was why he'd needed the others to leave. His cock had been rising for Carol, and he had no intention of displaying himself in front of other dragons.

"You are always wearing clothes," he said in frustration.

He tugged at buttons, but Carol put her hands on his shoulders and held him back. "You remember me, then?"

"Why wouldn't I remember you?" Seth yanked her blouse down her arms, and she slithered out of it. He was pleased to see that she wore nothing beneath it.

He cupped her breasts in his hands and lowered his head to run his tongue around each nipple. *Mmm*, he loved the taste of her.

"I didn't bring you back here for sex," she said.

She might think so, Seth thought. "No? Did you retrieve me to enslave me again?"

She cupped his face in her hands. "Never again, Seth, I promise. I brought you back to talk about your dragon fire, and to ask if you'll let me have a little. Not all of it," she said quickly. "But enough to give me the power to accomplish a task. Nothing that will kill you."

Seth gave her a long look, though his wanting urged him to stop talking and take her. "What task?"

"To banish the demon-god. Axel explained to me how to do it, and I can with the help of the other dragons. But I need your fire."

More memories came pouring back to him, memories of him speaking to the Dragon Master before Carol had freed him, of hearing the demon-god whispering from the darkness.

"You said you carried my offspring," he said. "Was it a lie to get me here?"

Her eyes widened. "We are going to have a baby—that's true."

Seth's heart beat faster, an incredible joy washing over him. "You would endanger our offspring by fighting the demon-god?"

"He'll get out eventually if we don't. There's a crack in the column."

"I know. I saw it." Seth pressed Carol back down to the bed and rested his body on top of hers. "That doesn't mean you have to head to battle to fight him. Let Lisa do it. She is very powerful, and you will stay safe here."

"I'm more powerful than Lisa is. I can command her power as well as that of the other dragons. Their magic will be orchestrated through me. Besides, Lisa has a family. I can't let her risk doing it alone."

Seth slid his hand to her warm belly. "We will have a family now."

Carol bit her lip. "The Dragon Master said I was the best chance we have of banishing the demon-god." She paused. "I don't want my friends to be hurt, and it would kill me if they were when I could have prevented it."

Seth drew a breath to argue—or rather, to stop her arguing, because he wanted to make love and forget everything else. But something in her face changed his mind. "There is more to this than who banishes the god, isn't there? What are you not telling me?"

She hesitated a long moment, then finally looked straight at him. "Axel explained what we have to do. He told only me, with the promise that I'd keep it to myself until it was time to fight. But the gist of it is, what's needed to banish a god like this is a strong collective will, which we have—I've never seen beings with stronger wills than dragons."

"This is your worry?"

"I didn't finish." She drew a breath. "Axel said there also has to be a sacrifice. He didn't specify, but Seth, I'm so afraid he means that one of my friends—or you—will be killed."

Seth made love to her slowly, lying inside her without moving. She stroked his face, so happy to be able to touch him again.

He kissed her, not speaking, not letting her speak. His lips were hot, a spark of his fire entering her mouth. She savored it.

Carol loved the way they fit together, he thick and hard in her, her body opening to take all of him. For a moment, nothing existed but Seth loving her in a pool of sunshine.

Seth twined their hands together on the pillow as he slowly rode her, and when they climaxed, fire sparked from his fingers to hers.

He rolled off Carol and gathered her against him. He slept, and she slept, too, curled up, feeling safe.

When Carol awoke, it was dark and Seth was gone, but she heard the shower running. Still naked, she rose from their warm nest and entered the steam-filled room.

Seth tilted his head back behind the clear glass doors to

let the water run over his red hair. Droplets gleamed on his biceps and streamed down his sculpted torso, gathering on the dark hair around his penis.

Carol folded her arms and let herself enjoy the sight. Eventually, he turned his head and looked at her while the water ran over his body.

She opened the door and got in with him. He caught her by her elbows and pulled her under the warm stream. She tucked her head under his chin and enjoyed leaning against his hard, strong body.

"Why didn't you try to kill me in Dragonspace?" she asked. They hadn't spoken since she'd told him about Axel's instructions for banishing the demon; they'd only made love and slept. "You rushed me to your cave, instead." She paused. "It was beautiful."

"To protect our offspring," he said as though he didn't have to think about it.

Offspring. Such a dragon way to look at things. She couldn't bring herself to ask, *Were you glad to see me?* Such a question smacked of weakness, of fishing for what she wanted to hear.

"You never told me if you'd let me have some of your dragon fire. I think I can control it now."

"No."

Carol looked up at him, but his eyes were enigmatic. "No, I can't control it or no, I can't have it?"

"You are my mate. Giving you my fire can hurt you, and letting you confront the demon-god will hurt you. So, no."

She pulled away. "Are all dragons this arrogant?"

"When it comes to protecting their mates, yes, especially when they want to do something stupid."

"But I don't think it's stupid," Carol said. "*I'm* being protective—I want to protect my grandmother and Shaiming and our child from persecution by the Order. The Order killed my mother because of their demon-god, and I don't intend to let them get away with that. I don't care if Fai insists it was so long ago we should forget about it."

She was breathing hard now, her fists clenched on her abdomen like she was ready to defend the child inside.

"I don't want to let them get away with it either," Seth said in a hard voice. "But I don't want to see you die for it. You are stubborn Carol, always thinking you have to do everything alone."

"I always have had to do everything alone." She thought of the long years she'd struggled, watching her friends have real lives and happiness while she worked. She'd done it so Shaiming and Ming Ue wouldn't have to worry, and she didn't regret it, but the path had been damn lonely, though she knew that was partly her own fault.

"You have me now." Seth touched her face. "You don't have to do anything alone."

"Because we need to protect the offspring?"

"Yes."

She smiled weakly. "Of course. It's good to know you won't be a deadbeat dad."

He looked puzzled. "A deadbeat . . . ?"

"Never mind." She closed her eyes as he continued to caress her cheek. "Do dragons fall in love?"

"We mate."

"Not quite the same thing."

She thought of how they'd been twined together almost constantly, his music and hers. That was gone now.

She wasn't certain how he viewed her—as a brood mare to be kept safe? Or as a Dragon Master who could easily enslave him again?

After Carol had the child, what then? It would be half-dragon, half–Dragon Master. How mixed up would the poor kid be?

"What is funny?" Seth asked.

Carol realized she'd hiccupped a laugh. "Just thinking of the future."

"I'm thinking of the now."

She found herself pressed against the cold tiles of the shower before she could draw another breath. Seth's eyes sparkled with his fire as he slanted his mouth over hers.

His hardness swelled against her, undimmed from an afternoon of sex. He lifted her against the wall and entered her, and she moaned at the thickness that slid into her.

Seth kept his gaze fixed on hers, the black of his eyes filling the whites. It was like looking into voids of darkness.

The water made holding on slippery. Carol grasped him as Seth drove in, sinking fingers and nails into flesh. It was wild, hot, and hard, and Carol rejoiced in it.

Her head went back, her wet hair sticking to her face. Seth's eyes were closed, his lips tight in a grimace of pleasure.

Carol knew what she had to do. She hated to do it, and she knew he'd hate her for it, but resolving this and keeping her friends and family safe were more important than her personal happiness. Hadn't she proved that all this time?

She cupped Seth's head in her hands, opened her mouth, and drew his fire into her.

Seth resisted. He snarled and growled, his dragon strength snapping the fire back to him. Just as he jerked her hands apart and made to shove her away, she called his true name.

The notes slid easily through Carol's mind, the melody familiar. The bathroom rang with it, the patter of the water adding a perfect counterpoint.

Seth drew back in horror. "No."

I have to. I need your strength.

"No," he shouted. He tried to twist away, but Carol held

him fast. Still singing his name in loud, strident notes, she kissed him again, taking all the fire she could hold.

No, damn you.

Carol's skin sparkled with heat, her body filling with incredible power. She *was* fire, and it sang through her, the Dragon Master in her delirious with joy.

He is mine. All mine.

She felt Seth's rage and his pain, and beneath it all incredible hurt at her betrayal.

I'm sorry, she whispered.

The fire seared her from the inside out, but she could stand it. She'd become strong enough to take it, thanks to Seth, and she could hold it without it burning her.

Carol left some of the fire behind for Seth, but he went slack in her arms, the look in his eyes like one of a wounded animal. She shut off the water and lowered his body to the tiles.

Carol didn't need to dry herself, because the fire evaporated every droplet of water on her skin. She stepped over Seth's body, raised her arms to the ceiling, and became *fire.*

The Dragon Master in her shouted with glee as her string of fire roared around the tiny room, then out through the apartment, seeking the night. She shot above the glittering, beautiful city that was her home, flying hard.

Along the way, she called to three dragons, who responded as they'd promised, the silver one streaking out like white fire to join her.

21

Seth crawled out from under the towels Carol had dropped on him, his body limp and exhausted. He used the marble vanity to pull himself painfully to his feet then leaned on the counter, unable to stand upright. His face in the mirror was pasty, his eyes sunk into bruised sockets.

Weak and sick, he held on to the walls to get himself out of the bathroom, then he collapsed on the bed, pressing his hands to his face. His name wound sharply around him, stealing what was left of his strength.

She'd betrayed him.

The sting of that bit deep. But over his fury, Seth's instinct to protect the offspring inside Carol rose like a bright moon.

He knew Carol had gone because she thought it was the right thing to do. Carol was like that—believing she had to be brave and strong and take care of everyone else.

Seth didn't like what she'd told him about the process of banishing a god, that a sacrifice would be required. Who would be sacrificed? One of the dragons? Carol? *Their child?*

He growled deep inside himself. He didn't even like the idea of the irritating Caleb as a sacrifice—dragons fought among themselves, but an outside force killing a dragon was anathema to them. The Order had once killed four dragons . . .

The same Order that would be standing by if Carol and her friends opened that column. *Hell.*

Seth could at least get to the warehouse and drag Carol out of the danger she'd decided to put herself square in front of. *Protect the offspring. Protect the mate.*

He pulled himself to his feet and willed his body to turn into a string of fire.

Nothing happened.

Seth tried again, with the same result.

He caught sight of himself in the mirror across the room, a tall, broad-shouldered man with wet red hair and wide, dark eyes. He gathered himself in, reaching for the fire that was an essential part of him—and didn't find it.

In panic, he swung around and looked over his shoulder into the mirror. The flame tattoo that had been etched across his hips was gone.

He stared at his bare back for a long time without any emotion registering, then he felt them all—shock, rage, dismay, fear.

She'd taken the core of his being. She'd left behind a shell of a man, a helpless human chained to the human world, a man who wouldn't be able to save her.

Seth still hadn't developed a knack for phones and phone numbers, so he dressed and made his way on foot to Ming Ue's Dim Sum. The little restaurant had closed for the night when he reached it, but pounding on the door brought Shaiming to peer out anxiously.

Ming Ue came downstairs from the apartment above, and humphed when Seth told her what had happened.

"My granddaughter can be such a foolish child. This is typical Carol, you know. When she came home from college, she had people begging her to come work for them. I told her, 'Take a job where you'll sit in a high-rise office in a cushy leather chair all day.' So what did she do? Started working my cash register day and night, lived in her old room upstairs, listening to the pipes thumping. Wouldn't dream of leaving us, started talking about ways of increasing cash flow. Stubborn girl."

"But she has made us rich," Shaiming said in his soft voice. "She is very smart."

"That isn't the point," Ming Ue broke in. "She feels responsible for me, because I had to raise her. As though it were her fault her mother died, her fault that I had to send her to school every day and make her dinner every night. She grew up determined to pay me back for everything, silly girl. Now she feels responsible for her friends and for you, and for keeping the Order of the Black Lotus under control. That's why she's done this, you know."

"And we must stop her before she kills herself," Seth said. "And our child."

Ming Ue blinked. "Child? Carol is pregnant?"

Pride welled up through his other emotions. "She is."

Ming Ue stared with her mouth open for almost a full minute, then tears began running down her face. "My Carol. My Li Mei. Did you hear, Shaiming? My great-granddaughter will have dragon blood."

Shaiming nodded, his eyes shining.

Ming Ue rubbed the tears from her cheeks. "Well, then, if that's the case, we must get down there and help her.

Shaiming, go and fetch the car. Pick up Zhen along the way—we might need him."

"You should not go," Seth protested. "I came here to ask you for a way to get there."

"That way is in our car. Which Shaiming is fetching, *now*. And if she's stripped you of your power, dragon, you can't do anything to stop me from coming with you."

Seth could still feel Carol through their bond. As Shaiming drove the small, slightly battered sedan through the streets, Seth sensed her gathering power. He also sensed the other dragons with her—Malcolm, Caleb, Lisa—and he felt the moment when she drew them into her power.

The difference was that this time, they went willingly. Carol kept her touch light, taking only a little from each of them. The two male dragons were wary, but the silver dragon trustingly joined in.

They were about to open the column.

Don't, he pleaded silently.

Carol didn't hear him. She focused all her strength and fire on the column, and the power of the other dragons fused with her.

Seth was so bound to her that when he closed his eyes, he could dimly see Caleb and Malcolm standing a few feet apart, hands joined, while fire and silver light twined around them.

The four of them together directed a stream of pure power into the column, which glowed as though lit from inside. The tiny crack at the base widened, then with a popping noise, bits of the column began to break away.

Seth groaned out loud. Zhen in the backseat sucked his breath between his teeth. "They have opened it?"

Seth nodded. He saw the faint outline of a man against

the brightness, then the man fell forward to the floor and lay unmoving.

Behind him rose a being of darkness. Black tendrils whipped toward Carol and the dragons, ready to kill. But the tendrils pulled away in frustration when they encountered a barrier in front of Carol. Seth felt confusion, then fury.

He opened his eyes. Shaiming was slowing to a stop at a red traffic light. "Can't you go faster?" Seth demanded.

Shaiming motioned helplessly to the line of cars ahead of him. The light turned green, and Shaiming gently slid the car forward again.

Seth had never felt more powerless in his existence. His fire was gone, and he was stuck in a tiny car with three small elderly people heading toward danger at a snail's pace. Meanwhile, when he closed his eyes, he saw the demon-god grow until his blackness filled almost every space in the room.

Shaiming did try to drive a little faster once traffic thinned, and finally, he pulled around the corner to the street where the small warehouse sat.

"Stop," Seth hissed.

The street and small lot in front of the building were filled with men. Most of them had weapons; all of them faced the building with gleeful expressions.

"We need to find another way," Seth said to Shaiming.

Shaiming lost no time reversing the car and steering it back around the corner. Half a block down, he turned into a narrow, inky black alley. The headlights sliced across garbage, filth, and bits that had fallen from the buildings around them.

When Shaiming couldn't get past a large pile of trash, Seth leapt from the car and ran the rest of the way on foot. He heard an argument in Cantonese start behind him.

The entrance to the building he wanted was locked, but before he could despair, he saw that the hinges had rusted through. He pulled the door out of the frame, leaned it against the wall, and quietly ducked inside.

The room was empty, but light and dark flickered from the hole in the corner, the battle commencing below. He ran to the opening in the floor and looked down.

The demon-god had grown, its body so dense that it had crushed the remains of the column. It took up most of the basement, with Caleb and Malcolm, Lisa and Carol, wedged into a corner by what was left of the stairs.

Near them, Axel and Saba crouched, drawing runes on the floor and chanting something in unison. A half circle of glittering stones separated the six of them from the demon-god, and Seth could see wards of protection shimmering above them. They'd dragged Sying the Dragon Master inside the stones, where he lay still, though Seth saw the rise and fall of his chest.

Seth sensed the three dragons and Carol building toward a climax, their energy pouring through one another and pooling into Carol as the focus.

A strong collective will, she'd said.

She was channeling that collective will toward the demon-god, trying to create a crack in the universe that would suck the demon-god inside. That's why Carol wanted the silver dragon, the magical being who could open doors between worlds wherever she wanted.

The gold and black dragons were there for strength and extra magic. But Caleb and Malcolm were limited in their human forms, and so Carol wouldn't even have the power that the Dragon Master had originally called to imprison the demon-god in the column.

Axel could help, but he and Saba were trying to work the spell that Carol would use to seal the demon-god in as well as the wards to keep the demon-god at bay.

Seth could feel the drag of his fire wanting to break from Carol and return to him. But he couldn't pull it from her now, or the demon-god would break free and slaughter them all.

A sacrifice, Carol had said. A death? In this room, the weakest one was Saba, who had magic but not as powerful as that of Axel or Carol or Lisa. Or the sacrifice might be the Dragon Master, who lay exhausted and limp on the floor.

Seth knew already that the fire Carol held wouldn't be enough. The two dragon-men's strength would eventually wane and drag on her. The silver dragon had a lot of power, but it was fire that would close the rift to the hell dimensions that the silver opened.

They'd soon have to contend with the Order, too. Seth heard the men outside approach. Before they opened the front door, Seth swung his body through the hole to the basement, held on to the edges, and dropped to the floor.

The Dragon Master sat up when he heard Seth, but the others were too involved in their tasks to notice.

"Fire dragon," the Dragon Master hissed, his eyes glittering in joy. He lifted his hand and sang the first notes of Seth's name.

Dark threads twisted around Seth's mind, but Carol's bright touch was still there, and Sying couldn't catch hold. But Carol felt the attempt and swung her attention to them.

The fire swirled and became Carol. She was naked, her body upright and beautiful, her hair damp with sweat.

She stared at Seth and the Dragon Master with wide eyes. "Seth, get out of here."

The demon-god rose, arching over the protected half circle.

"You need all of my fire," Seth said in a hard voice. "You don't have enough. It has to be a complete joining."

"He speaks true," Sying said.

"You told me it would kill you," Carol protested.

"It might. But didn't Axel say you needed a sacrifice? Maybe this is what he means."

He felt Axel's gaze on him, but the Baku didn't stop his chant.

"I was trying to save you from that." Carol's eyes were wet with tears.

"I know. You try to save everyone, but this time, save yourself."

The notes of his name rose like chimes in a fierce wind. "I'll send you away. Don't think I won't."

"That thing is out, the spell has started, and the Order is trying to breach the wards. They have guns; they'll shoot everything moving down here to save their master. You need to finish. Now."

"And you need to stop wasting time arguing about it," Malcolm snarled, opening his eyes. The orbs of them glowed silver. "He's right—we need more power. Let him go for it."

Seth shucked his coat and came to her. Lisa's silver lights swarmed over everything, and Seth felt a hot tingle on his body as they encompassed him. He slid his arms around Carol's waist and gently kissed her.

"Let me."

Tears wet her cheeks. "I don't want to lose you."

"Keep singing my name," Seth told her. "And I'll always be part of you."

The golden dragon swung to them, his eyes molten blue. "We have to do this now."

Seth pressed his face to Carol's neck, inhaling her sweet scent for the last time. Then he touched the fire that was in Carol and reached for the spark she'd left him. He felt the pain of it as they melded, pain that grew rapidly by the second.

"I love you," he heard her whisper.

I love you, too.

They were one. Carol felt Seth become part of her, his fire and his name mixing with her very essence. The Dragon Master in her scooped it up, and strength she'd never felt in her life flowed through her.

Then they were both fire, one being.

They felt the wards upstairs suddenly fall away. Footsteps and shouts sounded overhead, then men were dropping in through the hole, guns in their hands.

"No, you don't." Lisa the silver dragon whirled and stopped the barrage of bullets with a wave of magic.

The men lowered their weapons, but they waited. If their demon-god won, they would be more powerful than anyone in this room. None would stop them.

Lisa swung back to the swirling fire and focused her silver energy on a point in midair. Axel's and Saba's chanting grew louder, and the fire fused with Lisa's magic to rip a hole in the air.

The fire being caught the magic of the black and golden dragons, wrapped it with the silver dragon and themselves, and poured it into the hole. The opening began to drag the darkness toward it, but only a tiny bit.

I can do this, Carol thought. She felt the beautiful melding of herself and Seth, a heady joy like an orgasm, but better. They were one, fires joined, and a tiny flicker of a new life inside her drove her on.

The drag on the demon-god increased. He fought hard, grabbing the ceiling with huge claws and pulling part of it down. Axel dragged Saba and the Dragon Master closer to the other wall, and the men of the Order crouched there with them.

Carol knew she was stronger than the demon-god. She had the power of dragons, she had the fire of the most powerful dragon of all, and she had the silver dragon, the most magical creature in the universe.

Laughing, she pointed all their energy to the hole and the demon-god. "Go."

The hole grew wider, until suddenly it exploded into a void, sucking the demon-god into it in its entirety.

"Now," she screamed.

She sang Seth's name as the other dragons backed away. The being of fire that was Carol and Seth formed around the edges of the hole. The demon-god battered at them, trying to get out, trying to reach the humans of his Order.

The fire being swirled around the edges of the hole, burning brighter and brighter. Dimly, Carol sensed everyone else in the basement scrambling for a way out, Lisa and Axel carrying them quickly up, the men of the Order screaming for help.

The flames grew larger and brighter until they rivaled a small sun in incandescence. They burned their way inward, closing the hole a little at a time.

The demon-god reached out, sending sticky, black tendrils straight into the fire. He roared as he burned, but Carol felt the bond between her and Seth breaking.

She sang Seth's name with all her might, and heard Seth's answering music. The fire whirled into a violent vortex, pulling the last of the edges of the hole in on itself. With a sudden bang, the edges came together, then the hole vanished completely.

The fire dropped to the floor, a string of shooting flame, and then it burned out.

Carol felt her body solidify, and the hard, dank basement floor under her. She hurt all over, and her skin stung like she'd been sunburned.

She rolled over and saw Seth next to her. He lay flat

on his back, the flame rolling out of his body to dissipate into black smoke. He looked at her once, then the last of his breath left his body in a gasp, and his eyes went blank.

Carol screamed. She dragged Seth up to her, calling his name, both human and dragon, but he didn't respond.

She was dimly aware that the basement hurriedly filled again, her friends returning, but she couldn't see them. She held Seth's bruised body against her own burned flesh, rocking him.

He couldn't be dead. He couldn't have been the sacrifice. Axel had got it wrong.

"Carol, honey." Axel crouched next to her, trying to wrap a blanket around her naked body.

She clawed at him. "No, no, no. You're wrong."

"Carol." It was Saba, her dark eyes tired, but her hand cool on Carol's skin. "Let Lisa have him."

"No." She held on to Seth and sobbed into his red hair. "Don't take him away from me."

"I have to." Lisa's chiming voice flowed around her, the silver lights touching Seth's body. "I'll get him back to Dragonspace, where he belongs."

Carol couldn't let go of him. She continued to rock and sob, until Saba and Axel pried her hands away. Lisa flowed around Seth, lifted him toward a black rent that had appeared in the air, and then was gone.

Carol fell facedown on the floor, incredible grief spearing her. The Order had taken her mother and her father from her, and now they'd taken the only man she'd ever loved.

She wanted them all dead—every man in the Order should be slain. The darkness that was the Dragon Master in her began to call the other dragons, telling them to rise up and kill them.

"Stop her," she heard Malcolm grate. She wasn't sure whom he was talking to, and she didn't care.

She felt the blanket on her back again, and then Axel's voice saying things she didn't understand.

Slowly, the blackness eased away, and she found herself flat on the filthy basement floor, her face wet.

22

Carol sat at a table in Ming Ue's Dim Sum, staring sightlessly past the plate of ha gow that Shaiming had put in front of her. Shrimp dumplings were her favorite, but now the odor rising from them made her sick.

"You have to eat something," Ming Ue said, thumping down in the seat next to her. "You have to think of the baby."

Carol didn't answer. In the three days since Seth had died, she'd gone to the doctor, chivvied by Ming Ue, and discovered that she was indeed pregnant and also very healthy.

Of course she was healthy—the dose of magic Seth had given her had made her physically stronger than ever. She picked up her chopsticks and moved the dumplings around the plate, but couldn't make herself eat one.

Across the room, Zhen hovered around Sying, the Dragon Master, bringing him food and drink whenever the man waved his hand. The Dragon Master took this without embarrassment, and Carol realized that he was used to being waited on.

Ming Ue had insisted they bring Sying home and nurse him back to health. Carol had the feeling that a few weeks with Ming Ue would change the man's imperious attitude.

"Do not worry, Li Mei," Sying said around a mouthful of rice. "You can always call another fire dragon."

Carol bit back a retort. She realized Sying was trying to comfort her, much the same way a person might say, *You can always get another cat.*

"You brought him here in the first place," she said bitterly. "Why couldn't you leave him alone?"

Sying blinked. "I wanted to get out of my prison."

Carol opened her mouth for another rejoinder, but Ming Ue put her hand on Carol's arm and leaned to her.

"He'll come to understand. We must show him respect. He is our ancestor, after all."

Carol reflected that most people's ancestors were comfortably far away in oblivion, not sitting in the dining room eating their way through half a dim sum cart.

Shaiming came quietly in and brought Carol more tea. She thanked him, trying but failing to smile.

He patted her arm, and suddenly she thought of the many times he'd acted as her father, going to parent-teacher conferences with Ming Ue, holding her steady on her bicycle, or patting her arm as he did now when she was sad. Tears pricked her eyes.

She realized that she'd never truly known Shaiming, whose voice got drowned out by hers and Ming Ue's. At the warehouse, when they'd emerged from the cellar, it had been to find men of the Order with their feet fixed to the floor and their weapons inexplicably stuck to the ceiling. Carol had been too shocked at the time to pay much attention, but Shaiming had been holding his hands palm upward, chanting something under his breath.

When she'd gotten into his car for the long ride home, she'd looked at him curiously, and he'd nodded and smiled. "I, too, am a mage, Li Mei. It runs in the family."

She looked up at him now, and to his surprise, caught him around the neck and gave him a kiss on the cheek. He shuffled away, looking pleased.

The restaurant had closed for the evening, but the chimes on the door rang, echoing the slight music that touched Carol's mind whenever Lisa entered a room.

"Lisa," Ming Ue sang. "And Caleb. You are welcome. Let me see those babies." She held her arms out for Severin and Li Na, who looked perfectly happy to be transferred to Ming Ue's care.

Lisa came to Carol, leaned down, and hugged her.

"Please don't ask me how I am," Carol said before she could speak. "Everyone keeps asking me how I am."

"I won't." Lisa sat down, and Caleb stood behind her, putting himself between Lisa and the Dragon Master. "But I will ask you to look at your back."

Carol didn't register the odd request at first, then she blinked. "Look at my back? What for?"

"Humor me." Lisa reached behind Carol and tugged her blouse from her skirt.

Carol pushed away from her, but pulled the blouse a little way up her back and showed the sliver to Lisa. "There. Are you happy? What is all this about?"

Lisa put her finger on the waistband of Carol's skirt and eased it downward an inch. "There. I knew it would show up."

"What are you talking about?" Carol craned her neck to look, then she gasped. A flame stretched across her hips, one trickle of it inching up the small of her back.

"Carol," Ming Ue said in disapproval. "When did you get a tattoo?"

"I didn't. It wasn't there this morning."

It was Seth's tattoo, the same curls and licks of flame that had graced his beautiful skin.

"I thought it might take a few days to manifest." Lisa looked pleased with herself. "He buried it deep."

"He buried what deep? What are you talking about?"

"His flame. He knew he couldn't survive the melding, so he buried the last of himself deep inside you. You're a Dragon Master—you can hold the essence of a dragon."

Sying nodded as he lifted another dumpling in his chopsticks. "That is true."

Carol's heart squeezed. "Don't do this to me, Lisa. I'm not in the mood to learn all about dragon magic and Dragon Masters—not yet."

"No, this is a good thing." Lisa smiled again, taking on that look she got when the silver dragon had done something clever. "I need you to come with me to Dragonspace."

"I'd rather not."

Caleb turned around. "Lisa will insist, Carol. Let her take you, while I stay here and look after my children." He gave Sying a wary look.

"I assure you," the Dragon Master said. "My powers are drained for now. I can't call a dragon of any kind."

"I won't let him," Carol said. "I can do that much."

Lisa got up and held out her hand. "Come with me. Please. I want to show you something."

Carol had no desire to see Dragonspace ever again. It would remind her of flying over it with Seth, of enjoying the beauty of the place while she shared her bond with him.

But she found herself taking Lisa's hand and walking out into the alley behind Ming Ue's to the very spot she'd seen Seth the first time.

"We'll go from here," Lisa said.

The alley was deserted, and there was none to see Lisa swirl her silver lights around Carol and carry her through a slit of nothing to a bright world. Carol blinked at the sudden sunshine, incongruous with dark and cold San Francisco.

Lisa formed as the silver dragon and carried Carol, slip-sliding so smoothly that Carol barely noted the transitions—the rocky cliffs flowed into green meadows or white-capped seas without a jolt.

They emerged into a wide desert valley that Carol recognized. Her heart felt hollow, but she said nothing.

Lisa flew upward and slid through the crack in the cliff that led to the cave of jewels Seth had carried Carol to before. The silver dragon magic set the gems to dancing, and Carol slid to her feet among the pulsing light.

Lisa became the human Lisa, able to be human or dragon wherever she chose, but the cave was also filled with the dark hulk of a black dragon.

"Malcolm?" Carol asked. She touched his silver-black threads and found the first notes of a familiar name. Malcolm swung his gaze to her from far above, and she instantly backed off.

"He's here to help," Lisa said. "He thought it was possible, but we didn't want to tell you until it was time."

"Tell me what?" Carol asked in a hard voice.

"That you carried Seth's essence. Malcolm has been reading up on fire dragons and what happens when the fire meld occurs. He also helped me with this."

She led Carol around the large black wall that was Malcolm. Behind him, in a hollow at the back of the cave, the gemstones had been piled high. On them, encased in a bubble of silver light, lay Seth.

He was in his human form, his perfect male body lay out straight and utterly still, his eyes closed as though he were sleeping. Light glistened off his red hair and shimmered on his skin.

Carol gasped and stepped back. "Lisa, no."

"He's in stasis," Lisa said. "Exactly as he was the moment he drew his last breath."

The gems shone and sang, tingeing the silver with the colors of the rainbow.

Tears ran unheeded down Carol's cheeks. "Why isn't he a dragon?"

Stasis, Malcolm repeated from far above. *Lisa did it because she wanted to help him.*

"Help him what?" Carol asked in anguish.

"I didn't like seeing you grieve," Lisa said gently. "I know what I'd feel like if it were Caleb. I'm the silver dragon—the most magical being in the universe, as Caleb keeps reminding me. I thought I might be able to save Seth, but it turns out I can't."

"So you brought me here, why? To have me watch him die again?"

Malcolm answered, *Because you might be able to revive him. In my studies of fire dragons, I learned that when one is in danger of dying, he can bury his last spark of fire, his essence, in another, and if it is given back to his body quickly enough, it can save him.*

"If that's true, why didn't Seth mention it? He never said, 'Here's my flame for safekeeping, Carol. Put it back in my body if something happens.' "

"He might not have known," Lisa said. "It's an instinctive thing."

Unique to fire dragons. They always have to be a little bit different.

Carol thought of one of the last things Seth had said to her: *Keep singing my name, and I'll always be part of you.*

"He did know," she whispered. "Or he guessed."

"If you feed his essence back to him, it might work," Lisa said.

"Might," Carol repeated. "Lisa, don't do this to me."

"I can't force you. But I think it's worth a try."

Carol looked at Seth's inert body. She'd do anything to bring him back, anything to have him touch her again and say her name in his dark voice. But she also feared giving herself false hope.

At least, she thought, *I can kiss him good-bye.*

"All right," she said in a dull voice. "What do I have to do?"

"To be honest, I'm not sure," Lisa answered. "Even Malcolm's books don't say. Maybe the Dragon Master in you knows how, or Seth will be able to instinctively take it back."

Carol walked slowly to the pile of gems, gazing down at the man she loved. She reached to touch the glitter of silver, and it tingled on her skin like electricity.

I'll go, Malcolm said, his body moving surprisingly quickly across the cave floor. *If he wakes, he'll become a dragon, and if he finds another dragon in his lair . . .*

"Thank you, Malcolm," Carol said, still looking at Seth.

She heard Malcolm reach the slit and squeeze his huge body through, then sensed him take wing.

Lisa remained. She gave Carol an encouraging look. "Are you ready?"

"No. But let's do this and talk about how hard it will be later."

Lisa gave her a sudden smile and a hug, then she stepped back to let Carol be alone with Seth.

Carol had no idea how to reach him through the stasis bubble, but she found she could put her hand through without changing anything. She touched his face, drawing the ball of her thumb across his cheekbone like she'd always loved to do. His eyes were closed, his dark lashes resting on pale skin.

Carol brushed his hair back from his forehead, leaned down, and kissed his closed mouth.

A spark jumped from her lips to his, and she felt the

tattoo on her back sear and burn. She drew a sharp breath, then her mouth filled with fire, and she breathed it straight into him.

Seth's body jerked, then the flame outlined it, swirling with the jewel colors and the silver. He coughed once, then his eyes flew open.

"Carol," Lisa shouted.

She jerked Carol back from Seth just as the silver shimmer burst into shards that flew outward and smashed against the walls. Seth gasped, and then his human body twisted sharply and elongated into the iridescent hide of the fire dragon.

He filled the cave, breathing fire across the stones, which flared madly. He shot to the top of the tall cave then became living flame.

If he noticed Carol and Lisa huddled together far below him, he made no sign. His fire roared around the walls of the cave, lighting up gems buried in the rocks until the entire cave spun with color and music.

The fire dragon writhed in delight. He was a wild thing emerging from his chrysalis, spreading his wings to fly free.

Seth streamed toward the crack in the wall, flowed out, and was gone. The stones rang for a few moments in his wake, then quieted a little at a time.

The two women stood together, hand in hand, breathing the now heated air in silence.

"He'll come back," Lisa said to Carol. "He needs to get the shock out of his system, then he'll remember and come back."

Carol wondered if Lisa knew that for certain or if she was trying to comfort her. The truth was that Seth was a wild creature, not a human, and there was no predicting his reactions or what he'd do.

"Take me home, Lisa."

Lisa looked surprised. "You don't want to wait here?"

"No." Carol drew a breath, feeling her heart ache. "I want it to be his choice. I pulled him to me twice, and this time, I want him to choose whether he wants to see me again."

The Dragon Master in her sighed in disappointment, but Carol ignored it. She loved Seth, and she knew the best way she could show him that was to let him go.

"If you're sure," Lisa said quietly.

"I'm sure."

Lisa squeezed her hand and flowed her silver essence around Carol again. She flew with Carol through the gap in the rocks and out into the bright valley, morphing into dragon form to fly back across Dragonspace.

Carol scanned the horizon for Seth or his fire as they went, but she saw no sign of him.

It was late when Carol reached her apartment. Lisa didn't want to leave her alone, but Carol told her to go home to her babies.

Carol expected to break down and cry once Lisa was gone, to wash away her shock and grief and loneliness in a flood of tears.

Her eyes remained stubbornly dry. Maybe she'd cried too much in the last few days; maybe she had nothing left to give.

She performed her grooming ritual instead. She soaked in the bath, not wanting to enter the shower where she and Seth had made love so many times. She scrubbed and dried herself, trimmed her nails, rubbed lotion on her arms and legs. She did it all without feeling, going through the motions without truly registering what she did.

She'd bought herself a new robe, leaving the white silk dressing gown with the red dragons hanging in the closet.

She couldn't bring herself to look at the dragons' night-dark eyes anymore.

Pulling on the innocuous blue terrycloth, she made her way to the kitchen to fix a cup of orange blossom–infused oolong tea.

As she popped off the lid of the canister, a blinding white light flashed in her living room. The light died to a fiery flicker, and Carol rushed out, tea canister in hand.

A pillar of fire stretched from her rug to the ceiling, a string of flame that burned nothing. It swirled around itself, then coalesced into the form of a tall, naked man with rough red hair and eyes like midnight.

Carol froze, her mouth dry. Seth turned his head and looked at her, his gaze burning her all the way across the room.

He didn't speak. They stared at each other in silence, no thought threads, no music, nothing.

Carol set down the canister of tea, her hands shaking so hard she almost missed the table. She walked slowly toward Seth, not quite believing she hadn't fallen asleep and dreamed this.

Seth watched her without speaking until she was close enough to touch him. She reached for him, and her fingers brushed hot skin.

Now the tears flowed. "Seth."

His hand came up to cup her face, but with curiosity, as though he'd never seen her before. "I like when you say my name."

She wiped her eyes. "Do you remember me?"

He cocked his head, studying her with dragonlike intensity. "You are Carol, the Dragon Master. You summoned me."

"No, I didn't." She did a quick scan through her mind, but she wasn't singing a note of his name. She'd made herself not even reach for it.

His touch softened, and he traced her cheek. "Then why was my pull to you so strong? I returned to my cave and you were gone, and I went halfway across Dragonspace looking for you."

"Maybe it's the essence you gave me."

Seth looked over his shoulder at his back. "It seems to be there."

Carol peered around him, warming at the glimpse of his delectable backside and the flame tattoo stretched across his hips. "It looks like it did the first time I saw you."

"You have none of it now."

"Just whatever is in our child." Carol laid a fond hand on her abdomen, a gesture that was becoming familiar. "Maybe that's what called to you."

He also touched her abdomen, his hand gentle. "It was the strongest pull I've ever felt, and it was here." He touched his breastbone. "I wanted to see you, to hold you again."

Carol's tears threatened to spill out again. "I left because I wanted being with me to be your choice, not mine. Do you understand?"

He tilted his head to the side again. "I want to touch you and never stop touching you. I want to wake up with you and go to sleep with you. I want to hear your voice, and I want to hear your music in my head."

"I want all that, too." She smiled shakily. "Except the other way around."

"I want this because you're my mate."

"Or maybe that's why you want me to *be* your mate."

Seth blinked, and she saw the dragonness in him recede a little. "Or maybe I came back to ask you why you decided to steal my fire and charge out to face a demon-god."

She grimaced. "I thought we'd get around to discussing that."

"You did it because you didn't want me to die."

"Of course I didn't want you to die. Why did you come after me?"

Seth slid his arms around her waist, his hard arousal pressing against her. "Because I didn't want *you* to die." His breath brushed her lips. "Sing my name."

She stared. "No, I don't want to hurt you."

"Sing it. Like a mate would sing to her lover."

Carol wasn't certain if the Dragon Master in her would know the difference, but she touched his face and let her heart summon the notes of his name.

The syllables filled her head, the strange music that meant this man in her arms, her fire dragon, her Seth.

Their threads touched and wound gently together, no binding, no snarls. Seth smiled, and then he began to sing *her* name.

The notes sounded like a combination of *Carol* and *Li Mei* and other music she didn't recognize but now knew had been a part of her all her life. She realized some of the music came from the mother and father she'd lost, and from Ming Ue and Shaiming and the love with which they'd sheltered her.

Last, the music combined with a shimmer deep inside her that she knew was their child.

"Seth," she murmured, layering that name in with the music. "I love you."

He held her close, rubbing his face in her hair. "I love you, my Carol. My mate."

She held on to him while he kissed her, a spark of his fire warming her skin. She slid her hands to his firm backside, the warmth in her changing to heat and need.

She pulled her mouth from his, ready to suggest they adjourn to the bedroom, but Seth growled low in his throat, and she realized the bedroom was too far away.

The next thing Carol knew, she was on the carpet, laughing into Seth's mouth, as his hands made short work of the robe. He had it off and his skin against hers in seconds.

"I take it you missed me," she said.

"I missed you every second you were gone. I don't ever want us to be apart again."

"I'm not a dragon," she pointed out. "You live for thousands of years."

"You're a magical woman, and I'm sure Lisa will help you." He nipped her lower lip. "Too much talking."

She laughed. "I like that about you, Seth. You get down to essentials."

He growled long and low, and she closed her mouth. He opened it with kisses, then he slid his hand between them, finding her hot, wet, and ready for him.

As he slid inside her, she dared to say one more thing. "Thank you for coming back."

He kissed her again for answer and began to make love to her, until she cried out with the joy of it.

"I love you," he said hoarsely as he came. "I love you so much."

Those were the best words in the world, the only ones she needed.

Turn the page for a preview of
Allyson James's new
erotic paranormal romance

MORTAL TEMPTATIONS

Available January 2009!

Midtown, Manhattan

When Patricia descended to investigate the noise in her antique store, she found an unconscious man with a broken wing stretched across the floor.

He didn't have white angel wings or transparent dragonfly wings—they were a shiny, satiny black, feathers gleaming and glistening in the dawn half-light as they spilled around his body. One wing cradled his bare torso as though cushioning his fall, and the other was broken.

Patricia played her flashlight over him, taking in broad, muscular shoulders, a chest dusted with dark hair, narrow hips hugged by blue denim, and a strong throat encircled by a thin gold chain. He had dark hair long enough to flow over the store's ugly beige carpet and a square, handsome face. His eyes were closed, lashes resting on firm cheekbones. His legs were twisted, and one arm had been flung out to break his fall.

And wings.

The broken wing lay at a right angle to his back, the

ends fanning across the floor. Strewn about the feathers were things he'd swept from the counters when he fell—an entire stand of necklaces, a box of sparkling pins, and a bisque doll who'd landed a few feet from him with her legs wantonly in the air.

Patricia couldn't blame her. He was sexy as hell.

Her two cats, Red Kitty and Isis, sauntered in from the back room. They sat on their haunches and stared at him, probably wondering whether he was overlarge prey or someone with the potential of filling the food bowl. Either way, they couldn't lose.

Were his wings a costume? But no costume-shop creation could match those glorious feathers and the perfection with which they fit him. When she crouched down to carefully touch the feathers, they were warm and alive, the tips fluttering beneath her fingers.

Being psychic, Patricia was no stranger to creatures of the night, but she'd never seen anything like him. His psychic aura was incredible—hot and wild with lightning flashes that stabbed through the shields she usually kept in place. He didn't *feel* evil, but he didn't feel good either. Most humans were a mixture of both, but supernatural creatures tended to be one or the other.

Her flashlight took in the bruise that stained his temple blue and purple. He was a big man, and anything that could take him down would be—bigger. But he was alone in the shop; there were no other auras in the place but his, hers, and the tiny, vibrant ones of the cats.

When she touched the bruise, he moaned but didn't wake. She fetched her first aid kit from the tiny bathroom and doctored the bruise with Bactine, but she wasn't sure what to do about the wing.

It was broken halfway down. Her fingers found the thin middle bone bent. She had no idea how to treat it, but it couldn't hurt to carefully straighten the bone and wrap the whole thing with an Ace bandage.

The man twitched and moaned throughout the procedure, but the pain wasn't enough to wake him. She fetched a pillow and arranged the man's head gently on it, then covered him with a blanket.

That was all she could do for him. She was not a witch or a healer; her gift was the ability to read auras of people past and present and to detect the psychic imprints they left on objects. That was why she liked antiques—she could feel the history of the objects and the people who'd touched them. Antiques weren't dead pieces of the past to her but shadows of living, breathing entities.

Patricia curled up on a Belter gentleman's chair and tugged a second blanket over her knees. Red Kitty joined her; the long-haired tom never passed up the chance for a warm snuggle. Isis, the black-and-white female, stayed next to the man to keep watch.

Patricia settled in to wait. Was the entity on her floor good or evil?

Nico woke to a pounding headache. He seemed to be on a hard floor, but he felt a pillow beneath his head and a prickly wool blanket across his chest.

He knew the Dyon hadn't been kind enough to leave him with a pillow and blanket. The Dyon had been doing its damndest to beat Nico black-and-blue once they both figured out the ostracon and its inscription were no longer here.

The creature had thrown Nico across the counter. He hit his head on the way to the floor, and the Dyon had dissipated. It wasn't allowed to kill Nico.

Nico raised his throbbing head and met the intense stare of a sleek black-and-white cat. Its gaze bore into his as though the creature were trying a spot of telepathy, but Nico knew it was just a cat. Nothing supernatural about it, thank the gods.

The lingering stink of the Dyon in the room was quickly being covered by the aroma of percolating coffee. Nico tossed aside the blanket and climbed painfully to his feet.

He stumbled and caught himself on a glass counter, rattling the glitzy jewelry that glittered on its surface. He wasn't dizzy, despite the headache, but he couldn't get his balance.

He realized that his left wing was all wrong and saw in amazement that it was tightly bound. An Ace bandage held together with bright blue tape crisscrossed it, crushing the feathers.

"Shit," he said out loud.

He heard running feet and a woman emerged from the back room, a steaming mug of coffee sloshing in her hands.

Oh, fuck.

She was absolutely beautiful. Her hair was incredibly curly, a riot of dark blond ringlets that cascaded across her face and flowed down her back. She had a face neither too round nor too pointed, full red lips, and a lusciously curved body.

Her head would rest at his collarbone if she stood against him. He wanted her to, so he could lean down and inhale the warmth of her hair. He could whisper into her ear that he was there for her use—all she had to do was name her pleasure.

His cock began to lift, his balls warming and tightening against the fabric of his jeans.

He felt the familiar pull of longing, the compulsion of the spell kicking in. *Damn it, not now.* The curse beat on him at the most inopportune times, and this was a most inopportune time.

The woman started toward him, followed closely by a

fluffy red cat. The black-and-white cat leapt to the counter, scattering more treasures, and sat down to resume her watch on Nico.

The woman reached Nico and looked up at him, and something stabbed through his heart. Her eyes were blue green, an incredible oceanlike aquamarine that sparkled like the sea in the sun.

"What are you?" she demanded.

Not *Who are you? What are you doing here? What do you want?* No hysterics. She simply wanted to know what kind of creature had landed in her store.

"A customer," he said, forcing a smile.

"I don't open until ten. How did you get in?"

She wouldn't believe him if he told her, so he just winked. "Through the keyhole."

"What were you expecting to steal? I don't have anything valuable in here, just a sentimental jumble that reminds people of their grandparents."

"But you *had* something valuable?"

Her flush told him he was right, plus the thing's unmistakable presence still hadn't worn off. It had been here, but he and Andreas hadn't figured that out until too late. The Dyon hadn't known either—he'd been following Nico to see what Nico was up to.

"I didn't call the police," the woman pointed out.

"I noticed." He'd also noticed she wore a tight-fitting T-shirt that nicely outlined her braless breasts.

"I thought I'd have trouble explaining the wings to the cops," she said.

"Probably."

"So, what are you?"

He took the coffee she handed him and sipped it. Did it taste better because she'd made it? The curse wanted him to believe so.

"A man with wings," he answered.

"I'm psychic; I can tell you're not human. Your aura is—strange."

"Is it?" He finished off the coffee quickly, needing it. He also needed her to touch him again. The curse was kicking in fast this time.

"Would you mind helping with the bandage?" He asked her. "I'm off balance like this."

She looked doubtful but set down the empty cup. "The bone was broken in half. I think you should keep it still."

"I heal quickly." He steadied himself on the counter, and let her reach up and peel off the tape.

To unbind him, she had to step right into the flowing feathers of his wing. He couldn't stop himself snaking the wing around her, liking how good she felt cradled in its embrace. He could feel every hollow and crevice of her body with the sensitive tips as she plucked at the tape and started to unwind the bandage.

Her breasts brushed against his bare chest, and he wondered if she could feel his pulse hammering under his skin. Her hair smelled nice, clean and fresh, like she'd just washed it.

His already inflated cock was throbbing by the time she unwound the last of the bandage and stepped away. Nico flexed the wing bone, which had melded as he slept. It was a little stiff, but manageable.

"I can try to find a shirt for you," she said, her gaze fixed on his bare torso.

"That's all right. I brought my own."

Nico retrieved his T-shirt from where he'd dropped it when he'd unfolded his wings to fight the Dyon. The ceiling was too low for a good stretch, but he fluffed his wings all the way out, the feathers sleekly erotic against his back.

The feeling didn't help his erection die, especially when he imagined pinning her against him with his wings.

There was a sharp pull in his shoulder blades, then the wings slid away, vanishing. He sensed her gaze on the sharp black tattoo of wings that fanned over his back, the points of them disappearing under the waistband of his jeans.

As he slid the T-shirt over his head, the cloth pulled at the hated chain, reminding him what he was.

"Andre's?" The woman read the logo that slanted from his right shoulder to his left pectoral. A large cat's paw print splotched just under it. "Do you work there?"

Andre's was a trendy bar and club around the corner on West 56th Street that had opened a few months ago. It was packed every night.

"I own it with my friend Andreas," he said.

"Oh." She looked at him in surprise. "I haven't seen you around. Not that I get the chance to get out much." She sounded regretful.

"Come tonight and talk to me. I'll waive the membership fee."

She fixed him with a stare as penetrating as her cat's. "Does everyone there have wings?"

"No, just me."

"I'll think about it."

Nico pulled a shining black card with white lettering out of his back pocket. The name he used, Nico Stanopolous, was printed at the bottom. "Show that to the doorman, and he'll let you in. Tell him I sent you."

She took the card, giving him a suspicious look. He flicked a more staid, matte white card out of the little holder on her counter. PATRICIA LAKE, PROPRIETOR. "Nice to meet you, Patricia. Thank you for fixing my wing."

"You still haven't told me what you were doing here. Even if you didn't take anything, you knocked half my jewelry stock onto the floor."

Nico gathered up the pins and earrings and a tangle of

necklaces and replaced them on the counter. "I came to find something," he said. "It wasn't here."

"Would you mind telling me what?"

He hesitated. He could hear Andreas's roar if Nico decided to trust the woman, but that wasn't what made him reticent. She'd be in danger if she had too much knowledge, making her a target for things she couldn't possibly understand or fight.

She had magic in her, obviously, because she easily accepted that a man with wings had entered her store without breaking in or triggering the alarm. She hadn't called the police; she'd put a blanket over him and waited for him to wake up.

"Come to the club tonight, and we'll talk about it."

Patricia cocked her head, looking more adorable by the second. "And I should do this because . . ."

"You're curious." He tickled the black-and-white cat behind the ear, and the creature purred. "If you weren't, you'd have called the police by now. I took nothing. You can search me if you want."

He spread his arms, warming when her gaze flicked up and down him. She was a beautiful woman, and part of the reason he wanted to wait to tell her was so he'd have the chance to draw this out. His body throbbed with need, and his cock hadn't deflated since she'd walked into the room.

He knew damn well why he wanted to see her again, and the knowledge both excited and depressed him. She found him attractive, and she'd find him even more attractive tonight. It was an even bet that she'd want his hands on her, the compulsion affecting her, too. He looked forward to it, and at the same time resisted it.

He suddenly wished with all his heart that with her this could be real. But the thought only brought more depression because he couldn't trust his heart.

"Come by if you're interested." He shrugged. "I have

to go before Andreas rampages Manhattan looking for me."

Andreas rampaging was bad. The man had a temper, and he'd give them away if he wasn't careful.

"I'll have to let you out."

The grates were still firmly over the doors. Patricia unlocked a box with a small key and punched a code. There was a loud click, then she opened the door and slid the grating back a few feet for him.

Nico turned sideways so he could slide through, letting himself brush against her as he went. She had a lovely, soft body, and he wanted to bury his face in her riotously curling hair and breathe her in. He craved it with an intensity that wasn't quite normal.

Outside, Manhattan was stirring. Early morning commuters poured up from the subways and spilled across the sidewalks in a sea of black and dark gray. He had to go.

He brushed the tip of her nose with his fingertip and slid all the way out the door. She rattled the grating closed behind him without saying good-bye.

Nico chuckled as he moved into the crowd. Their relationship was going to hurt like hell when it was over, but first, it would be very, very good. He'd suck as much as he could from that and pretend it wouldn't break his heart when she finished with him.

Patricia arrived at Andre's at nine, right before it opened.

Andre's was a private club, memberships sold online and through other businesses. Patricia had debated all day whether she should go, but in the end she knew she'd not be able to pass up the opportunity to see her winged man again. Nico had hit it right when he told her she was too curious to resist.

She still had no idea what he'd been looking for. She'd

searched her record books for whatever valuable items she'd moved in the past few weeks, but couldn't decide which one he'd come to find. The eighteenth-century writing desk; the ostracon—a small slab of limestone with Egyptian hieroglyphs on it; the carnelian earrings belonging to one of Queen Victoria's daughters; or the bone-handled letter opener from 1675? She'd found buyers for all of them from her list of people who paid her to keep an eye out for "special somethings."

Patricia handed Nico's card to the doorman, telling him that Nico had invited her. The women in line behind her wore tight dresses that showed mountains of cleavage and sharp-heeled shoes that bared miles of legs.

In her neat black jeans and blouse Patricia felt woefully out of place. She'd put on antique earrings and a cobwebby antique necklace that earned a few envious glances, but the ladies behind her were surprised when the doorman nodded gruffly and opened the door half a foot so she could slide inside.

A second doorman wearing an Andre's T-shirt and sporting a phone on his ear took the card and jerked his head for Patricia to follow him. He led her through the dark club and up a flight of stairs. At the top he touched a buzzer beside a door and waited until the door clicked open. The doorman gestured her inside but didn't follow her in.

Nico waited for her at the end of a plush-carpeted hallway. His Andre's T-shirt was crisp and clean, and there was no sign of his wings. He'd obviously shaved since their last encounter, and his dark hair was damp from a shower.

He wore black jeans instead of blue and sandals. Patricia had never liked sandals on a man, but she decided she'd make an exception for Nico. They seemed to go with him, giving him the aura of an ancient god.

He smiled at her, his dark eyes promising. "Hello, Patricia. I'm glad you came."

He took her hand and led her into the room behind him.

She'd expected an office but found a suite. It had a living room done in trendy minimalist décor and a small kitchen tucked behind a shining granite counter. Through an open double door, she saw a bedroom with an iron-poled canopy bed and cubelike shelves.

A man came in from the bedroom, also wearing an Andre's T-shirt. He was not quite as tall as Nico, but his body was as well built and bulged with muscle. He had mottled black-and-white hair and eyes of clear ice blue. While Nico's eyes could melt a woman like ice cream on a hot sidewalk, this man's eyes chilled her through.

The one thing the two men had in common, besides powerful auras, was the thin gold chain around their necks.

The two of them looked completely wrong in this room, which must have been decorated before they moved in. This suite was for men in expensive corporate suits, not these beautiful males with auras of wild magic.

"This is Andreas," Nico told her. "At least that's what he calls himself. Andreas, Patricia Lake of Lake Antiques."

Andreas swept Patricia a dismissing glance and started talking to Nico like she wasn't there. "Does she have it?"

"Not anymore."

"Have what?" Patricia asked. "I can't help you find something if I don't know what you're looking for."

"The ostracon." Andreas fixed her with a chill blue gaze that had fiery rage behind it. "Give it to me, and Nico and I will fulfill your deepest desires. Anything sexual you've ever wanted to try, we'll do it for you."